one
Summer
night

Caridad
Pineiro

sourcebooks
casablanca

Published by Sourcebooks Casablanca, an imprint of Sourcebooks, Inc.
P.O. Box 4410, Naperville, Illinois 60567–4410
(630) 961–3900
Fax: (630) 961–2168
www.sourcebooks.com

Printed and bound in Canada.
MBP 10 9 8 7 6 5 4 3 2 1

Chapter 1

Sea Kiss, New Jersey

TRACY PARKER WAS IN LOVE WITH BEING IN LOVE.

That worried her best friend and maid of honor, Maggie Sinclair, more than she cared to admit.

In the middle of the temporary dance floor, Tracy waltzed with her new husband in a satin-and-lace designer gown, gleaming with seed pearls and twinkling sequins. But the sparkle dimmed in comparison to the dreamy glow in Tracy's eyes.

The sounds of wedding music competed with the gentle rustle of seagrass in the dunes and the crash of the waves down on the beach. The fragrance from centerpiece flowers and bouquets battled with the kiss of fresh sea air.

Connie and Emma, Tracy's two other best friends and members of the bridal party, were standing beside Maggie on the edge of the dance floor that had been set up on the great lawn of Maggie's family's beachfront mansion on the Jersey Shore. Huddled together, Maggie and her friends watched the happy couple do a final whirl.

"She's got it *so* bad," Maggie said, eyeing Connie and Emma with concern past the rim of her rapidly disappearing glass of champagne.

"Do you think that this time he really is *The One*?" Connie asked.

"Doubt it," Emma replied without hesitation.

As the DJ requested that other couples join the happy newlyweds, Maggie and her friends returned to the bridal party dais set out on the patio. Grabbing another glass of champagne, Maggie craned her neck around the gigantic centerpiece piled with an almost obscene mound of white roses, ice-blue hydrangea, lisianthus, sheer tulle, and twinkling fairy lights and examined the assorted guests mingling around the great lawn and down by the boardwalk leading to the beach.

She recognized Tracy's family from their various meetings over the years, as well as some of Tracy's sorority sisters, like Toni Van Houten, who in the six years since graduation had managed to pop out a trio of boys who now circled her like sharks around a swimmer. Although the wedding invite had indicated *No Children*, Toni had done as she pleased. Since Tracy had not wanted a scene at her dream beachfront wedding, Emma, who was doing double duty as the wedding planner for the event, had scrambled to find space for the children at the dinner tables.

"Is that Toni 'I'll never ruin my body with babies' Toni?" Connie asked, a perplexed look on her features. At Maggie's nod, Connie's eyes widened in surprise, and she said, "She looks...happy."

A cynical laugh erupted from Emma. "She looks *crazed*."

Maggie couldn't argue with either of their assessments. But as put-upon as their old acquaintance seemed, the indulgent smile she gave her youngest child was positively radiant.

Maggie skipped her gaze across the gathering to

take note of all the other married folk. It was easy enough to pick them out from her vantage point on the dais, where she and her friends sat on display like days' old cakes in the bakery. They were the last three unmarried women in an extended circle of business and college acquaintances.

"How many times do you suppose we've been bridesmaids now?" Maggie wondered aloud. She finished off her glass and motioned for the waiter to bring another.

"Jointly or severally?" asked Connie, ever the lawyer.

"Way too many," replied Emma, who, for a wedding planner, was the most ardent disbeliever in the possibility of happily ever afters.

Maggie hadn't given marriage a first thought, much less a second, in a very long time. She'd had too many things going on in her life. Not that there hadn't been a few memorable moments, most of which revolved around the absolutely worst man for her: Owen Pierce.

But for years now, she'd been dealing with her family's business and its money problems, which had spilled over into her personal finances. As she gazed at the beauty of the manicured grounds and then back toward her family's summer home, it occurred to her that this might be the last time she hosted a celebration like this here. She had mortgaged the property that she had inherited to funnel money into the family's struggling retail store division.

Unfortunately, thanks to her father's stubborn refusal to make changes to help the business, she spent way too much time at work, which left little time for romance. Not to mention that none of her casual dates had piqued her interest in that direction. Looking down from her perch, however, and seeing the happiness on so many faces suddenly had her reconsidering the merits of married life.

"Always a bridesmaid and never a bride," she muttered, surprising herself with the hint of wistfulness in her tone.

"That's because the three of us are all too busy working to search for Prince Charming," Connie said, her defense as swift and impassioned as if she were arguing a case in court.

"Who even believes in that fairy-tale crap?" Emma's gaze grew distracted, and she rose from her chair. "Excuse me for a moment. Carlo needs to see me about something."

Emma rushed off to the side of the dance floor, where her caterer extraordinaire, Carlo da Costa, raked a hand through his thick, brown hair in clear frustration. He wore a pristine white chef's jacket and pants that enhanced his dark good looks.

Emma laid a hand on Carlo's forearm and leaned close to speak to him, apparently trying to resolve a problem.

"She doesn't believe in fairy tales, but her Prince Charming is standing right in front of her," Connie said with a sad shake of her head.

Maggie took another sip of her champagne and viewed the interaction between Carlo and Emma. Definitely major sparkage going on, she thought.

"You're totally right," she said with an assertive nod.

Connie smiled like the proverbial cat, her exotic green-gold eyes gleaming with mischief. "That's why you hired me to represent your company as soon as I finished law school. Nothing gets past me."

"Really? So what else do you think you've seen tonight?"

Raising her glass, her friend gestured toward the right of the mansion's great lawn, where some of the fraternity brothers from their alma mater had gathered. One of the men slowly turned to sneak a peek at them.

"Owen has been watching you all night long," Connie said with a shrewd smile.

"Totally impossible, and you of all people should know it. Owen Pierce has absolutely no interest in me."

She set her glass on the table to hide the nervous tremble of her hand as her gaze connected with his for the briefest of moments. Even that fleeting link was enough to raise her core temperature a few degrees. But what woman *wouldn't* respond like that?

In his designer tuxedo, Owen was the epitome of male perfection—raven-black hair, a sexy gleam in his charcoal-gray eyes, broad shoulders, and not an ounce of fat on him, which made her recall seeing him in much, much less on a hot summer night on Sea Kiss Beach. She had been staying in the quaint seaside town on the Jersey Shore with her grandmother that summer, much as she had all her life. As they also had for so many years, the Pierce boys had been residing next door for the entire season.

The two beachfront mansions had been built side by side decades earlier, before the start of the Pierce and Sinclair rift. The cost of waterfront real estate had escalated so drastically since their construction that neither family was willing to sell their beloved home to put some distance between the warring clans.

Well, make that the warring fathers, because as far

as Maggie was concerned, she had no beef with Owen. They had played together down on the beach as kids. She couldn't count the many sand castles they'd built or the time they'd spent out in the surf.

But after her mother had died, things had changed, and the carefree spirit of those halcyon days had disappeared. The Pierce boys had stopped coming down to the Shore for the next few years, and combined with the loss of her mom, it had created an emptiness inside her that hadn't really gone away.

By the time the Pierce brothers returned years later, the feud had gotten worse, and Owen and Jonathan had been instructed to stay away. But an ill-timed and half-drunk kiss with Owen on a moonlit summer night had proved that staying away was impossible. It had also helped the emptiness recede for a bit. Since then, Fate had seemed to toss them together time and time again in both their business and personal lives, keeping alive her fascination with him. She felt not quite so alone when he was around, not that she should get used to that.

Owen Pierce had left her once before when she'd needed his friendship the most: right after her mother's death. His on-again, off-again presence in her life proved that she couldn't count on him.

Owen stood next to his younger brother, Jonathan, who couldn't be more different. While Owen was clean-cut and corporate, Jonathan had the scruffy hipster look going on. It was appealing in its own way, but not to her.

"Trust me, Maggie. Your families might be at war, but Owen would clearly love to sleep with the enemy," Connie said.

She blew out a frustrated sigh. "More reason to avoid him. You know I'm not the kind to sleep around."

Emma returned, color riding high on her cheeks, but not in a good way.

"Something wrong?" Maggie asked.

Emma kneeled between the two of them and whispered, "It seems the groom had a bit too much to drink and Tracy caught him being hands-on with an old flame."

"Not Amy? Tracy always lost it if she spotted him with Amy," Maggie whispered.

"Definitely Amy. Now Tracy is refusing to come out and cut the cake. I have to say, this takes the cake, literally. Married a few hours, and already there's trouble."

"Ever the hopeful romantic, Em," she kidded.

"If you think you can do better, why don't the two of you come help me talk Tracy off the ledge?"

—⁓—

With keen interest, Owen Pierce took note of the three women as they hurried away from the dais and into the Sinclair mansion.

"Put your eyes back in your head, Bro. She's nothing but trouble," Jonathan warned in low tones.

Owen bit back the retort that if anyone knew about trouble, it was his brother. Jonathan had always marched to a different drummer and had set out on his own as a teenager to explore what he wanted out of life. Now a successful entrepreneur, he had captured the media's attention with his innovative designs and daring adventures. That left Owen to shoulder most of the burden of the family's real estate business, as well as deal with his father's anger over Jonathan's latest newsworthy escapade.

He envied his brother's carefree spirit and determination, especially as Maggie Sinclair marched back onto the patio with her friends, an angry bride, and an obviously inebriated groom. Both the bride and groom looked far from happy as they approached the elaborate, multitiered wedding cake that had been wheeled out to the middle of the makeshift dance floor.

He worried the bride might plunge the long knife she held into her new husband, but luckily for the newlyweds, Maggie directed the blade toward the cake.

Jonathan playfully elbowed him. "Seriously, Owen. She's not for you. Father declared the Sinclairs off-limits ages ago. He would have a stroke if he thought the two of you were involved."

Involved with Maggie Sinclair, Owen thought and sighed with regret.

In a way, he'd been involved with her forever. He'd like to chalk it all up to a sloppy, hurried, and stolen kiss at eighteen and the allure of forbidden fruit. But since that kiss, he'd watched her mature into a smart, beautiful woman. One who was willing to work hard for the town and business she cared about as well as friends and family. With every encounter, he'd grown more intrigued with the person Maggie had become.

But his father had come down hard on them about mingling with the Sinclairs right after Maggie's mother's death. For years, they'd been unable to come to their Sea Kiss home, and even when they'd returned, they'd done so without their father, who refused to be so close to the family he thought had wronged him.

Not that Owen expected that Jonathan would kowtow to such rules, since his brother was the kind of man who didn't hesitate to take what he wanted.

He arched a brow and met his brother's blue-eyed gaze, which glittered with a mix of undisguised challenge and amusement. "Do you think you're the only one entitled to a little adventure in your life?" he said.

Jonathan chuckled. "My kind of adventure is way safer than what you may be considering."

"Why's that, Li'l Bro?" he asked, appreciating the sight of Maggie in a dusty-rose gown that hugged dangerous curves. Her chestnut-brown hair fell to her shoulders in soft waves and framed ice-blue eyes and a sassy, sexy face that snared his attention every time he saw her.

Jonathan took a last sip of his champagne and barely stifled another laugh. With a shake of his head, he replied, "Because all I risk is an occasional broken bone, but that…" He jerked his head in Maggie's direction as she stepped back beside Connie and Emma. "*That* will break your heart."

Chapter 2

THE BRIDE AND GROOM HAD DEPARTED HOURS EARLIER FOR their honeymoon. The guests had lingered to enjoy the beautiful midsummer day at the beach but had cleared out shortly before midnight. Connie and Emma were staying for the weekend, as they had so many times before. The two of them and Maggie had sat on the patio, sharing a final glass of champagne and listening to the peaceful lullaby of the ocean. The sweet noise of the sea had swept away the tension and stress of the day. One by one, with a simple wave and smile, they'd gone their separate ways to their bedrooms.

Maggie was finding it hard to sleep with all the thoughts rampaging through her brain. Image after image of profit and loss statements raced through her mind followed by scenes of out-of-business signs on their storefronts.

She cursed, threw back the covers, and slipped out of bed, intending to walk off the disturbing thoughts. Jerking on jeans, a T-shirt, deck shoes, and a hoodie to fight the chill that sometimes swept in along the shore, she stole out of the house like a thief in the night. Outside, the susurrus of the ocean beckoned to her.

At the end of the great lawn, she strode across the short boardwalk and down to the beach, pulling the hoodie closed against a strong ocean breeze and a misty fog that had settled all along the beachfront. She paused to look back at the home she loved so well. The fog had shrouded the mansion, making it nearly disappear. For a moment, it was almost as if she had already lost the place she loved so well.

Swiping at an errant tear, she tucked her head down and walked the familiar way southward, but as she did so, the faint scent of cigar smoke caught her attention. She glanced around and, in the dim light of an almost moonless night, saw the glowing tip of the cigar and the shadow of a man sitting on the steps of the boardwalk leading to the Pierce family mansion.

"Owen," she sighed as the man rose and she recognized his silhouette. She stopped, unsure whether he would acknowledge her, but he smiled and walked toward her. She noticed that he had changed into casual clothes, not that they lessened the sense of power that always seemed to surround him.

"Maggie," he said with a dip of his head as he sidled up to her. "You're up late."

"You too." She started walking again, alternately worried and excited that he would join her for her walk.

"Too many thoughts in my head." He matched his pace to hers, taking an occasional puff on his cigar as they strolled down the beach.

"Me too," she said, but then they fell silent. They had known each other all their lives and had been friends at one time, but in recent years, they'd kept an awkward distance. Even with the silence, there was something comforting about his presence beside her during the walk. Maybe it was that aura of innate strength and assurance in the way he carried himself. Maybe it was that she felt not so lonely with him. Regardless of the

why of it, the quiet as they walked side by side along
the beach soothed the riot of thoughts that had kept her
from sleep.

With a half glance in his direction, she noticed that he
seemed more relaxed as well, and a part of her wondered
what it would be like if they could be more than just
distant acquaintances. Deciding to breach that distance,
she said, "Will you be at the lighthouse rededication at
the end of the month?"

She and Owen had worked on their town's committee to repair the destruction done by Hurricane Sandy
years earlier. Federal and state funding had helped to
rebuild most of the public areas, like the boardwalk.
Their fundraising efforts had gone toward fixing the
damage to the Main Street business area in time for
the first summer season after the horrific storm, but
it had taken much longer to raise the funds to fix the
lighthouse and a nearby pier. The committee was still
working on how to help repair the many private homes
and cottages not covered by insurance and that still lan-
guished years later.

"I hope to be there. It all depends on some business
items that need to be wrapped up." He paused as they
neared the long rock jetty that marked the end of Sea
Kiss and the start of the next town. She hadn't realized
that they'd walked nearly a mile together in companionable silence. With a wry smile and a wave of his hand,
they turned and started the walk back up the beach.
Every now and again, he would meet her gaze and hold
it, almost as if to reassure himself she was still there.

"Is that what kept you from sleep?"

"Possibly. What about you? Will you be there? Seems

like we should attend, considering how much time we put into the committee."

"I've got some things I need to do as well, but it would be nice to be there to celebrate. It took so long to reach this point."

"But we did it. The town was ready for the first season. We helped a lot of people get back into their homes, even if we still have a long way to go to set everything right."

"You led most of that, Owen. I was hard-pressed to know one end of the hammer from the other," she said with a laugh, recalling her tortured efforts when they had volunteered to do some construction work on one of the damaged homes.

Owen chuckled. With a sexy grin, he said, "You did okay, and more importantly, you were there to help. People appreciated that, and they won't forget it anytime soon."

"That's not why I did it," she said.

He nodded. "I know."

His easy reply and the warmth of his gaze confirmed that he understood what had motivated her to volunteer, and in truth, she'd always known that he'd helped for the same reason. They both loved Sea Kiss and considered it home, even though they both worked and had residences in New York City.

They fell quiet again until they reached the boardwalk for the Pierce mansion. Maggie waited for him to head there, but Owen kept on walking beside her.

"No need for you to see me home," she said.

He rolled his eyes and shook his head. "I always see a lady home," he replied and did just that, going so far as to walk her up the boardwalk and across the great lawn. When they reached the patio, he looked back toward the dunes and jerked his head in the direction of the corner of the lot.

"I see you rebuilt the gazebo that Sandy took out."

"I couldn't imagine not putting it back up." When the storm surge had gouged away huge pieces of the protective dunes behind the house, it had swept the old boardwalk and gazebo out to sea.

"You always spent a lot of time there reading," he said, surprising her.

"I didn't realize you'd noticed," she replied, but as she glanced toward the Pierce mansion, she recalled that he would often sit on the second-story balcony where he would have a clear view of the gazebo.

"I've noticed a lot about you, Maggie," he said and then walked with her again until they reached the french doors to her home.

Maggie faced him and stood there awkwardly, wondering how to end the night. A handshake was way too formal given the situation. A hug way too friendly. A kiss was...unfathomable.

That Owen was feeling the same way was obvious as he rocked back and forth on his heels and then shoved his hands into his jeans pockets. With a very masculine head nod, he said, "I guess I'll see you around."

She dipped her head in agreement and said, "See you around."

He forced a smile, pivoted on his heel, and walked away, but as he did so, she called out to him.

"Owen."

Turning, he stared at her, a perplexed look on his face.

"This was nice. Thank you."

His smile was brilliant in the dark of the night. "It *was* nice. Get some sleep, Maggie."

"You too, Owen." As she headed through the french doors and up to her bedroom, she suspected her thoughts would once again keep her from a restful slumber. Only this time, those thoughts wouldn't be about her family's business problems and losing the home she loved. They would be about something much more pleasurable.

—◆◆◆—

Maggie Sinclair had been on Owen's mind a lot in the weeks since the wedding and their unexpected, enjoyable walk along the beach. He had been looking forward to seeing her at the lighthouse rededication this past weekend, only he hadn't been able to make it due to a surprise strike at one of the Pierce company's construction sites.

Owen had just settled that issue after a meeting at the union's offices, and the summer day was too nice not to take the time for the crosstown walk to his office. As he strolled up Fifth Avenue, it occurred to him that he would walk right past Maxwell's, the Sinclair family store, and he did need a birthday gift for his administrative assistant.

It was a long shot that he'd run into Maggie there, but he was willing to take the risk.

He rushed past the smaller retail stores and restaurants on Fifth Avenue in the Twenties but slowed as he neared the Empire State Building and the Maxwell's store diagonally opposite the New York City landmark. As he stood on the corner, he appreciated the elegant look of the big, shiny windows with their displays and the graceful blue awnings above them. The navy blue was as true as it had been years earlier. At each entrance, a uniformed doorman in Maxwell blue and gold greeted shoppers and assisted them with hailing taxis and managing their bigger packages.

The building itself looked like it had been recently cleaned, the stone a pale gray that shone in the bright summer sun. Planters with flowers in a riot of colors were placed at various spots all around the building, which stood tall against most of its neighbors.

Prime real estate, he thought, although he knew that for Maggie and her family, Maxwell's was way more than that.

He crossed the street, nodded at the doorman, and pushed through the entrance and onto the main floor. He paused there for a moment as he was transported back in time. Suddenly, he was eight again, and he and his brother were in the store with their mother to visit Santa. It had been one of the last times with his mother before she left them, never to return. It wasn't difficult to picture the store as it had been back then, all done up for the holidays. He remembered seeing Maggie there with her mother during that visit, waiting in line like everyone else for her turn at Santa. She'd peeked around her mother's skirts and waved at him, a friendly smile on her face. Even at eight, her smile and bright blue-eyes had made his heart beat a little faster.

Christmas was still months away, however, and the store was bedecked in flowers and bright colors in honor of the summer season. While the decor might be lively, the activity on the main floor was nothing like it had been twenty years earlier during the holiday season. Far fewer patrons were strolling through the aisles, but Maxwell's still gleamed.

Ambling through the store, he peered at one display case after another, telling himself it was because he was in search of his assistant's gift and not because he was hoping to see Maggie. Luck wasn't on his side as he finished perusing the various items in the first aisle and doubled back along the second where some scarves caught his attention.

He was fingering one lightweight scarf, considering whether his assistant would like it, when, from the corner of his eye, he saw Maggie coming down the aisle with an older woman. Maggie was clearly in work mode, the sleeves of her pristine white shirt tidily rolled up and her hair done in some kind of fancy braid. Wisps of hair had escaped confinement and curled around her face, highlighting eyes the color of the ocean by Sea Kiss and the creamy skin along the straight line of her jaw.

Maggie walked behind the counter, moved some of the items on the display, and spoke to the woman, earning a smile and a nod. She grinned at the woman and turned to walk away when she noticed him. Her smile dimmed, and the happy look on her face turned to one of puzzlement. She strode toward him, her movements brisk, efficient, and totally businesslike, and yet no less enticing. She stopped a foot away from him and, with a slow nod, said, "Owen. It's a surprise to see you here."

"Because of the feud?" he asked. He shifted his gaze back to the scarf, because the sight of her beautiful face was just too distracting.

"In the women's section," she clarified. "I didn't

realize you were seeing someone," she replied but then murmured a sharp curse beneath her breath as a becoming stain of color blossomed on her cheeks.

He was secretly pleased she might be keeping track of whether he was involved, not that he was. In fact, being a type A workaholic, he hadn't been involved in some time. He couldn't resist teasing her and said, "Actually, we see each other almost every day, and I can't imagine not having her in my life."

"Oh, that's nice," she said.

It pleased him even more that he detected a hint of disappointment in her tone. Despite that, he couldn't keep up the deception. "She's my administrative assistant and a very lovely lady. Her birthday is coming up, and I wanted to get her a gift, but I'm not sure this is right."

Maggie blew out an obvious sigh of relief and skimmed her hand along the scarf he had been examining. "This is nice for an older woman, but if she's younger—"

"She's a grandmother but quite a fashionista."

With a nod, Maggie picked through the other scarves and pulled out one in a light-taupe color with alternating bars of metallic gold and navy blue. She handed it to him, and their hands brushed, causing her to jump back a bit.

Stammering, she looked down and said, "It's raw silk, and the fabric and colors will work well with either a suit or jeans."

He placed his thumb under her chin and applied gentle pressure to urge her gaze upward. "It's lovely. Thank you," he said. When she locked her gaze with his, he hoped it was clear he was referring to something other than the scarf.

"You're welcome. If you don't mind, I have to finish my walk-through," she said and pointed toward the far side of the floor.

"Not at all," he said and held out his hand for a handshake.

She looked at it and then back up at him before finally placing her hand in his. As he closed his fingers around hers and held her hand for way too long, he decided to take another gamble. He leaned forward, brushed a fleeting kiss across her cheek, and whispered, "It was nice to see you again, Maggie."

Before she could respond or he totally embarrassed himself, he hurried away, smiling, pleased both with the gift and with himself. He might work way too much and his father might have a ridiculous hatred of the Sinclairs, but he didn't have to be shaped from the same mold. Especially when the reward was a possible relationship with Maggie.

Chapter 3

MAGGIE ALWAYS ENJOYED THE PEACEFULNESS OF EARLY morning in her mother's old office in the Chrysler Building, now her main workplace. Her father hadn't changed a thing since her mother's death over twenty years earlier, which made it easy for Maggie to remember how she'd come and visited her mom as a child. She would play on the mahogany coffee table in front of the silk-upholstered settee while her mother sat across the way, working at her Victorian pedestal desk.

She could feel her mom's presence here as well as at their Sea Kiss home and the store. It was why she would do almost anything to keep from losing them. Even though her mother had been gone from Maggie's life for more years than she'd been in it, she knew that her mother would have wanted her to fight to keep the business alive and to safeguard the jobs of the many employees who had been loyal to them for years. Plus, she had her own dream to put her stamp on the upscale stores her mother's family had founded nearly a century ago.

A job made harder by the fact that her father not only hadn't changed a thing in the office, but he also refused to consider modifying any aspect of how the stores operated.

With a heartfelt sigh, Maggie rose from her mother's desk and walked to the windows. From their location fifty-some floors up, she could see all the way downtown to the new World Trade Center and the Verrazano Bridge at the mouth of the harbor. The eastern-facing windows brought a view of the United Nations and, stretching beyond that, Queens and Long Island. From her father's office on the opposite side of the floor, the vistas of the New Jersey Palisades and Hudson River were equally spectacular.

Prime real estate, her father would say, and if there was one thing her father knew about, it was real estate. His wedding gift to his new bride had been six fabulous locations in upcoming suburban areas that his wife had used to expand the reach of her family's signature Fifth Avenue department store. That real estate was one of the few things left to bargain with to help keep the stores afloat and to help her make the modifications necessary to compete in a world filled with cheap fast-fashion establishments, big-box stores, and the internet.

Returning to her desk, she sat down and opened the file folder with the earnings report that had been unofficially released, probably by a disgruntled board member and minority shareholder. As a closely held corporation where she and her father owned over fifty percent of the shares, they had far fewer reporting regulations to worry about, but they still had to have audits and reports on their financial status. She had gotten a tip from a friendly reporter that the information would be made public later that morning.

Her stomach clenched at the sight of the losses stemming from the retail division. The numbers had caused her many a sleepless night the last few weeks. Especially since she had mortgaged the family's Jersey Shore mansion for money to keep the stores running for the next few months. She was already in talks with another bank for a loan against the New York City town house she'd also inherited and lived in when she wasn't in Sea Kiss. If she couldn't turn the stores around…

For months, the other half dozen or so shareholders had been pressing for them to close the retail division, add the valuable properties to their real estate holdings, and focus solely on the real estate division in order to cut their losses. But Maggie was determined to save that part of the company for her mother, herself, and their many employees.

Closing the folder, she opened a bottom drawer in the pedestal desk and took out another portfolio, thicker by far than the earnings report. Flipping open the file, she skimmed through her notes and the collection of photos and rough designs she'd sketched to transform their signature Fifth Avenue store.

Little by little, a smile crept onto her face as she ran through her idea file and sipped the latte she had picked up on her way to the office. By the time she flipped the last sheet of paper, her latte was done, and the first sounds of activity were filtering in from the outside work space.

A knock at the door had her collecting her papers and closing the file before she called out, "Come in."

Her administrative assistant entered, a wary smile on her face and another cup of coffee in her hand, because she knew Maggie fueled her mornings with nonstop doses of caffeine.

"Good morning?" her assistant said with some trepidation, aware of what would happen that day.

Maggie smiled and accepted the large mug the young woman offered her. "You're a godsend, Sheila, and yes, it's a good morning for now."

She checked her watch. The morning business shows would soon be turning their attention to various earnings reports, and she had no doubt that the Sinclair Corporation would be a topic of discussion. Whoever had released the report without authorization had likely done so to publicly embarrass her father in the hopes of getting him to take some kind of action regarding the stores.

"Do we have to worry, Maggie?" Sheila asked while wringing her hands.

Her assistant was a single mom, loyal, smart, and highly responsible. It was why Maggie had chosen her for the job as her right-hand woman. She wouldn't violate Sheila's trust by sugarcoating what was happening. If they had to sell the stores to pay off the debt they had accumulated, many people would lose their jobs, including those in the office area, since they wouldn't need as much staff to run only the real estate division.

"It's going to be a rough day, Sheila. The numbers aren't good, but I really believe we can still turn things around."

The hand wringing stopped, and Sheila smiled. With a nod, she said, "If anyone can do it, you can, Maggie."

The weight of such unfailing belief was a difficult burden, but as Sheila left the room, Maggie stiffened her spine and flipped on one of the morning business shows. The commentary from the talking heads was harsh, but it could have been worse. One reporter even made a positive mention of some of the cost savings Maggie had accomplished by renegotiating one of their union contracts and another with a delivery firm. As they finished with their discussion about the Sinclair Corporation,

Maggie shut off the television and prepared herself for what would follow now that people knew that the grand old lady of Fifth Avenue was in trouble.

The first email hit her inbox seconds after the financial reporters ended their talk. She muted her computer speakers in an effort to ignore the *bing-bing-bing* as a deluge of messages flooded her mailbox, and she phoned Sheila to warn her that she didn't want to be disturbed in case anyone called.

She hung up and leaned back in her chair. There was no doubt the situation had become dire in the last year. While her father was a whiz when it came to real estate transactions, retail had been her mother's gift, making for a good partnership at the time. But the retail arena was different now. To save the stores and the employees' jobs, not to mention the Sea Kiss home she loved, they needed to make changes in how the stores were operated. And they needed cash and lots of it. With the leak of the report, it would be difficult to get a loan from any of the banks, and worse, it was possible some of their vendors would start cutting off their lines of credit.

Opening her personal folder once again, she ran down the list of prospective white knights she had identified. After this morning, she could cross a number of names off the list. Only a few viable candidates remained, including Owen Pierce.

She didn't know why she had recently added him, except of course that she had no issue with him personally. If anything, she had long felt it was time to end the rift between the families. Maybe even explore her fascination with Owen in order to get past it.

Owen had been on her mind a lot since Tracy's

wedding and their assorted meetings in the last few weeks: the late-night beach walk, their local gym, her favorite neighborhood Italian restaurant, and, last but not least, during her walk-through at the store the other day. That barely there kiss on her cheek had held the promise of so much more.

Or is that just wishful thinking on my part?

She shut her eyes tightly, picturing him in his tuxedo at the wedding and jeans afterward. Remembering him in his elegant suit as he stood in the store, thoughtfully looking for a gift for his assistant.

"Ignoring me?"

She jumped as she realized her father stood before her desk, a bemused look on his handsome face. Shaking her head, she rose and invited him to take a seat. "Sorry, Dad. I was lost in thought."

Guilt bit into her that she wasn't being completely truthful by omitting what she had been thinking about. Or rather, *who*.

"I know it won't be easy to handle the reporters or the other shareholders after this morning," her father said.

"I don't mind, except there's one question that is sure to keep popping up: What do we plan to do about the stores?"

Her father's features tightened, and his lips thinned into a disapproving slash.

"I don't want to discuss this again, Maggie. You know my position on it."

With frustration, she raked her fingers through her hair, pulling the shoulder-length strands away from her face. "It's been a very long time since Mom died, Dad. It's time to let go and honor her memory in another way," she urged.

"Really, Maggie? How do you propose we do that?" he challenged, ruddy color erupting on his cheeks. A nervous tic pulsed along his clenched jaw.

"We make the changes we need to so that the stores can be successful again. We make Mom proud of what we can do together."

"Maggie, I'm not sure—"

"Can you do that, Dad? Are you willing to take that risk with me?" she pressed, trying to make her father understand that they were almost out of options. As she met his shuttered gaze, however, she knew he was unconvinced, and that left her with few prospects for the future. As much as she wanted to honor her mother's memory and save the stores, she wouldn't do it by dishonoring her father by getting the other shareholders to give her their votes in order to have control of the board.

It was why she had mortgaged so many of her personal assets to provide loans to the company, but she was close to the end of her rope. She had to do something to convince her father to change his mind or risk losing everything.

Maggie had thought that the day couldn't get any worse, but then a tearful Tracy phoned near midday.

"I hate to bother you. I know you're busy," she began.

Maggie quickly jumped in. "I'm never too busy for a friend. What can I do?"

"Lunch would be nice. Are you free?"

Although she had a lot of work to do, she could use the break after the kind of morning she'd had. Besides, when a friend needed her, she couldn't say no. "You know that Mexican place at Forty-First and Third? How about I meet you—"

"I'm in the lobby. The security guard wouldn't let me up."

"I'll be there in a few minutes," she said. After letting her assistant know that she was going out, she headed down to the lobby where her friend waited in the large space, looking decidedly lost. As she approached Tracy, she examined her friend and immediately recognized the signs of a major Tracy tragedy. The nearly opaque sunglasses probably hid tear-reddened eyes and dark smudges from a lack of sleep. Tracy's bottom lip was bitten clean of lipstick, and her hands gripped her Prada purse so tightly, her knuckles were white from the pressure.

There was just one big difference from all her earlier romantic tragedies: this time, it was about a husband and not just a boyfriend.

Maggie hugged her friend. "Whatever it is, it's going to be okay."

A watery sniffle escaped Tracy, and her friend nodded. Maggie slipped her arm through Tracy's, and they walked quietly to the Mexican restaurant where they were seated quickly, since it was early for lunch.

Tracy finally slipped off her sunglasses and laid them beside her on the table. Her eyes were red and puffy, just as Maggie had guessed.

Leaning closer over the narrow width of the table, her friend said, "I think he's cheating on me, Mags. Tell me what to do."

Maggie considered her friend at length before laying her hand over Tracy's as it rested on the pristine white tablecloth. "What do *you* want to do?"

Tracy looked away, avoiding Maggie's scrutiny. "I want it to work, only… Maybe this marriage was a mistake," she said softly. "You *all* knew, and you *all* tried to tell me in dozens of ways, but I didn't listen."

No, you didn't listen, Maggie thought.

Gently squeezing Tracy's hand to comfort her, she said, "Whatever you want to do, we're here for you. We understand what you're going through."

Tracy shook her head and twisted her lips into an angry smirk. "How could you? How could any of you? When have you ever taken the time to fall in love? You're all so…"

"Independent," Maggie filled in when her friend hesitated.

Tracy leaned forward once again and fixed her gaze on Maggie's. "Afraid. You're all so frickin' afraid."

Maggie jerked away, as taken aback as if her friend had slapped her. "Afraid? Who says I'm afraid?"

In an accusatory whisper, Tracy said, "I saw you kiss Owen that night at your grandmother's. I saw how the two of you looked at each other at my wedding, only you're too afraid to defy Daddy. Connie's too afraid of being like her unwed mom. And sweet Jesus, don't even get me started on Emma, because that girl's got major mommy and daddy issues and who knows what else going on."

Tracy's voice had escalated. Maggie knew it was soul-deep pain talking, so she didn't take offense, although it bothered her a little that her friend might be right about some things.

"I know you're hurting, so I'll forgive you for being a bitch just now. And you know that no matter what you decide, we'll all be here to help you."

At that moment, the waitress brought over the margaritas they'd ordered. Tracy picked up her drink and eyed Maggie over the salt-laced rim. With the hand that held the glass, she pointed a perfectly manicured finger at Maggie and said, "You're always there to help, Mags, but the bigger question is who's going to help you?"

Maggie narrowed her gaze and, slightly puzzled, said, "What do you mean?"

"The business. Your love life—"

"I don't have a love life."

"Exactly," Tracy said with another wave of her hand.

Maggie was about to protest again but snapped her mouth shut, because in the emotional state that Tracy was in, it would do little good to argue. But as the meal came, she wondered how a lunch that was supposed to be about making her friend feel better had ended up making her feel so miserable.

Chapter 4

THE LETTERS STARTED DOING A LITTLE JIG ACROSS THE PAGE.

Or maybe it was a moonwalk, Owen Pierce mused as he closed his eyes and scrubbed his face with his hands.

It had been a long, tiring, and frustrating day spent negotiating a new lease agreement for one of their commercial Midtown properties. Now he was trying to make up for the time he had lost by burning a little midnight oil to review a contract for another location the company wanted to acquire in Queens. With properties in Manhattan and Brooklyn running at a premium, they needed to be in the next most likely hot location.

Unfortunately, the letters continued to dance across the paper in a blur, a clear sign it was time to stop for the day. Besides, Queens wasn't going anywhere overnight.

As he closed the file, he leaned back in his leather executive chair and laced his hands behind his head. All he could think about was going to his favorite restaurant for a quick dinner followed by a relaxing night sitting in front of the television, watching the ball game. Especially since it looked like the Mets would make the postseason this year.

Surging from the chair, he slipped his suit jacket back on, straightened his tie, and headed out of his corner office and into the main space of his family's real estate business. There were a few ambitious souls huddled at their desks on a Friday night, but for the most part, the staff had gone home to start the weekend.

Outside the building on Sixth, traffic streamed uptown while across the street, a crowd of tourists mingled in front of Radio City Music Hall, waiting for a show.

He sauntered eastward to Fifth where he was lucky to grab a cab to take him downtown to the restaurant near his condo in the Flatiron District, although he reconsidered just how lucky as the cabbie swerved and dodged other cars and trucks at breakneck speed before jerking to a sudden stop only inches shy of a pedestrian who had been paying more attention to his cell phone than to traffic.

The cabbie muttered a curse under his breath and shot off again as the light turned green, tossing Owen against the seat back and yanking a curse from him as well. Not that the cabbie took note of that or slowed his speed.

The city went by in a blur of noises and smells. Horns honking and a distant siren. The riot of colors from the neon and lights on buildings and the summer clothing the tourists wore to walk around. The pungent scent of the hot dog vendor's cart was quickly replaced by the sweetness of cinnamon rolls from a food truck parked on the next block.

Owen was infinitely relieved when, a few minutes later, the taxi dropped him off in front of the Italian restaurant on Park Avenue South. He flipped the cabbie the fare and told him to keep the change, earning a "Thanks, man."

When he glanced through the plate glass window of the restaurant, he muttered another curse when he realized how crowded it was. He hoped it wouldn't be too long a wait, although with the kind of luck he was having today, he wouldn't bet on it.

He walked in and froze. There was no ignoring who stood in front of him, elegant and feminine in a dove-gray designer pantsuit. Her thick, dark hair hung loose to her shoulders, and pearl earrings winked from beneath the lush strands. A pearl necklace graced her long, slender neck while a slim gold watch completed the classic look.

Maggie.

She turned, and the heat of embarrassment snaked through him as he realized he'd said her name aloud.

Surprise colored her crystal-blue gaze as it swept over him, and she stumbled through her reply. "O-O-Owen. Hello. I just came by for a quick bite."

He looked past her to the packed restaurant where only one table for two was free. "Me too, but it looks like I may have to wait. So much for quick."

The hostess rushed over and blurted out, "I'm so sorry, Mr. Pierce. We've just seated a number of the other guests, so it may take an hour or more for the next table to free up."

He gestured to the sole empty table and locked his gaze on Maggie's. "Would you mind sharing?" he asked, arching a brow. It occurred to him that maybe today was going to be his lucky day after all.

———

It was on the tip of Maggie's tongue to refuse, but Tracy's words from earlier that day challenged her.

Hell no, she was not afraid of Owen, their family feud, or her father.

Besides, the temptation of all that was Owen Pierce was too much for her to resist. Plus, she was hungry, and he could be really charming. A part of her even wondered if she could feel him out about the loan she needed, although after the kind of day she'd had, the business, the mortgage on the beach house, and the possible mortgage on her town house were the last things she wanted to think about.

"I wouldn't mind at all," she said, offering Owen a grin to dispel any doubt he might have about her sincerity.

With a broad smile, the hostess picked up two menus and led them to the table in the back. As she did so, a couple of heads in the restaurant swiveled around to follow them.

Tracy's friend Toni Van Houten was dining with her husband sans her trio of boys. Toni and her husband kept a pied-à-terre in Chelsea.

One of the morning show financial reporters sat at another table with his brother, a sportscaster at a local television station. They were rambling far from their Uptown studios, but this restaurant was popular with the local media.

After they were seated and the hostess stepped away, Maggie unfurled her napkin and said, "You know there will be gossip all over by the morning."

Owen's broad shoulders shot up in a nonchalant shrug that stretched the deep, navy-blue merino wool of his bespoke suit jacket. "How about this? For tonight, no talk about our businesses or our families. Just about us."

She exhaled sharply, although humor tinged her words. "I thought we were all about our businesses and families. What's left?"

He grinned, and his startling charcoal-gray eyes lightened to a rich slate color marbled with gleaming silver. "How about baseball? Please tell me you're not a Yankees fan, because that's one thing I could never forgive you for."

She threw her head back and laughed as he had intended. "I'm a Mets fan through and through," she said. She watched with too much interest as he jerked open his tie and undid the top two buttons of his shirt, clearly intending to relax during dinner.

Mimicking his actions, she eased out of her jacket, and with it gone, it seemed as if a huge weight had been lifted off her shoulders. Funny how she had never thought of her business suit as being a kind of burden, but in the short time since lunch with Tracy, she'd become somehow more sensitive about her situation.

The waitress came over quickly, barely giving her time to recover from that revelation.

"Would you like a drink while you make up your minds, or have you decided what you'd like?" the young woman asked.

Maggie was a creature of habit, and the chicken parmigiana here was the best she'd ever had. Since Owen had closed his menu, she ordered it, and when Owen ordered the same thing, she smiled. "Two things we have in common: chicken parm and the Mets."

With a smile that awakened a dimple that made him look infinitely more boyish, Owen replied, "That's a good start."

She wanted to say there was nothing to get started because there was nowhere they could go, but that would be lying to herself. For way too long, Owen had played an on-again, off-again role in her fantasies, only tonight, he was no fantasy.

He was there right across from her, mouthwatering flesh-and-blood male wrapped up in a hand-tailored custom suit that totally amplified his aura of power. Everything about him said that he was a man used to getting what he wanted.

Her heart beat triple time in her chest as she wondered if he might want her. For tonight, she was going to take advantage of this opportunity to find out more about the man who fascinated her more with each encounter. Maybe even to find out how much he'd changed from the young boy who'd once built sand castles with her and then left her.

The waitress brought over their salads and a bread basket wafting yeasty goodness that was impossible to resist. They both reached for the bread at the same time, but Owen gallantly demurred.

"After you," he offered.

She nodded, picked up a slice, and waited until he had grabbed one as well. "Sorry, I'm a carboholic," she said in explanation as she tore a piece off the bread and popped it into her mouth.

That wicked dimpled grin erupted again. "Guilty as well. Nothing better than a good hunk of bread, some cheese, and wine. Which reminds me."

He motioned to the waitress and ordered a bottle of the house red, but then quickly said, "If that's okay with you?"

"I'd love some. It was a tiring day." She gave him dating brownie points for asking her about the wine, belated as it was. But then again, the dating rules didn't apply if one wasn't on a date…only this was starting to feel too much like a date.

"Anything you'd care to talk about that would make your day less difficult?"

Owen would probably know what she'd faced today. She had no doubt he and his father were closely watching the Sinclair missteps. Particularly his father, who had likely been gleeful about their situation.

"We said we wouldn't talk about either business or family. My miserable day would definitely fall into both categories."

"What if I wasn't who I was? What if I was a friend? What would you tell me about your miserable day?"

Maggie had been eating her salad, but now she laid down her fork as she considered him. His features were serious, his gaze intense as it settled on her face, waiting for her answer. She smiled reluctantly and said, "We are friends, kind of. I mean, we've known each other forever. We've spent summers together, kind of. Went to the same college. We've been on the same committees in Sea Kiss."

"And I carried you to your dorm room after our first frat party when you thought that was only fruit punch," he said with a wry grin.

"Spiked with grain alcohol." She dragged a hand through her hair and looked away as heat warmed her cheeks. "That was so embarrassing."

"It could have been worse. At least you didn't toss your cookies all over me."

She chuckled, and Owen pressed ahead, clearly not dissuaded about her reluctance to share. "So tell me what's up."

She hesitated for a second before the words spilled from her mouth in a rush. "My father is driving me crazy, and overall, today has to be one of the suckiest days of my life, but it's nice to be able to relax and enjoy this meal."

He frowned, and that drew her immediate response.

"Something wrong with that?"

"I was hoping you'd say that it was nice to have dinner with a handsome, intelligent, and really funny—"

She cut him off with a slash of her hand. "Don't push it, Owen. I don't know you well enough to say whether you're intelligent and funny, much less *really* funny."

"But you'll give me that I'm handsome," he said, dimples blazing in a big grin.

"And modest, I see," she said with a pointed laugh and smiled, making it clear she was just teasing.

"*Can* you see, Maggie? Can you see past this sexy facade and everything that stands between us to the real me?" His words were almost wistful, but he flashed that playful smile at her again and fluttered his lush eyelashes in mock flirtation.

She laughed out loud, totally amused by his demeanor and the easy repartee. "*Damn*, Owen. This is a very different side of you that I hadn't noticed before."

He forked up the last of his salad and stopped with it halfway to his mouth. "Really? I thought I was a goofball as a kid also. But I guess you noticing is a good thing, right?"

"Definitely."

Chapter 5

"ARE YOU SURE YOU DON'T WANT DESSERT?" OWEN ASKED, loath for the night to end so soon.

"I wish. I've got to watch what I eat." Maggie covered her midsection with her hand and grinned.

The smile was one that was free of the earlier worry and brightened the blue of her gaze. It reminded him of the way the blue had shone when they were kids, playing on the beach.

He decided that her eyes were a barometer for her feelings, changing with her moods. He tucked away the memory of the happy hue so that he might draw it out again. It also occurred to him that he liked their earlier banter, and hunger grew inside him for more. He forged ahead, the tone of his voice low and slightly rough but still striving to be lighthearted. "From what I can see, it's all good. *Really* good."

Her gaze skipped over his face, as if she was trying to figure out just where they stood, and he hoped that she got the hint that the last place he wanted to be was in the friend zone. That was funny, considering that they'd started the night with a sort of friend truce because of the fight between their fathers. But for some time now, he'd been wondering about the sense of continuing with a feud that was decades old and really had nothing to do with either him or Maggie. It was all about a business deal gone wrong and a friend's betrayal.

Not to mention that lately, he'd been chomping at the bit to spend less time working and more time having a life. So why waste this opportunity that Fate had provided?

"If you're not up for dessert, how about some coffee?" he pressed.

She hesitated, her gaze questioning, but then she relaxed. "It's only a few blocks to my town house, and I just bought this new espresso machine since I'm addicted to lattes. I haven't had a chance to try it out."

"Too busy, huh? You know that all work and no play is not a good thing, right?"

"Says the man who is probably going to the office tomorrow," she teased as the waitress came over with the check.

Heat washed across Owen's cheeks. "Says the pot to the kettle," he shot back playfully, snared the check, and tucked his credit card inside.

Maggie leaned toward him and said, "This isn't a date, Owen. You don't have to pay my share."

"I know. Feel free to treat me to dessert, but I'm warning you. I have a ferocious sweet tooth."

"Yes, I remember the infamous cotton candy incident and the stomachache that followed after the annual Sea Kiss carnival."

The increase of heat across his cheeks felt like the touch of a blowtorch, but then again, that she remembered their fun times together was a good thing.

The waitress returned with the check, and Owen quickly signed it, stood, and held out his hand to Maggie. She slipped her hand into his, and as they strolled out, hand in hand, Toni and the two reporters followed their passage once again, but he didn't care. There would be talk, and it was sure to get back to their fathers, but he was enjoying his time with Maggie too much, and the feeling was obviously mutual.

He tightened his hold on Maggie's hand as they exited the restaurant, and a sharp gust of wind warned that a summer storm might be on the way. Applying gentle pressure, he drew her close and eased his arm around her waist. She fit perfectly against him, her rounded hip bumping his thigh while her equally flawless breast brushed the side of his chest as they walked.

Another gust of wind sent strands of her thick, wavy brown hair fluttering along his jaw, and the scent of a clean and flowery perfume filled his senses.

Gazing down at her, he noticed the peaceful smile on her face, so different from the slightly agitated look she'd had when they first sat down to eat. Her eyes were the deep blue of calm sea waters at night. It pleased him that their time together had accomplished that.

They walked in amiable silence, and when they passed a bakery a couple of blocks away, they decided to get dessert after all. Since there were just too many luscious items to choose from, they picked an assortment of sweets. Another block or so and they were at Maggie's town house right across from Gramercy Park.

It was quiet in this part of town, far removed from the Midtown business districts and tourist areas. A little haven that somehow suited her, he thought as she turned and walked through the wrought-iron gates enclosing a small garden in front of her brownstone. The garden was filled with an assortment of pots bursting with flowers in full summer bloom that spiced the air. The area reminded him of the gardens Maggie's grandmother had planted every year down at the Sinclair home in Sea Kiss. He wondered if that was why Maggie went through the trouble of creating this little oasis in the city.

As she walked through the space, she stretched out her hand and skimmed it across the blossoms closest to the stoop, rousing a lemony-sweet fragrance from them.

He followed her up the steps, enjoying the enticing sway of her hips as she walked and wondering where this unexpected encounter was going to lead.

Inside, she faced him and motioned to the living room. "Make yourself at home," she said as she peeled off her suit jacket and hung it on a coat rack in the front hall. She laid her keys in a bowl on a foyer table and walked into the space.

He did as she asked, following her to the kitchen where he placed the box with the pastries on the breakfast bar, whipped off his jacket, and draped it over one of the high stools tucked beneath the bar.

She immediately began fiddling with the gleaming and obviously new espresso machine on the counter on the opposite side of the kitchen. As she did so, Owen pulled out a stool and sat, then swiveled around to inspect her home, looking for more clues to the mystery that was Maggie.

It was definitely a home and not just a place where she hung her hat before returning to the office.

A long, narrow sofa table along one side of the room held a half dozen or so framed pictures of her mom and dad, as well as of her friends. A large glass vase boasted a collection of seashells, and as he examined the space, it occurred to him that while the room was elegant, it had a beach-house feel.

The walls were painted a weathered blue-gray shade like you'd find on the outside of a Sea Kiss cottage, and pops of bright yellows, whites, and an occasional coral red on seat cushions and pillows added to the coastal vibe.

The kitchen area was a sunny shade of yellow with gleaming white cabinets reminiscent of a beach cottage. The quartz counter was white, offset by a glass-tiled backsplash in soothing shades of ocean blues and greens.

The inside of her home, much like the garden outside, was designed as if she had wanted to bring a little piece of the Shore to Manhattan. And unlike his gleaming, modern-designer decor, her town house made him feel decidedly at home.

"I like your place," he said and gestured to the living room.

She glanced up from the espresso maker and snuck a quick look at him and then beyond to her space. With a smile, she said, "Thanks. It's been in the family for a long time. I know it doesn't have a fancy city feel—"

"I like it. It reminds me of Sea Kiss," he said.

"Yeah, it does. That's why I did it, I guess. I love being there, and I can't get down as much as I'd like."

"Me either," he said with a regretful sigh.

She shook her head and chuckled. "We're two of a kind, and not in a good way."

Definitely not in a good way, but change is always possible, he thought.

He popped open the bakery box, grabbed a cannoli, and walked to where she was making the coffee. He leaned against the counter alongside her and held the confection up to her mouth.

As she pushed a button on the coffee machine, she

faced him and glanced at the pastry, and then his lips, and then the pastry again. She took a tentative bite that left powdered sugar and ricotta cream all over her lower lip.

Tempting. Way too tempting, he thought as he finished off the rest of the pastry in two quick bites, all the time wondering if she would taste as good. He bent his head but stopped just short of her mouth.

"Since we seem to have so much in common," she began, meeting his gaze from beneath half-lowered lids, "I suspect that right now you're thinking way too much about how crazy this is, because that's exactly what I'm thinking."

"You'd be right," he admitted without moving, enjoying the way her fresh, warm breath spilled over his lips. His groin tightened at the thought of that luscious mouth doing delicious things as they made love.

"But what would be *really* right is exploring whatever is happening between us."

Before he could utter a word, she closed her mouth over his, her kiss light at first as she skimmed it across his lips but growing more urgent.

She opened her mouth on his, and she was so warm, so soft. Smooth.

When she teased him with a quick lick, he groaned and cupped the back of her head, keeping her close so he could return the caress. Licking her lips before dropping a line of kisses from the corner of her mouth to the center of her full lower lip.

It tasted as sweet as he'd imagined it would, and he deepened the kiss, nearly eating her up with the intensity of his lips exploring hers.

Maggie breathed in the scent of him, so clean and all male. She opened her mouth and accepted the slide of his tongue. Danced hers across his as he pressed his body close, and the long, hard ridge of his erection brushed the soft flatness of her belly.

Heat and wet filled her center, and she shifted her hips back and forth across him, an invitation for more. As insane as it might be to give in to the temptation, she needed to explore why he moved her as no one else ever had.

He groaned and bracketed her hips with his hands, pressing her near as he rocked his hips along hers.

"Maggie," he whispered, and she didn't need to hear more to understand what he wanted, because she wanted it too.

She hopped up and wrapped her legs around his waist, whispering, "Living room."

With long, easy strides, he moved them around the breakfast bar and to the center of the sectional sofa, but he never stopped kissing her.

As he eased her down to the sofa and stretched out over her body, something crashed to the floor, and they bolted apart, breathing heavily.

Maggie looked down at what Owen had knocked off a side table by the sofa—a crystal bowl filled with seashells. Shattered glass and shells were strewn across the polished wood floor like a portent of lives broken by careless action.

Like carelessly giving in to the temptation that was Owen.

"I'm sorry," he said, then he pushed off from the sofa and bent to pick up the shells and bits of broken glass.

Maggie sat up abruptly and dragged her fingers through her hair to draw the strands off her face. She could feel the heat there, both of desire and growing embarrassment.

"You're sorry? About the bowl or about something else?" she said defiantly.

The woeful look he provided spoke volumes.

She shot to her feet and grabbed hold of his hand as he reached for another piece of broken glass.

"Leave it. I can take care of it," she said.

As his gaze met hers, she knew he understood what she wasn't saying: that he could leave because she was a big girl and could take care of herself.

He clearly wasn't about to let it go without getting his two cents in. "As much as I want to explore this attraction between us, we both know that this is where it could lead." He motioned to the bits of broken and scattered shells on the floor. "Our lives, in pieces, for all the world to see."

"I didn't take you for a coward, Owen," she replied with a cheeky tilt of her chin.

A dull flush erupted across his cheeks at her challenge. "And I always suspected you were stubborn, Mags."

She lifted her chin another rebellious inch. "Only my friends call me Mags."

"A long time ago, we used to be friends," he said, and the side of his mouth quirked up with the hint of a determined smile.

"We used to be, but then you left," she said, recalling the loss she had felt at his absence.

"I never wanted to stay away, but I didn't have a

choice," he said and then hesitated, clearly torn before leaning toward her. He kissed her again, hard and demanding. Almost bruising with the intensity of it before he jerked away and said, "You'll thank me in the morning."

Without waiting for her reply, he strode to the door and left.

Maggie winced as the door slammed shut. She hugged herself tightly, a sudden emptiness within her now that he was gone. If Owen could have her feeling like that with just a few amazing kisses, what would it feel like if they did take it further and the world around them shattered just like the shells and glass littering the floor?

As she bent and started picking up the pieces, it occurred to her that maybe she should thank him for being so sensible.

That maybe he had been right to stop when he did—until the little voice inside her head said, "Coward."

Only that little voice wasn't referring to Owen.

Chapter 6

INSIDE HIS SKULL, A THOUSAND CON ED JACKHAMMERS were pounding away at what little was left of his brain. Owen had spent a very restless, sleepless night thanks to erotic thoughts of where last night could have led with Maggie if he hadn't allowed common sense and responsibility to rule.

That's who he was, Mr. Boring and Reliable, as his brother, Jonathan, liked to chastise way too often. Owen Pierce, always the one you can count on to do the right thing, Jonathan would say and then jet off to Paris or Antarctica or wherever to promote another of his company's innovative designs.

But even his brother, who thought Owen needed more excitement in his life, knew that anything to do with Maggie was far riskier than racing electric cars on the Bonneville Salt Flats or flying across the Atlantic in a solar-powered plane.

Although he'd always wondered why it had become so risky. As he'd told her last night, they'd been friends a long time ago when they were both so young, and he hadn't wanted to stay away. But then her mother had died, and his own family life had started going to shit. They'd stopped visiting the shore for years until their mother had left and his father had sent them back to Sea Kiss for the summer season, either unable or unwilling to deal with two active boys who were off from school. That return to the Shore had come with a warning about mingling with the Sinclairs and the threat of not being allowed to return to Sea Kiss if they defied their father's wishes.

Hurting from the loss of Maggie, his mother's desertion, and his father's bitterness, Sea Kiss was the one stable thing in his life, and he hadn't wanted to risk its loss.

After that and their one ill-fated summer night's kiss at eighteen, both he and Maggie had been consumed with their studies and mindful of their fathers' wishes. But their more recent encounters had sent heat and protectiveness and need and way too many other sensations cascading wildly over him, making him want to forget common sense for a change.

Jonathan had been right over a month ago when he'd warned that getting involved with Maggie could only lead to pain. *And a whopper of a headache*, he thought as he picked up a supersize cup of coffee and a bagel at a local deli before entering the skyscraper where his family's business was located.

With a forced smile at the guard in the lobby, he keyed himself through the security turnstiles and walked to the elevators. Forty-some floors later, he let himself into the Pierce Holdings' offices and was eternally grateful that no one had decided to come into work.

What idiot would on a gorgeous Saturday like today? the little voice in his head chastised, but he ignored it and kept up the march to his office.

Once there, standing at his windows and staring down at the huge expanse of Central Park, he couldn't argue with that annoying little voice anymore about being an idiot. From his office high above the city, he had a multimillion-dollar view. Central Park. Uptown to where a brand-new Pierce Holdings condo complex sat right on the edge of the Harlem Meer.

But that amazing view was a pricy perch that somehow made him feel like a caged canary. Especially on a beautiful Saturday like this one, when he could have been out for a run on the beach or riding a nice wave. Or maybe just sitting on the great lawn, having a coffee while reading a good book and soaking up some sun. Only he couldn't even remember the last time he'd read anything other than a business journal or taken a Saturday off for that matter. Which just served to remind him of Maggie again and how she had teased him the night before about coming to work today.

He wondered if she was also at work or enjoying some time off. He considered how the day might have started pleasantly for both of them if last night had ended differently. How it would have gotten better if it had started with some very satisfying good-morning sex and breakfast in bed followed by maybe even more sex.

All those thoughts had him getting hard with visions of naked Maggie that, in turn, had the jackhammers going off in his skull once more, reminding him of how complicated it could get to have Maggie in his life.

He shook his head to clear away the noise, winced, and hurried to his desk where he put down the bag with breakfast and reached into a drawer for some aspirin. After downing the medicine with a mouthful of way too hot coffee, he opened the file with the agreement he had started reviewing the night before and grabbed his bagel, wishing that the local deli would carry pork roll to add some flavor, but that was just too Jersey for the city folk.

He mindlessly gobbled down the bagel as he read the

document. When he was done hours later, the jackhammers in his head had dwindled to the occasional thud of a pile driver. He grabbed his tablet, put his feet up on his desk, and flipped through assorted financial websites to check up on how the markets had finished and what people were saying about the Sinclair earnings report. He'd known it hadn't been good, judging from Maggie's mood, but he hadn't really expected that it would be that bad. Whoever had leaked the report clearly had an ax to grind with the Sinclairs.

The retail division losses were eating up any profits from their real estate division. Worse yet, the projections indicated that those losses were going to increase in the coming year. Shareholders who weren't reaping any rewards were not going to want to continue shoring up the retail division against those losses, especially since they could be making a tidy sum instead on the real estate business and on the sale of the store locations.

My father must be ecstatic, he thought. Like conjuring an evil spirit by daring to say its name, his father appeared in the outer office, a newspaper tucked under the arm of his dark-blue pinstriped Brooks Brothers suit. He wondered if his father owned any other type of clothing or if he'd popped out of the womb in a dark-blue suit.

As he watched his father stride toward him, it hit him that his father hadn't always been that uptight and anal. Not that he had been the fun dad or even the cool dad when he and Jonathan were little. His father had always been on the demanding side, with rarely a smile on his face.

Although Owen could remember a few times he'd seemed happy. Usually at Sea Kiss when they'd run into

Maggie and her mom on the beach. A memory came unbidden of one of those days.

He, Jonathan, and Maggie had just finished building an immense sand castle, complete with a moat that was slowly filling as the tide moved in. Maggie's mom had been with them, praising their accomplishments, when his dad had marched down in his suit and dress shoes, a dour expression on his face until...

Until he'd seen Maggie's mother with them. He'd stopped calling their names and curbed his pace until he stood by them, and slowly, ever so slowly, a smile had crept onto his face.

He suddenly remembered Maggie's mom teasing his father about ruining his dress shoes as the wash of a wave inched toward the expensive leather. It had dragged a chuckle from him and a promise that he'd dress more appropriately next time.

They'd lingered there together, the children trying to protect the castle from the encroaching water. Maggie's mother and his father had stood there, chatting amiably, like old friends. The animosity between the families forgotten in the bright sun of a summer's day on Sea Kiss Beach.

Special times like that one had been few and far between. After their mother abandoned the family, his father had gotten far worse with his demands and hostility.

Owen was pulled back to the present as his father marched to Owen's desk and eyeballed Owen's casual clothes and relaxed stance with disdain. With a grim smile, he yanked the newspaper free and slapped it onto Owen's desk.

"I thought my day was perfect when I heard about the Sinclair earnings reports, and then I saw this."

"Good afternoon, Father," Owen said, eased his feet to the floor, and slowly straightened in his chair. As he did so, he realized that the paper was open to the gossip section. The first article was about his impromptu dinner with Maggie and featured a grainy cell phone photo of them smiling and holding hands as they walked out of the restaurant.

"So is it true? You and that Sinclair woman had dinner? Together?" his father said, icy derision chilling every word. It was a tone Owen knew well but that was usually reserved for one of Jonathan's newsworthy escapades. Come to think of it, this was Owen's first time as the center of attention in the gossip column, which was both uncomfortable and exciting.

Take that, Jon. Not so boring and reliable anymore, he thought before answering his father calmly.

"Maggie and I had dinner. Big deal."

His father's bushy, silver-gray eyebrows flew upward. "Maggie now, is it? When did the two of you get so chummy?"

"Father, we've known each other since we were kids. Of course I call her Maggie," he replied, his frustration growing with every word.

Cold, gray eyes narrowing, his father considered him carefully, making him feel like the proverbial bug under a microscope. A bug that his father delighted in squishing in one way or another whenever he could. It made him worry, because his sharp-eyed father was sure to notice that something was different, even if, at the end of the day, nothing had really happened with Maggie, though a part of him wished it had.

"You're up to something, Owen. You never were

a good liar." His father beat an angry rhythm with his hands on the arms of the chair, and a tic pulsed along his jaw as he ground his teeth together.

No, he wasn't, but if he was going to deal with what was happening or not happening with Maggie, he'd have to think of something and quickly. That's when it hit him.

"You always told me that, Father. You also told me time and time again that I wasn't very ruthless considering I was your son."

"You're not. If you were *truly* my son, you'd have found a way to put the final nail in the Sinclairs' coffin."

While his father didn't actually wring his hands like the evil villain in a bad B movie, Owen could picture him doing just that. His father had become as one-dimensional as one of those movie villains with his focus solely on one thing—destroying the Sinclairs.

"Why do you still hate them so?"

His father jerked back as if struck, but then regained his composure and glowered at Owen as he said, "You know why. Her father was my best friend. My partner. Those properties were very valuable to the business we had together."

But the properties hadn't gone to the business the two men had owned together at the time, Owen thought. Bryce Sinclair had gifted the real estate to his newlywed wife for the expansion of her family's stores.

Glancing away for a moment, because his father's unwavering scrutiny was becoming unsettling, he said, "The banks won't be loaning them any more money, so Maggie needs someone who can provide the funding. Someone like me, but Maggie's not stupid."

His father wagged his head, a confused look on his face. "I'm not following you, Owen."

"Maggie needs to believe that I'm a friend. That I care about her and want to help. Once I accomplish that, I'll offer her a deal she can't refuse," he said, formulating a plan on the fly and hoping that would be enough to convince his father.

A heavy silence followed as his father continued examining him, looking for any telltale signs about what Owen truly intended. But then, surprisingly, his father relaxed, smiled, and actually did rub his hands together with villainous satisfaction.

"I didn't think you had it in you, Owen. But I'm not sure you can pull it off."

"I can, Father. I'm your son after all," he said, even if the words made his gut twist with disgust. He didn't like lying, but being able to explore what was happening with Maggie was worth the deceit.

His father rose from his chair and jabbed a pointy finger in Owen's direction. "Make sure that you do, because if you don't—"

"You'll do what? Disown me? Cut me off the way you cut off Jonathan?" he said, but the answer was clear from his father's face.

"Don't disappoint me, Owen," he warned, but his voice wavered a bit, almost as if he was fearful that Owen would.

Hope sprang into Owen that his father might actually reconsider, but then with a sharp glare, he tacked on, "You're the only son I have left."

Without a second's pause, his father stomped out of Owen's office, leaving him to consider his father's threat. Seven years earlier, his father had disinherited Jonathan after he had refused to return to college and begun his adventurous ways. His father's parting shot and cold stare confirmed that he would do the same if Owen defied him.

Could I handle that? he wondered. For too long, his identity had been tied to his position at Pierce Holdings. His income had been tied to the company as well, although because he was as anal and responsible as his brother teased, he had built a tidy little nest egg for himself. He had enough to survive being disowned if money alone was the issue, but it wasn't.

He liked what he did. He wanted to steer the course of the company for the future, and to do so, he had to please his father.

Even if it keeps you from having a real life? the little voice in his head challenged.

Sadly, Owen wasn't sure if he'd know what a real life was if it bit him on the ass, but he sure would love to find out what it might be like, especially if it included Maggie Sinclair.

Chapter 7

WHEN THE GOING GOT TOUGH, THE TOUGH CALLED FOR AN emergency meeting of best friends, minus Tracy of course, since she was the reason for the emergency meeting.

The bottle of cabernet was open and breathing on the breakfast bar. A backup bottle was close at hand, along with champagne, just in case some celebrating was in order. Connie's West Coast trip had been for a client trying to finalize a merger. Maggie hoped the meeting had gone well.

Grabbing a tray with cheese and crackers, she strolled to the coffee table and placed the tray there. She hesitantly sat on the sofa and nervously rubbed her hands across her thighs as she remembered what had happened there days earlier. If one soul-searing kiss—okay, make that more than one—could make her feel so awkward, what would happen if they had taken it further?

Would she have to redecorate to erase the sinfully delicious memories?

As it was, she'd had to repurpose another bowl to hold the shells that had survived that night's misadventure. The shells she'd once gathered with such love on Sea Kiss Beach now mocked her failure with Owen.

Owen, she thought, and her gut roiled with a mix of need and fear.

Damn it, fear, she acknowledged, hating that Tracy had been right.

She was afraid of her fascination with Owen. Afraid of dealing with it the way anyone would when they were attracted to someone else. Well, at least how anyone would if they weren't a coward.

But then again, she had reason to be afraid. She'd lost her mother, and the pain of it was still with her. She knew it was still with her father. On the heels of her mother's loss, there had been the absence of Owen and Jonathan for years and the distance between them. Add to it the fear that if Owen and she became close again, it wouldn't last, or that, if it did, it would be messy and complicated.

If she wasn't so concerned about Tracy and her situation, she'd want to strangle her for creating the brain equivalent of an ear worm. Forcing that recurring thought from her head, she tidied the cushions on the sofa. Again.

By the time she'd brought the wine and glasses over, someone was ringing the doorbell.

She hurried over and threw open the door.

Emma was there, hands loaded down with an overnight bag and a tray of pastries that she thrust at Maggie.

"Connie always wants sweets, and we had a bunch left over from the afternoon engagement party. Lots of women trying to lose weight for the wedding means more goodies for us," she said with an easy smile.

"Did Carlo make them?" Maggie asked as she brushed a kiss across Emma's cheek.

Emma's smile brightened, and a dazzling gleam erupted in her gaze. "Of course. Who else but my fabulous caterer?"

"Who else?" Maggie repeated with a knowing grin and walked to the kitchen to put the pastries in the fridge.

When she returned, Emma had already tossed her bag by the side table and comfortably plopped herself on the sofa, her legs tucked beneath the hem of her dress. She reached for the wine, poured herself a glass, held the bottle up in the air, and said, "Want some?"

"More like need some," Maggie replied and took a spot in the chair opposite her friend.

"Rough week?" Emma asked, although her observant, green-eyed gaze normally didn't miss a thing. That perceptiveness had served her well in her wedding planner role.

"Rough few days," Maggie said, but she didn't get to expand on it further as the doorbell rang again. She stood to open the door, but Connie tossed it wide and marched in, bag in one hand, bottle of Cuervo in the other.

She waggled the bottle in the air. "Definitely going to need this. Working on a Sunday's always a bitch. Having to deal with Tracy on top of that…"

Maggie hugged her friend hard, snared the bottle from her, closed the door, and steered her toward the couch. "Take a load off and start with a glass of wine."

Connie walked to Emma, bent, and embraced her before settling into the spot next to her on the sofa.

"Does the fact that you're still in your suit mean you came straight from the office?" Emma asked.

Connie nodded and eyeballed her friend. "And you look done up for a big gig. I'm assuming you came straight from there, which I hope means Carlo goodness for us."

Emma grinned and ran her hand across the very feminine and yet demure floral motif dress. The bright summer colors were the perfect foil to her strawberry-blond hair and cat-green eyes. "It does, and I can see you need it after the Tracy thing."

Maggie walked to the breakfast bar separating the kitchen from the living room, placed the tequila bottle there, and hurried back to her chair. "Tracy was in rough shape when I saw her on Friday," she began. "Any better today?"

Connie shrugged and grimaced. "She's still hurting, and who can blame her?"

Although the question was rhetorical, Emma shot up her hand. "We tried to warn her. Repeatedly. She wouldn't see what was right in front of her face."

"She was in love. You know how much Tracy wants that happily ever after," Maggie said in defense.

"I got the feeling she was kind of cured of that kind of fairy tale after today," Connie said and looked down at the wineglass as if searching for an answer.

"What do you mean?" Emma asked.

With another shrug, Connie raised her gaze and skipped it from Maggie to Emma, and then back to Maggie again. "She's different this time. More settled. Less Tracy."

Something clenched in Maggie's gut with that statement. As much as Tracy's romantic spectacles had been alternately amusing and worrisome, there had always been something uplifting and hopeful about Tracy's unflappable belief in romance.

"Will she be okay?" she asked.

"Yeah, will she be okay?" Emma chimed in, worry darkening the green of her eyes to an emerald hue as she bit her lip. Emma might seem tough on the outside, but when it came to those she loved, she was all marshmallow gooeyness.

Connie sipped her wine thoughtfully and eyed the two of them with a penetrating stare. "She said I could share our discussion with you because we will be there for her."

Maggie and Emma both nodded and said, "We will."

Connie did a slow bob of her head and continued. "She and Bill had a long talk, and they've agreed to go to counseling together. She said she's tired of being the drama queen and wants to make the marriage work. That she needs to grow up."

"Not your typical Tracy response, is it?" Emma said with obvious concern.

"No, not at all," Connie replied. "It makes me wonder if she's really serious this time about changing. She was so much more…"

As Connie's voice trailed off, Maggie jumped in with "Thoughtful?"

"Tracy? Thoughtful?" Emma said, sarcasm finally leaking into her tone.

"At lunch, she admitted that she should have listened to us. She also told me the same thing. That she was determined to make this marriage work." Deliberating whether to continue, Maggie finally added, "She said something else too. Something that got me to wondering."

"About what?" Connie pressed when Maggie hesitated.

"About us. About men or our lack thereof. She said we're still alone because we're all afraid." She avoided their gazes as she delivered that message, because she feared what she might see there.

After a stunned minute of silence, Connie and Emma finally fought back.

"No way," Emma said at the same time as Connie complained, "She doesn't know what she's talking about."

As much as Maggie wanted to join her friends in that denial, since the lunch, she had been thinking about Tracy's observation and that maybe there was some truth to it. "I'm not sure she's so wrong. If I'm honest with myself, it scares me to think about losing someone the way my dad lost my mom," she said, her voice tight with emotion.

Connie and Emma both leaned toward her and offered their hands to hold. She took hold and graced them with a teary smile. "I'm okay, but it was tough back then. Mom was gone, and I felt like I had lost my dad as well. He was always working and hardly ever around."

She kept to herself the loss she'd felt as a child when Owen and Jonathan had not returned the summer after her mother's death. If not for her grandmother and Mrs. Patrick, their housekeeper, she would have been all alone to deal with her losses. The two older women had been there for her in Sea Kiss, providing support throughout her life.

"That's not unreasonable," Emma said and gave a reassuring squeeze of Maggie's hand.

"Just like it's not unreasonable that after what you went through with your mom and dad's breakup, you'd be a little leery."

A flush of angry color rose to Emma's cheeks. "Who wouldn't be? You think you know someone after eighteen years of marriage, and they up and leave you. Steal every penny you have."

Maggie nodded and stared at Connie, who had gone silent once again. "I know you worry about being like your mom."

"I love my mom," she shot back, her features filling with a maelstrom of anger and guilt that she had been the reason for her mother's dreams going unfulfilled. Connie's mother had sacrificed going to college in order to care and provide for her newborn child.

"I know you do, but you don't think you can have a successful career and a relationship too, right?"

Yet more silence greeted her until Connie gazed at her shrewdly and said, "I think Tracy's comment challenged you to do something crazy, like test the waters with Owen. So what's up with him?"

Emma chimed in with, "Yeah, you looked real chummy in that photo."

"Nothing happened, but I can't deny that he's handsome. Smart. Funny, but not *really* funny." She stopped and smiled, recalling the carefree exchange during dinner.

"OMFG, she is *really* hot for Owen. Smart women, foolish choices," Emma said with traces of awe and concern in her tones.

"What normal woman wouldn't find him attractive? I mean, he's like a *GQ* god. Romance novel billionaire sexy," she said and fanned her face.

"And he's the son of your father's enemy," Connie added, worry coloring her every word.

Maggie considered her friend's admonishment and shrugged. "Since I have no intention of my thing with Owen going anywhere, there's no sense in talking about it anymore."

"Smart woman," Emma said with a confirming bob of her head and took another sip of her wine.

Maggie did the same, but as her gaze briefly crossed with Connie's, there was no doubt that her friend sensed there was a lot more to the story that they hadn't heard. But that was just too much information and still too fresh and confusing in her own mind, because no matter how much she wanted to deny it…

She was wondering what it would be like to be foolish for a change.

Chapter 8

I'M NOT LOOKING FOR HIM, MAGGIE TOLD HERSELF AS SHE peered into the mirror in the weight room and did a set of bicep curls. Behind her, fellow gym members came and went, many of them familiar, since they all seemed to exercise at the same time on a regular basis. Just like Owen did.

She had seen him on the Monday after their fateful encounter, and they'd exchanged a smile and hello head bob, but nothing more. They both seemed to understand that starting anything would be difficult, and yet, she couldn't stop thinking about starting something.

Tuesday had come and gone with no sight of him, as had this morning.

She finished her weight training and headed to the treadmills for a quick jog. The noise was louder here with the *slap-slap-slap* of a flat-footed runner, the smells a little sharper thanks to runners' sweat.

She was about to step onto one of the treadmills when Owen hurried in and spotted her.

Her heart raced as he walked toward her, a very sexy and masculine swagger in his step. He was wearing fitted running shorts that hugged lean and beautifully sculpted legs. A sleeveless T-shirt exposed toned arms and hung loose over his flat belly.

"Hi, Mags," he said.

The *lub-dub* of her heart tripped a beat.

"Hello, Owen. It's good to see you," she said but stepped back from him, earning a puzzled look.

"Then why do you seem so skittish? Does this mean our friend truce is over?"

She scrutinized the gym and noticed a few acquaintances who would recognize both her and Owen. Maybe even some who would report to their fathers or another of the gossip rags.

"The truce isn't over, but this isn't really a good time or place, Owen."

"Time or place for what?" he asked with a sexy grin, arched a midnight-black brow, and leaned closer.

She laid her hand on his chest to urge him to keep his distance. His body was hard beneath her palm, and he was close enough that she could smell his cologne mingling with his very masculine scent.

"For this. For you and me. I'm just here to work out," she said. Not entirely true, since she had been looking for him and wondering about their relationship.

"Does that mean there might be another time that would be right for this? For you and me?" he asked, motioning between the two of them with an index finger.

She shook her head. "We said it was possible to be friends. Maybe that's all this should be," she said, repeating his move by pointing between the two of them.

"Just friends, huh?"

"It's what makes sense, Owen. You were right the other night when you stopped."

"What if I was wrong? What if this is something worth exploring?"

The thought of more was enticing but scary. "I've

really got to go. I've got an early morning meeting," she said and rushed past him.

———〰———

Owen watched her go and, on some level, understood.

After all, he'd walked out on her days earlier when common sense had intruded on their very pleasurable interlude.

In the days since, she'd stayed on his mind, in large part because he wasn't sure he wanted to be just friends with her. Another part, the one he really didn't want to acknowledge, was the lie he'd perpetuated with his father. A lie necessitated by Maggie's allure and his desire to see more of her.

And not just as a friend, he thought, recalling the passionate way she had responded to him and just how close they'd gotten to exploring that passion.

The pressure building inside his tight running shorts warned him to get his mind off Maggie before he embarrassed himself in front of the whole gym.

He took a deep breath to wrestle his need under control and hurried to the treadmill, hoping that he could run thoughts of Maggie right out of his brain.

———〰———

"This doesn't make any sense, Dad," Maggie said as she reviewed the terms for the deal her father wanted to finalize.

"We've been buying from them for years, Maggie," her father said in a tone both indulgent and firm.

"They sell these very same products to Macy's and JCPenney, only they get better pricing because of the volume of their buy. We have to sell them for more or do a deep discount that eats away at our profits. If we can't get the same pricing, we need to consider another vendor."

Her father raised a gray-haired eyebrow in challenge. "Do you think you can do better on the pricing?"

"I think we can go with a more upscale brand at a slightly higher price. People used to expect better quality at our stores, and they were willing to pay a little more for that quality. Since they haven't been getting it lately, they're going to our competitors for the cheaper prices," she said and boldly tossed the contract to the edge of her desk.

Her father placed his hands on his knees and slowly pushed himself to his feet. "I'm sorry you feel this way, but I've already committed to this deal."

"It's not signed yet from what I can see. No reason you can't go back to them and explain our concerns. If you don't want to do it, I will. I have no problem playing hardball with them."

He folded his hands before him and met her gaze, his blue eyes, so much like her own, simmering with anger. "What makes you think they will agree to different terms?"

With an indifferent shrug, she tilted her head up rebelliously. "It doesn't matter to me if they don't. I have another vendor with better merchandise who'd be ecstatic to be in our stores. It's what we have to do, Dad. We need to restore our image of better quality at competitive prices."

It was an argument they'd had more than once, and as he had repeatedly done, he'd shot her down. Today was no different.

"I can't risk losing this vendor. We've had too long a history with them, and anyone else would be an unacceptable unknown." He swept the contract up off her desk and walked out, leaving her fuming as she stared at his retreating back.

She was so angry she was trembling and had to sit down to keep from running after him and snatching the contract out of his hands. After a few calming breaths and a quick look at her watch to confirm the time, she picked up the phone and dialed Connie. Since her friend's law firm office was in the annex to the Chrysler Building, they regularly got together for lunch.

"Lunch? Tudor City Greens?" she said, more curtly than she intended, when her friend answered.

"Another bad day?" Connie asked.

"Another one. I'll meet you in your lobby?"

"Give me five minutes, and I'll be there."

She grabbed her purse from a bottom desk drawer and walked to the anteroom of her office.

"I'm taking a break for lunch, Sheila. Please don't call me on the cell unless it's urgent, and by urgent, I mean—"

"Someone is bleeding or about to die," Sheila said with a smile. "I get it, boss lady. You deserve a break."

She deserved something else. *Anything else*, she thought as she took the elevator down to the lobby and then walked through the underground arcade connecting the Chrysler Building to what had formerly been the Kent Building. It was now the annex to the expanded Chrysler Center.

She greeted the security guards in the lobby as she waited for her friend, and as promised, Connie joined her just a few minutes later.

They hugged, and that simple embrace immediately

loosened some of the tension in her body caused by the confrontation with her father.

"Thanks. I needed that," she said.

"Anytime, my friend," Connie replied.

Tudor City was just a short two-block walk, and as they strolled down Forty-Second Street, they stopped at one of the sandwich shops and bought food and drinks for a picnic lunch in one of the parks in that area.

When they were halfway between First and Second Avenues, they climbed the stairs up to where Tudor City Greens was located, walked into one of the parks, and luckily found a bench beneath some shade trees. When the weather was nice, it was sometimes tough to find a free place to sit down.

The leaves on the trees were lush and thick, providing protection from the strong summer sun. The scent from a nearby honeysuckle vine spiced the air, and mounds of flowers filled the beds of the park.

They sat slightly apart, leaving room on the bench between them for their sandwiches, chips, and sodas. Because Connie understood her all too well, she waited until Maggie had eaten some of her sandwich and calmed down a bit before speaking.

"You really shouldn't let him get to you like that."

Maggie nodded and took another bite of her sandwich. With some of her upset subsided, she was able to enjoy the flavors of the Black Forest ham, creamy brie, arugula, and honey mustard. After she swallowed, she said, "I know. It's just that I've reached the breaking point with my dad. He won't listen to a thing, even though it's a reasonable suggestion. He just wants to do things the way he's always done things."

"The way he thinks your mother would have done things," Connie said intuitively, dragging another nod from Maggie.

"Yes, only my mother would have been smart enough to evolve as the market changed. Or at least I think so based on what others have told me about her." She'd barely been eight when her mother had died in childbirth, leaving Maggie with only distant memories of what she'd been like.

A thoughtful silence followed as they both ate again, a bit of sandwich followed by salty chips, soda to soothe thirst. She was almost done with her lunch when Connie said, "There may be things you can legally do if your father won't listen."

Maggie mulled over Connie's statement but feared the repercussions on both personal and professional levels.

Every day, it seemed more and more that Tracy had been right about what was holding her back.

"Do you think we let fear keep us from doing things?"

"Things?" Connie said. "Like what kinds of things?"

"Like my standing up to my father. Taking the time to find Mr. Right."

"I get the sense that you're ready to deal with your father. There's too much at stake for you not to," Connie said and finished off her soda with a large gulp. "And neither of us has the time for romance right now."

"Is it really about finding the time, or is it that you don't want to be like your mom?"

"I love my mom, but she made a foolish choice that stole her dreams," Connie said, looked down, and fiddled nervously with the fabric of her suit pants.

Maggie placed her thumb and forefinger beneath her

friend's chin and applied gentle pressure to urge her face upward. "*You* were that choice, and I don't think your mother regrets having you for a single moment."

"I know she loves me, and I love her. I just don't want to be *like* her, which means staying on course until I get what I want."

"A partnership in your firm," Maggie said.

"A partnership. I'm this close," she said and, to demonstrate, sized an almost nonexistent distance between her thumb and forefinger.

Maggie nodded. "I hope you get what you want." But she also hoped that if love came along, her friend wouldn't ignore it. A partnership didn't keep you warm on a cold winter's night. Which made her think about her own complicated situation.

"Do you think Owen is a foolish choice?"

Connie delayed for a bit, obviously giving the question a good amount of thought. With a shake of her head and a light laugh, she said, "Owen may be a difficult choice, but he isn't a foolish one. On the other hand, his brother, Jonathan? Totally foolish choice. That bad boy spells 'trouble' with a capital T-R-O-U-B-L-E."

A loud chuckle burst from Maggie. "Jonathan does have that whole James Dean rebel thing going on. Totally not my type."

"Or mine," Connie shot back quickly.

Maybe too quickly, Maggie considered as she examined her friend. Connie had always been über-responsible and über-determined. Jonathan was just the kind of man to shake up all that über-by-the-bookness.

"So what should I do, Counselor?" she asked.

"About your dad or Owen?" Connie replied as she

gathered up the trash from their picnic lunch. Some potato chip crumbs hit the ground, and in a burst of activity, a few industrious sparrows swooped in to eat them, dragging laughs from both of them.

"We should be more like those birds and just seize the moment when it happens," Maggie said.

"And after you seize Owen, Emma and I want a full report on all the sexy smoochies," Connie said and rose from the bench.

Maggie rolled her eyes, stood, and walked with her friend to the entrance of the park. As they reached the gates to exit, she stopped and faced her friend. "You do remember that whole Romeo and Juliet thing ended badly, right?"

Connie held up her hand and started counting down. "One, they were teenagers. Two, you're not in Verona. Three, you don't have to rely on a monk with a donkey to deliver your message. You can just text him. Or better yet, sext him."

She wrinkled her nose. "I hate sexting."

Connie grinned and nodded. "Yeah, it's much better to reach out and touch someone. So reach out. Touch. A lot."

Maggie playfully elbowed her friend. "You're incorrigible."

"It's why you love me," Connie said and slipped her arm through Maggie's. She urged her out of the park, down the block, and to the footbridge that ran across Forty-Second Street.

They paused in the middle to take in the view of Queens and Long Island on the East Side and turned to see all the way westward along the street to the Palisades in New Jersey.

With a sigh, Connie said, "I love this view. Sometimes, I imagine I can see my place in Jersey from here."

Connie's condo wasn't all that far as the crow flies. Just right through the Lincoln Tunnel and to her place in Jersey City. Not all that far from Union City, where her grandparents had settled after escaping Cuba and where she and her mother had both been born and bred.

"Always a Jersey girl," Maggie teased.

"Always, just like you. You may live here, but your heart is in Sea Kiss."

Since she couldn't deny it, she said, "Yes, it is. Maybe we can head down there this weekend for a girls' retreat." She drove from her mind that those weekends might come to an end if she couldn't repay the mortgage on the home.

"You say the word and I'm there," Connie said with a smile as they walked across the rest of the footbridge and down to the street below. They strolled slowly up toward the Chrysler Center and their offices.

"In the meantime, I need your help with the stores."

Her friend stopped short and stared at her shrewdly. "You really want to know what you can do legally?"

"I do. I need to be able to run the stores in the way I think will work, and I'm tired of giving in to my dad. I need to seize the moment," Maggie said, and inside her, something broke free. Her spirit grew lighter at the thought of finally doing what she knew in her heart to be right, as painful as it might be.

Connie nodded. "Okay. I'll take a look at everything and call you to discuss."

Maggie nodded firmly. "That sounds like a plan."

They walked along in silence, but when they reached

the lobby of Connie's building, her friend faced her, smirking.

"You know what else you have to seize, don't you?" Connie said.

Maggie shot her hand up to foreclose any further discussion. "Call me when you're ready to talk about the stores."

Connie pointed at her. "And you call me if there's any MagOwen action going on."

She rolled her eyes. "For God's sake, we're not a celebrity couple."

"You're rich and beautiful, so you're tabloid worthy. Would you prefer OwenMag? Or what about SinPierce? Maybe…"

Maggie raced off, leaving Connie playing around with mash-up names while she waited for the elevator.

As she reached her own bank of elevators, she decided no mash-up was necessary. Just Owen. Very seize-worthy, sexy Owen.

But as she had told him just that morning, the two of them together just didn't make any sense, and she prided herself on being sensible and responsible. Plus, if there was one thing about which she intended to defy her father, it was the stores.

Carpe Owen would just have to wait for another *diem*.

Chapter 9

SINCE MAGGIE HAD BASICALLY TOLD HIM TO LEAVE HER BE, he had done just that when he had run into her at the gym the last few mornings. Just a casual greeting before each went their separate way to either the weight room or cardio center. Although he had to admit to positioning himself at one of the treadmills where he could watch her do her strength training.

He allowed himself an office daydream about the sight of her toned but lushly curved body. Thoughts of her were just too hard to resist. A loud, gravelly cough and the sharp exclamation of his name dragged him from his workplace reverie faster than you could say, "Hello, Father."

Owen planted his feet firmly on the floor and swiveled to face his dad, who stood before his desk, bony, age-spotted hands clasped before him tightly. Those telltale markings made him take a moment to scrutinize his father, and when he did so, it occurred to him that his dad had aged quite a bit in the last few years. Even though he had just turned sixty, he looked far older thanks to his thinning hair and the sallow complexion of his skin. The forward hunch of his head and shoulders had shaved a few inches off his six-foot-plus height. The dark, lifeless suit he wore not only worsened his complexion, but also hung loose on him, increasing the impression of sickliness.

It showed what bitterness and unhappiness could do to a person physically.

"Are you feeling okay, Father?" he asked, genuine concern pushing aside any anger he might have about the way his dad generally behaved. No matter what, family should come first, which just added another reason to why he had to make sure everything worked out. He could risk his own assets in a new company, lose his place in a business he'd helped build, but he couldn't walk away if his father was not well.

"I'd be a lot better if I knew what was going on with you and that Sinclair girl," he said, impatience dripping from every word.

Deep breath, Owen, he told himself and braced his hands on the arms of his chair. After a second deep inhalation, he slouched back into the leather and adopted what he hoped his father would see as an "I don't give a shit" posture.

Tone neutral, features displaying what he trusted was calm restraint, he said, "Nothing is going on at the moment, Father."

Head dancing up and down on his scrawny neck, reminding Owen of one of those bobblehead dolls they gave away at baseball games, his father smiled smugly. "I guess you're not as charming as you thought, Owen."

He dug his fingers into the arms of the chair and resisted the urge to wipe that arrogant smile off his father's face. After another controlled breath, he said, "If I came on too strong too fast, Maggie would get suspicious. She's not a stupid woman."

"No, she isn't. She's a lot like her mother. Bright. Stubborn," he said almost wistfully before anger hardened his features once again. "Do you think I'm a stupid man? Or that I won't go through with tossing you out on your ass if you fail?"

Barely restraining himself, Owen said in a strangled voice, "I understand your expectations and the risk of failure."

His father harrumphed and sank into the chair in front of Owen's desk, clearly in no rush to leave. Unlike Owen, who was itching to be away from his father and his condescension.

"Talk on the street is that Maggie's trying to find some financing, but if she is as smart as you say, she'd realize no one is going to give her that kind of money."

"Contrary to what you believe, there are some people who might be willing to lend her the funds."

His father sniggered. "Like who?"

Owen steepled his hands before his lips and weighed what he thought were Maggie's possible options. He could personally loan her the money without any of the consideration his father might think would be appropriate as collateral, but he didn't tell his father that.

Owen was sure he'd be disinherited if his father found out the truth about his feelings for Maggie or if he lent her the money outright: his father wanted not only the Sinclair properties, but also to watch the Sinclairs grovel.

He was beginning to think that such anger held on to for so long was about something more than a friend's betrayal. He kept that to himself as he said, "There's Ryder Pemberton. Maybe a few other personal friends Maggie could reach out to." In their social circles in New York and New Jersey, Maggie had the connections necessary to drum up the money she needed.

"Pemberton is too smart to pour money into the Sinclair money pit," his father said with a dismissive wave of his hand.

"Ryder wants those properties as badly as you do. He'd take the risk if it meant getting them." It was a worry that had been bouncing around in his head since seeing Ryder at Tracy's wedding. The other man had casually mentioned Maggie's problems, clearly trying to elicit some kind of response from Owen, but Owen hadn't taken the bait. Much like when they occasionally played poker together, Owen wasn't one to reveal his hand and always kept his cards—and his thoughts—close to the vest.

With another harrumph, his father stood and said, "Then maybe you should be more like your brother for a change."

"Be like Jonathan?" he asked, slightly dumbfounded that his father would mention the son he'd already disowned. Even more so because there had been a hint of pride there toward Jonathan.

Firing a final salvo, his father said, "At least he has the balls to go after what he wants."

Owen was too taken aback to respond and could only sit there, mouth open, as his father stormed from his office.

Be like Jon, he thought and couldn't help but chuckle. Wouldn't his brother get a kick out of that?

As much as he hated to admit it, his slow approach toward Maggie was possibly progressing a little too slowly, while Jonathan never took anything at other than breakneck speed. Even as a kid, Jonathan had always been the one to accept any dare, whether it was racing down a hill on his tricycle or surfing the biggest wave.

On some level, Ryder Pemberton was like his brother.

His old friend and sometime nemesis wouldn't hesitate to go after both Maggie and the Sinclair properties, but unlike Owen, Ryder wouldn't give two shits if doing so would hurt Maggie.

He couldn't allow that to happen. He yanked his smartphone from his jacket pocket and hit the speed dial for his brother.

Jonathan answered after the first ring, slightly out of breath. "Yo, Big Bro. How's it going?"

"It could be better. How are you doing, or maybe I should ask, what are you doing?"

"Just finished a jog on the beach. I needed some time away from a certain lady who was getting too attached. Came down to Sea Kiss so I could avoid her. Want to come for a visit?"

Since their father hadn't returned to Sea Kiss in years, Jonathan stayed at their shore home often when he needed a break. Just like Owen needed to get away. It was early enough on Friday to accept his brother's invitation, but he still had a load of work on his desk and a staff meeting in an hour. It would take him a few hours to finish the more important items, but with a quick detour to his condo for some clothes and his car, he could be on his way before six.

"Definitely. I'll be there in time for a late dinner."

"Beer and meat will be waiting for you, Big Bro."

He grinned. "Knew I could count on you, Jon."

"Always," Jonathan said before disconnecting.

Maggie braced her hand on the dashboard and muttered a curse under her breath as Connie narrowly avoided the car in front of them when it jerked to an abrupt stop.

"Sorry. So close and yet so far," Connie kidded as traffic slowly crawled along on the Garden State Parkway. Not typical for a Friday at noon, but the day was gorgeous, and the weekend promised to be just as nice.

"Not to worry. I called ahead, and Mrs. Patrick is prepping the house. Emma can't join us until close to eight. We've got plenty of time to get there."

Connie blew out an exasperated breath. "Now I know why they call it a 'park' way," she said, taking her hands off the wheel to add some bunny quotes for emphasis. "We should just leave the car here and walk the rest of the way."

Maggie laughed and good-naturedly jabbed her friend in the arm. "It's probably just an accident."

"Or road work. There's always some kind of frickin' road work going on," Connie complained.

"At least we saved some time by meeting at your condo. I can't imagine what it's going to be like to get through either of the tunnels later today."

"True that," her friend confirmed and changed lanes when a break in traffic gave her a little space. That lane moved a trifle faster, and before long, the bright-orange cones and portable traffic signs confirmed that an upcoming lane closure was responsible for the gridlock. Once they had done the Jersey merge and cursed a New Yorker who cut them off, they cleared the bottleneck and were moving along nicely.

Soon, they were leaving behind the industrial areas close to New York City and the sprawl of suburbia farther south. Up and across the massive Driscoll Bridge over Raritan Bay, and little by little, the area grew greener, leading to the wetlands and the marina close to Cheesequake State Park. Another thirty miles or so and they were pulling off for Sea Kiss and the smaller roads rambling eastward to the shore. Homes and businesses spread fairly far apart until the first of the Victorian homes welcomed them to the edges of Sea Kiss.

As they entered town, Connie took her time, mindful of the pedestrians strolling in and out of the many small shops on Main Street and across the street before heading to the beach. At the end of Main Street, she turned onto Ocean Avenue with its mix of Victorian homes and inns across from the boardwalk. As they moved farther away from the heart of Sea Kiss, the dunes loomed ever taller, with their seagrass and beach roses. Once the boardwalk ended, the homes grew more scattered and varied, with a mix of small beach cottages tucked in between the larger mansions and inns. After Sandy, some of the homes in the areas hardest hit by the hurricane had been rebuilt on stilts to prevent future flood damage. Many of the small beach cottages still needed work to get them back into livable shape.

In the early 1800s, the Pierce and Sinclair family mansions had been small beach cottages much like those nearby. The larger mansions had gone up in the early 1900s. During Prohibition, the homes had expanded immensely, prompting some to speculate that the two families had used ill-gotten gains from selling liquor during that time. Especially since the Jersey Shore had been a favorite spot for bootleggers to unload alcohol from Canada, Ireland, and the Caribbean.

Over the years, the homes had been lovingly preserved,

but restorations shortly after Maggie's mother's death had forever changed the look of the two homes.

While her father had opted to bring back the bright colors that had earned Victorians the name of "painted ladies" in honor of his wife's vibrant love of life, the Pierce mansion restoration had painted the structure in deep eggplant and gray tones, almost as if the home had gone into mourning.

The landscaping of both homes matched the moods of their colors. Serious and meticulously groomed boxwoods and other bushes adorned the Pierce home, while the beds of Maggie's family home were a riot of colors thanks to various annuals and perennials, as well as an assortment of flowering trees and bushes.

As Maggie and Connie pulled into the driveway, it was impossible to miss the lovingly restored, vintage Willys Jeep that Jonathan Pierce had been driving for as long as Maggie could remember and that was now sitting in the circular drive of the Pierce home.

Connie mumbled something beneath her breath, but Maggie couldn't quite make it out.

"Problem?" she asked.

Connie shook her head vehemently. "Not at all, but what are the odds that Jon would be down this weekend?"

"It could just be his car," she said, but not a second later, Jonathan walked out the front door, grinning, a happy bounce in his step until he caught sight of their car and stopped short. The cheerful disposition that had been there just moments earlier fled the way the summer sun did with a coming storm.

He forced a stiff wave before he hopped into the Jeep, gunned the engine, and tore off down the drive.

"Boy, he was not happy to see us," Maggie said, wondering at the chilly reception. Things had always been civil between the two of them and…

She paused in her thoughts and carefully examined her friend. "Something up with the two of you?"

"Nothing. Absolutely nothing," Connie replied and jumped out of the SUV.

Clearly something is up, Maggie thought, but she didn't press. When Connie was ready to talk, she would. Her friend never kept secrets from her and Emma.

She exited the car and grabbed her bag from the back. As they neared the front door, Mrs. Patrick opened it and stretched her arms wide, welcoming them home.

"My girls," she said, wrapping a meaty arm around each of them and dragging them close for a group hug. She was doughy soft and smelled of vanilla from the sugar cookies she always baked for them. Tightening her hold on them, she added, "I'm so glad you're home."

"We're glad too," Maggie said and kissed the old woman on the cheek.

Mrs. Patrick had been at the Sea Kiss house as long as Maggie could remember. The housekeeper had been a young girl when she had first started working for Maggie's paternal grandparents and had stayed on after Maggie's parents married, and Maggie had come along a few years later. Maggie's grandmother had out-lived Maggie's mother by nearly two decades, and in all that time, the two women had resided in this beachfront home. Maggie had come to spend every summer with them as well as an assortment of holidays and weekends during the rest of the year.

After she had met Connie and Emma in college,

all three would transplant themselves to the Shore for the summer months and take part-time jobs. Her grandmother and Mrs. Patrick had made sure that they had good meals and toed the line to avoid any kind of trouble.

Maggie would make sure that if the mansion had to be sold, Mrs. Patrick would have a safe and comfortable place to live and work with either her, if she didn't also lose the town house she had mortgaged just a week earlier, or her dad.

As they broke the embrace, Maggie held out a gift bag to the woman who was like a second grandmother to her. "We brought your favorite."

The older woman eagerly took the package and peered inside at the bottle of Irish whiskey. "Thank you. You girls are always so thoughtful."

"And so are you. I bet you have lunch for us," Connie said.

Mrs. Patrick beamed at them, highlighting the laugh lines on a face otherwise free of wrinkles considering her seventy-plus years of age. "I do, my girl. If you want to get settled, I'll set it up on the back patio since it's such a lovely day."

"That sounds heavenly," Maggie said. She shouldered her bag and followed Mrs. Patrick into the house. As the older woman walked off toward the kitchen, she and Connie trudged up the stairs to the second-floor bedrooms. Almost by rote, they went into the same rooms they had occupied every summer.

Since she was a light sleeper, Connie took a quieter bedroom in the middle, leaving the two corner rooms for Maggie and Emma. Maggie's father and guests used the two remaining bedrooms on the floor if they came to visit. The bedrooms shared bathrooms on one side of the house, and on the other, french doors opened onto a balcony that ran the whole length of the back of the building.

At her end of the balcony, an enormous, decades-old wisteria vine climbed up from the ground floor to the second. When the gnarly vine was in bloom, the flowers perfumed the air with a delicate floral scent that the sea breeze would waft through the rooms.

From her side windows and balcony, she had an amazing view of the beach, but also the Pierce mansion next door. On more than one summer night, she'd been up here and seen Owen and Jonathan next door with their father and mother, before their mother had given up on her marriage and abandoned the boys to their father's care. That had happened just a few years after her own mother had passed, leaving her with just her father, grandmother, and Mrs. Patrick.

She, however, had been lucky to be surrounded with love and acceptance and not an embittered and dour man who never had anything but complaints about his young sons. When he'd stopped coming down to Sea Kiss, she knew it had been a welcome thing for the boys. Even though they'd kept their distance, she could tell they were happier thanks to their father's absence.

In retrospect, it seemed that she and Owen had a great deal more in common than just the Mets and chicken parm. Their fathers' feud and their long-gone mothers had probably shaped their lives in many similar ways.

"I don't see much unpacking going on," Connie said as she walked in.

Maggie shrugged and finally placed her overnight

bag on the upholstered bench at the foot of her bed. "Just thinking about old times."

Connie sat on the bed to watch as she unpacked. "Not good thoughts from the look on your face," her friend said.

"Some good, some not," she admitted, then folded a pair of jeans and tucked them into a drawer. There were some pants there already, but she always liked to bring fresh clothes when she came.

She faced her friend and braced her hands on the edge of her dresser. "We've had a lot of fun here."

"Summers with you were always awesome, and even work wasn't so bad. We had a good time and got lots of helpful experience."

Maggie nodded. She had taken a position at a local department store, getting real hands-on retail knowledge to add to what she was learning in school about the business end of things.

Connie had interned with a lawyer who specialized in real estate transactions. He had provided a recommendation that helped get her into law school and earn a scholarship.

Waitressing put a pretty penny in Emma's pockets, but when an upscale bridal shop in Sea Kiss had needed an assistant, she had jumped at the chance. She had been working there ever since, moving her way up the ladder until she was now their top wedding planner.

"Lots of fun, just like we're going to have this weekend," Maggie said and held her hand out to her friend.

Connie slipped her hand into Maggie's and swung it like a young girl skipping through a playground. "Totally. Let's get started with lunch. Maybe some mimosas."

"For sure," she said.

They hurried down the stairs and to the kitchen. Mrs. Patrick was just tossing a salad when they came in. On the breakfast bar, a platter with an assortment of sandwiches rested beside a pitcher of orange juice and an ice bucket with an open bottle of champagne.

Maggie wrapped her arms around Mrs. Patrick's waist and brushed a kiss across her cheek. "You think of everything."

"Always for my girls."

"Take a rest. Please join us for lunch," she said.

The older woman shook her head and shushed her. She put down the salad tongs and grabbed the bowl, turned, and handed it to Maggie. "I wouldn't think of it."

Maggie took the bowl but gestured a go-ahead motion with her head to Connie.

"We won't take no for an answer," Connie said. She took hold of the older woman's hands and urged her out to the back patio.

Maggie watched through the french doors as Connie guided Mrs. Patrick to the wrought-iron table and sat her down. The older woman was still protesting but laughed at something Connie said, and with that, she finally relaxed.

Her friend could be a shark when she needed to, but she could also beguile people with her disarming charm and down-to-earth good-naturedness.

Maggie put another place setting and champagne glass on the tray Mrs. Patrick had prepared and went outside. Connie eased the tray from her hands and started setting the table while Maggie returned to the kitchen to bring out the sandwiches and salad. Within a few minutes, the mimosas were prepped and they were all eating, drinking, and chatting in the warm sun of an August summer day.

It couldn't be more perfect, Maggie thought.

Chapter 10

IT COULDN'T BE MORE PERFECT, OWEN THOUGHT, STARING UP at the sprinkle of stars shimmering across the night sky. The smell of meat cooking wafted over from where his brother was grilling their dinner at the outdoor kitchen on one side of the patio.

He reached down and grabbed another beer from the ice-filled bucket nestled between the two Adirondack chairs Jonathan had set out on the great lawn behind their home. Snagging the can opener, he pried off the lid, tossed it into the bucket, and chugalugged a good portion of the perfectly chilled beer.

"Easy there, Bro," his brother said as he sauntered over with two plates loaded with food. Jonathan handed him a dish that he balanced on his lap as his brother straddled the ottoman of the chair beside him before plopping down onto the seat.

Grabbing his immense burger, Owen took a big bite and groaned with pleasure. "This is delicious. Fuckin' delicious," he said, prompting an inquiring glance from his brother.

"Just how many beers have you had?" Jonathan asked and bit into his own burger.

"Not enough to help me forget our fuckin' father," he replied around a mouthful of food.

"Too many obviously," his brother muttered as he continued eating.

Owen didn't respond, eager to forget about all that had happened that week. Work. His father. Maggie. His father. Just the thought of his old man killed some of the pleasant buzz he was feeling from the beer, food, and good company.

He dug into the meal his brother had prepared with gusto, incredibly hungry after the time he'd spent in traffic on the parkway. *Thirsty*, he thought as he slugged back another mouthful of beer to wash down the burger.

He forked up some of the potato salad on his plate and sampled it. Flavor burst in his mouth, a sweet-sour combo enhanced by the smokiness of bacon. He quickly devoured more. "This is really good. Where did you get it?"

Jonathan smiled and ate some of it himself before he said, "I made it, Bro. I'm a jack-of-all-trades, didn't you know?"

His brother never ceased to amaze him, and it saddened Owen that his father couldn't see how wonderful his son was. But then he recalled his father's comment of the other day, and it occurred to him that maybe he could see it but ego kept him from acknowledging it. Which killed a little more of his pleasant buzz.

"You're da bomb," he teased and tried the macaroni salad. It was equally delicious. Smooth, creamy, and with just the right balance of pasta to a variety of other ingredients.

"It's a beautiful night. Perfect," he added, grabbed his beer bottle, and waved it in the air in a toast of sorts. And then a very feminine squeal pierced the relative quiet of the night and was quickly followed by additional female sounds unmuted by the row of thick privet hedges that separated their property from the Sinclair home.

He bolted up in the chair and peered into the hedges, trying to make sense of the shapes and colors barely visible through the dense foliage.

"Is that—"

"Maggie, Connie, and I guess the excited noises are because Emma just got here," Jonathan said and grabbed another beer from the bucket.

Fuck, Owen thought and tried to school his emotions, because his brother was too sharp-eyed not to notice that something was up with him. He leaned back into the chair and picked up the last little bit of his burger. He ate it slowly, thoughtfully, wondering why the gods had chosen to deposit Maggie just yards away on a weekend when all he wanted to do was forget about her for just a moment.

As if he could, he admitted to himself.

"You know what I think about this supposed family feud?" his brother said pensively.

"That it's horseshit," he said, paraphrasing what Jonathan had said to him when an eighteen-year-old Owen had come back after a magical kiss with Maggie in the dunes.

"Definitely horseshit. Who even knows why those two old bastards are fighting?" Jonathan said.

Owen took another long swallow of his beer. "They're fighting about the properties."

Jonathan fervently shook his head. "It's more than that. No one stays angry for that long just about some dirt."

"Not *just* dirt. Bryce Sinclair was a friend, and he betrayed our father when he bought those store locations for his wife," he clarified.

Jonathan laid his empty plate on the ottoman and

faced him. "Are you saying that you think he's right? 'Cause if you are, you're just as crazy as he is."

"He" being their father, who Jonathan refused to accept as his father since the day their old man had decided to disown him. Much like the bastard refused to admit that his youngest son was a truly unique and wonderful individual.

Another burst of feminine laughter came through the privet hedge, snagging Owen's attention.

"It's crazy, Owen. Seriously crazy. Just go for it already. Find out if it's just an itch or something more," his brother urged and motioned toward the Sinclair property.

Because his brother was like a great white shark that wouldn't release its bite on a swimmer, he admitted, "I'm already working on it."

Jon's eyebrows shot up in surprise. "Seriously? You're not fucking with me, are you?"

Owen chuckled and wagged his head. "I'm not fucking with you. So here's to scratching that itch," he said and held up his beer bottle for a toast.

His brother hesitated for a moment, then grinned and knocked his bottle against Owen's.

"To going for it."

―⁓―

The night air was warm but not too muggy. Maggie stood on the edge of the balcony, enjoying the peace and solitude of a Sea Kiss night.

A slight breeze from the south kicked up, and the scent of cigars wafted to her. She glanced across the way to the great lawn behind the Pierce mansion. There was just a sliver of moon tonight, but it cast enough light for her to see the silhouettes of the two men reclining in the

Adirondack chairs, sharing a smoke. Their faces were in shadow, and she was far enough away to ignore the two, but suddenly, one of them raised a hand in greeting. The gesture was followed by a whispered discussion, and then the second man slowly lifted his hand, mirroring his brother's gesture.

Jonathan reluctantly followed by Owen, she surmised.

She waved back, feeling a little awkward with the whole Owen situation unresolved. Feeling exposed thanks to the light spilling from the room behind her, making her highly visible to the two men.

It should have occurred to her to be more discreet since they'd realized that Jonathan was in residence. Later, when Emma had gotten there, she'd caught sight of Owen's Lightning prototype car sitting in the circular driveway just behind the Jeep. It was one of the electric vehicles that Jonathan Pierce's company hoped to release to the public shortly.

Pushing away from the edge of the balcony, she entered her room and closed the french doors behind her. She had been looking forward to leaving them open to enjoy the sounds of the sea and the breeze, but the slight perfume of the cigar smoke would just lead her to thinking about Owen. Owen being one of the things she had wanted to avoid thinking about by coming down this weekend.

She grabbed a romance novel to help her relax and was climbing into bed when something rattled against the glass of the french doors. Narrowing her gaze, she peered toward the opening, searching for the source of the sound, when a second round of rattling came from the glass.

She rose, walked to the doors, and noticed the dozen or so pieces of pea gravel outside on the wooden balcony. Pea gravel like the mulch beneath the long row of privet hedges separating the Pierce and Sinclair mansions. As kids, they'd dodged in and out of the hedges and grabbed handfuls of gravel to toss at each other.

When the third barrage hit the glass, she had no doubt just what was causing the noise. She hurried out to the balcony, leaned over the edge, and looked down. Owen stood in the shadows, holding another handful of the small stones, ready to launch them yet again, presumably if she failed to respond.

"What are you doing?" she said in tones barely above a whisper, hoping that her friends would not hear what was happening.

"I wanted to get your attention," he shouted out, much louder than she hoped.

Grimacing, she held an index finger to her lips in the age-old sign for quiet and whispered, "Shh. Everyone's asleep."

He looked up and across the balcony, wavered a little on his feet, and said, "You're not asleep."

"Go home, Owen," she urged.

He shook his head with a bit too much vehemence and wobble. "We need to talk," he said and walked toward the wisteria vine at the base of the balcony.

"What are you doing?" she said, louder and more insistently, as he grabbed hold of one thick branch of the vine and pulled upward.

"What does it look like I'm doing?" he shouted back, finding a foothold in the twisted wisteria branches and boosting himself up a few more feet.

"Shit, Owen. Climb right back down, do you hear me?"

Despite her instructions, he continued his way up, fumbling for purchase on the branches, losing his grip at one point, which had him precariously flailing for a hold until he managed to wrap his arm around a thicker bough of the vine.

Luckily for him, it was late summer, and there weren't any of the fragrant purple blossoms that attracted a host of bees in the early spring. It was also lucky for him that with some of the leaves starting to fade, he could get a more solid grasp on the gnarly limbs. Because she feared the possibility of his falling and getting seriously hurt, she said nothing else until he climbed over the railing and landed unsteadily on the balcony.

Then she attacked, her hands fisted. Her voice was hushed to avoid others hearing but still crackled with anger. "What the hell were you thinking?"

With a dimpled, boyish grin and eyes that were slightly unfocused, he said, "I was thinking you and me on the balcony, romantic-like. That is if we can hash out what is happening between us."

She slashed her hand through the air. "Nothing is happening, remember?"

"Because of some stupid family feud," he replied confidently, but his words were slightly slurred. He tried to cross his arms in a sign of bravado, she guessed, but it took him a few tries.

Leaning closer, she sniffed him. The scents of cigar, bourbon, and Owen filled her senses.

"You're drunk. Jesus, Owen, you could have fallen and broken your neck!"

"Doesn't God watch out for children, drunks, and fools?"

"And you're two of the three right now. Can you imagine how you hurting yourself would have added to the damn feud?" Despite her comment, it was hard not to smile at the almost goofy, self-satisfied grin on his face that was dimming her upset.

She just couldn't resist those damn dimples.

"I didn't fall, Mags." Stretching his arms out wide with a flourish, he said, "And I'm here. In one piece. What do you plan to do about that?"

Shit, she thought and rolled her eyes. She couldn't send him back down the vine in his condition, but she also didn't want to keep him out on the balcony. Connie and Emma could step out at any second, and if they did, there was no telling what crazy ideas they'd get into their heads.

She grabbed hold of Owen's hand and hauled him through her open french doors.

"Whoa, I kind of like where this is going," he said, a little too loudly.

She laid her index finger on his lips, shut the doors, and pulled the lightweight curtains closed to keep away any prying eyes.

"Even better," he said when he realized it was her bedroom. He reached for her, sloppily laying his hands on her waist. Shifting them to her arms where he lightly trailed his fingers across her bare skin.

She slapped his hands away and fought to ignore the shiver of need his touch caused down her spine. "Stop, Owen. You're drunk—"

Raising one finger, he said, "I only had one bourbon."

If she knew Jonathan at all, they'd probably had a few beers as well and that one bourbon had likely been a water glass full and not just a couple of fingers over ice.

"You're a cheap date, then," she teased and placed her hand on his chest to guide him toward an upholstered divan in the sitting area of her spacious bedroom.

"Cheap and easy," he said as he threw himself onto the divan, and the delicate, antique furniture creaked with the weight of his big body. He shifted to one side of the divan and patted the space beside him. "Come on, Mags. The least you can do is listen to me after I risked life and limb to come see you."

He faked a pout, and she imagined him as a little boy, using that pout to wheedle something from his mom and, later, the assortment of caretakers who had watched the boys over the years. "That," she said as she sat beside him and circled her finger around his mouth, "won't work with me. But if you want to have an adult conversation about our situation, I'm game."

Her words seemed to have the effect of a cold bucket of water being tossed on him, since he sobered up for an instant. "Seriously? You're willing to discuss it?"

She had to laugh at his surprise. "Seriously? Yes, I am. We've been avoiding each other for too long—"

"Since that night when we were eighteen?" he jumped in, focusing his charcoal-gray gaze on her attentively.

Heat surged across her cheeks as the memories swamped her. She covered them with her hands to avoid his scrutiny. "*That* was a mistake. We were both young and inexperienced. A little drunk as well, if I recall correctly."

Owen loved the blossom of pink across her cheeks and her obvious discomfiture. While they may have both been young and maybe a little tipsy, he recollected her response, and it had not been lacking in any way.

"Funny, but I remember it was kinda nice," he said, closing his eyes for a moment to drag up that memory. Maggie in her bikini, her body lean but with all those curves he itched to touch. Her blue eyes, bright like a summer sky, darkening with pleasure as he'd caressed her cheek and urged her closer for a kiss.

"Owen, wake up," she urged, and he slowly opened his eyes to meet her questioning gaze. Then he dipped his gaze down and hers followed. Another layer of color painted her cheeks as she noticed what was happening in his jeans.

"I'm more than awake, as you can see," he teased and cradled her face. Urging her gaze back up, he said, "You were beautiful then, and you're even more beautiful now."

"Is that all this is? Physical attraction?" she said and gestured to the very obvious bulge visible beneath the denim.

He stroked a thumb across the stain of pink on her cheek before dipping his thumb down to trace the edges of her lips. "It's a good start," he said, because as much as he wanted to tell her how much he liked her intelligence and poise, his brain couldn't find a way to say it just right. He wanted it to be just right with her in every way that it could be.

"Kiss me, Maggie. Please," he said and eased his

hand behind her neck to apply gentle pressure and draw her closer.

Her soft sigh of resignation spilled across his lips a second before the moist warmth of her mouth covered them.

Sweet lord but he loved the feel of her. The taste of her, he thought as he met her kiss. He accepted the mingling of her breath with his and the fluid brush of her lips across his. As the kiss deepened, he opened his mouth and licked her lips, silently pleaded for her to open to him, and she did, accepting the slide of his tongue. Meeting it with her own.

He groaned, his head whirling with everything that was Maggie and that he'd wanted for so long.

———

Maggie drew away slightly at his ragged sound and explored his face, slightly flushed now from their kisses. His eyes, those startling, dark eyes shot through with threads of silver, had darkened to nearly black, but they were a little sleepy, making her reconsider what was happening at that moment.

"You're more than a little wasted, you know."

He grinned, and two deep dimples erupted at the sides of his mouth. With a shaky nod, he said, "Just a bit."

More than a bit, and surely enough to cloud his judgment. As for her, that one steamy kiss they'd just shared had her picturing where this could lead, but not when she felt like she might be taking advantage of him.

"Just enough," she said and sat up.

"Are you seriously not going to…you know," he said and levered himself up on one elbow so they were eye to slightly unfocused eye.

"And the fact that you can't even call it what it is at this moment is reason enough for us to wait until you're back to normal," she said.

He did that little-boy pout again, only it wasn't an act this time. "Normal Owen is boring and responsible."

She so knew where that was coming from and cupped his jaw. "Normal Owen is just my cup of tea. I don't need a shark like your dad or an all-action guy like Jonathan."

He chuckled and said, "Jon was the one who dared me to climb up here like he used to for Connie."

Now it was her turn to be surprised. "What? Connie? When?"

Owen cursed and shook his head. "Shit, it was supposed to be a secret."

Maggie had thought she and her friends never kept any secrets from one another.

Sensing her upset, Owen laid a hand on her thigh and stroked it reassuringly. "It was a long time ago. When we were kids. Whatever they had flamed out ages ago. It's probably why she never mentioned it."

"Yeah, probably," she said but rather unconvincingly.

Trying to ease her past her distress, he lightheartedly said, "Please don't make me climb back down that vine."

A small laugh escaped her, and she shook her head. "I won't." She paused for a second and heard the sounds of Connie and Emma out in the hall.

Owen must have heard them as well. "Your friends are still awake."

Biting her lip, she said, "You may have to wait to leave."

He arched a raven-dark brow. "Keeping secrets?"

"I don't keep secrets from my friends," she said,

more sharply than she wanted, but she was still stinging a little from what he'd unintentionally revealed about Connie and Jonathan.

He lifted his brow another condemning inch. "But you want me to wait here so they don't see me, and that's not a secret?"

She hated that despite the influence of both beer and bourbon and Jonathan's challenge, he could still be relatively logical. "I will tell them when the time is right, which is not now. I'll be right back."

She dashed from her room, leaving him lying on the divan, and raced down to the current source of the noise—the kitchen.

Connie sat at the breakfast bar while Emma placed perfect little scoops of cookie dough on a baking sheet. Both her friends looked up at her arrival.

"Damn, now you ruined our surprise. We were going to bring you up some of Emma's famous chocolate chip pistachio cookies," Connie said and drew out the stool beside her, obviously intending for her to join them.

Maggie bit back that if anyone was going to be surprised, it was her friends. But as much as she wanted to get back to Owen and their discussion and what might follow, there was no way she could refuse an offering of Emma's cookies. If she did, her friends would definitely know something was up, because she had never, in all the years that they'd been friends, refused any of Emma's delicious cookie creations.

"I'll get the milk," she said and busied herself with that and setting out plates and glasses for when the cookies were ready. She hoped that by doing so, she could avoid anyone noticing that something out of the ordinary was up.

Her hopes were dashed when eagle-eyed Connie asked, "You feeling okay? You look a little flushed."

"My room's too warm. I had to open the french doors to catch a breeze," she said and hated lying to her friend, but it might explain if they'd noticed anything earlier. She averted her gaze, poured the milk, sat on the stool beside Connie, and waited for Emma, who joined them after popping the baking sheet into the oven.

"It won't take long," Emma said and likewise scrutinized her. "You are red, Mags. Are you sure you're not coming down with something?"

"I'm fine," she said. To take the heat off herself and see what if anything remained of the attraction between Connie and Jonathan, she said, "Did you get a load of Jon out on the waves today? He still looks great out there."

"He's a show-off," Connie complained, grabbed hold of her glass, and slid it back and forth on the counter in a nervous gesture.

"Say what you will, he's way hot," Emma said.

Connie's head jerked up in shock. "You think he's hot? Really?"

Emma shrugged in a nonchalant way. "He's definitely got that bad boy, surfer dude thing going on in a major way. Have you ever watched him when he peels off his wet suit?" Emma fanned her face and grinned. "A Chippendale dancer couldn't do a better striptease."

"I never noticed," Connie said and continued with the uneasy juggling of her glass.

"Wow, Con, that's hard to believe," Emma said and glanced toward Maggie. "You've seen him, right?"

In truth, Maggie had been busy thinking about Owen and how he used to surf. He didn't get out on the water as often as Jonathan did, but he hadn't been a slouch when they were teens. Earlier that night, just before dusk fell, Owen had managed to catch a few nice waves beside his brother, and if Jonathan had done a stripping act, she hadn't noticed because she'd been too busy watching Owen peel off his wet suit.

"She's all googly eyed, so she's probably dreaming about Owen," Connie said, very effectively turning the tables and attention back to Maggie.

Emma peered at her, narrowing her green-eyed gaze to assess the impact of Connie's statement. With a shake of her head and an explosive laugh, she said, "No way. Maggie is just not the googly-eyed type, but…any change from our last chat?"

Because the new round of smoochies had not changed anything yet, she could honestly say, "If there was any change, you two would be the first to know."

When she was done, she pointedly looked at Connie, who clearly took the hint that Maggie knew more than she was saying.

The ding of the kitchen timer dragged their attention to the oven, and she finally noticed the enticing aroma of the buttery, nutty cookies and chocolate.

"Smells delicious," she said.

Emma brought over the baking sheet and a cooling rack. She placed the hot sheet on a trivet she had laid out earlier. When Maggie reached for a cookie, wanting to move the night along and get back to Owen, Emma smacked her hand playfully.

"Don't be a pig. You know they have to cool a little."

"In a rush? Got a hot date?" Connie asked, her perfectly manicured eyebrows raised in challenge.

"I've got a case of midnight munchies," she said, and it wasn't far from the truth. The tempting smell of the cookies had awakened her hunger. She didn't have long to wait as, within a few minutes, Emma moved the cookies to the cooling rack and, after another few minutes, announced that they were free to indulge. The warm cookies were, as always, delicious, especially when paired with the ice-cold milk.

"You really should think about selling these," she said and grabbed a second cookie that she immediately devoured.

"I just like to play around with them. Besides, I'm too busy with the wedding planning."

"And Carlo," Connie interjected and reached for another cookie.

Emma rapped her hand and said, "You can't tease me and expect to have another treat."

Connie brought her hands together in a pleading gesture. "Pretty please. No more mention of your Carlo."

With a playful pout, Emma said, "You're excused."

Which gave Maggie the perfect opening she was looking for. "Speaking of excused. I'm kind of tired. I've been up since five, and that ride down did me in. I'm going to head up to bed."

Although both of her friends seemed a little taken aback by her comment, they recovered quickly.

"Sure, it was a long day with the traffic and all," Connie said.

"I'm a little beat from the event today too. I'm looking forward to sleeping in tomorrow," Emma added.

"Sounds great. Good night, you two," she said and hugged both of them before hurrying back to her bedroom. And Owen.

He was right where she left him. Only he was fast asleep on the divan, snoring softly.

She walked over and considered waking him up, but she could still hear Connie and Emma downstairs. It would be just as easy for him to sneak out in the morning, and she was tired. She hadn't lied about that.

Grabbing the crocheted throw that she kept on the bench at the end of her bed, she covered him, walked to her bed, climbed in, and shut off the lights. But as tired as she was, it was a long time before she could drive away the memory of that night's kiss and the realization that if she wanted more, Owen was just feet away.

Those thoughts chased her into sleep and a long night filled with sexy dreams of being with Owen. Of kissing him and having him touch her. Feeling the weight of him pressing her down into the mattress. But as she gradually woke to the very pleasant sensation of his lips on hers and his warmth tucked along the length of her body, she realized it was no fantasy.

She broke away from the dreamy kiss and dragged a hand through her sleep-tousled hair.

"What are you doing here, Owen?"

A sexy smile stole slowly across his lips. "I must not be doing it right if you can't tell."

She chuckled despite herself and wagged her head. "I mean here, in my bed."

He bopped his head in the direction of the divan. "That thing is frickin' uncomfortable."

"So you just decided to hop into bed with me?" she asked with an imperial lift of her brow that usually worked to dissuade a response from others. But not from Owen.

"You looked too good to resist," he said, bent, and

kissed her again, a leisurely exploration of her mouth that yanked a murmur of pleasure from her and a groan from Owen.

"I love that sound, Mags. I love the way you feel," he said, and reaching up, he cradled her breast in his hand.

She wanted to protest, but the press of his hand on her felt way too good, and when he dragged his thumb across the tip, her nipple beaded into a hard point for him.

"Owen," she said breathlessly and laid her hands on his shoulders, her gaze locked with his as he played with the sensitive tip, circling it with his fingers and making it even harder. Tweaking it gently and drawing another gasp of pleasure from her.

"I want to see, Mags. Taste. Feel you against me," he said.

"So do I, Owen," she whispered.

In a flurry of action, he ripped off his polo shirt, exposing the broad expanse of his chest and lean six-pack abs. But he took his time with her, nudging down the shoulder of her loose nightshirt to expose her breast and touch her again before bending to take her into his mouth.

She closed her eyes against the sensations he created with the lick of his tongue and the tender pull of his mouth. With the heat of his skin beneath her hands and all his hard muscle along the length of her body. Damp heat exploded between her legs, and she wrapped her arm around his shoulders, dug her fingers into the smooth muscles of his back as he gently teethed the tight nipple before soothing that love bite with a kiss.

Urging him on with soft cries of pleasure, she cradled the back of his head and held him close while he shifted his hand down her body and beneath the hem of her nightshirt.

―――――

Owen groaned as he found the soft curls at her center and realized she had nothing on under the nightshirt.

As she pressed her hips against his hand, his dick jumped in anticipation, but his über-responsible side reminded him that he had forgotten protection. But that didn't mean he couldn't bring her pleasure. He parted her and swept his thumb across the sensitive nub at her center.

She jumped beneath him and held on to him tighter.

"I want to make you come, Mags. I want to hear you scream my name."

"Owen," she said, her tones urgent, almost demanding, and he nearly came himself at the thought of hearing her say his name as he entered her.

"Just like that, Mags," he said and stroked her clit. He eased a finger inside her and stroked gently at first, building her passion. Increasing the pressure of his caresses against the sensitive nub and inside her. Bending to take her breast in his mouth again, he licked and sucked the tender flesh until, with another powerful thrust of his fingers, she bucked up off the bed, climaxing beneath his hands, and called out his name.

A harsh breath escaped him as he fought not to embarrass himself by coming in his pants. Especially when she urged him over her body and spread her legs to straddle his thighs.

"Maggie, I can't. I didn't bring protection," he said, apologetic. Frustrated that in his very buzzed state of excitement the night before, he hadn't planned ahead.

The knowing smile she cast his way nearly undid him. "I'm sure you're aware that there are other ways—"

"I know, but it doesn't have to be tit for tat," he said, hoping he wouldn't rue his patience.

She smirked and glanced down at her exposed breast, still hard from his caresses. "I think you already got the tit part," she teased.

He thought he detected a very feline purr of satisfaction in her words. Heat poured through him, and he just couldn't resist. Bending, he took her breast into his mouth again, sucking the tight tip deep before reluctantly releasing it with a tender kiss.

"I need to go before I lose the last of my common sense," he said and pushed off the bed. He grabbed his shirt from the floor where he had tossed it and jerked it back on.

—∿∿—

Maggie watched him dress but didn't hurry to put her nightshirt back to rights.

Let him look, she thought, eager to explore the power of their mutual attraction. Hoping he wouldn't take too long to come back for another round. When she finally left the bed and slipped on a robe, he walked to where she stood and placed his hands on the slope of her hips, the gesture possessive and erotic. It was too easy to imagine his hands there, guiding her as she rode him.

"About today… Would you and your friends like to come over for dinner?" he said.

And there went desire, she thought. She hadn't really imagined that he was going to propose a group dinner, but maybe that's what they needed to let things cool down and allow calmer heads to prevail.

"Sure. What time?" she asked, taking hold of one of his hands and twining her fingers with his as she led him toward the door of her bedroom.

"I'll call you later to let you know." He paused by her door. "Are you okay with your friends seeing me now?"

Truth be told, she was hoping that they were still asleep, but if they weren't…

"I'm okay with it. They're going to wonder what's up anyway when I tell them about dinner."

With a nod, he followed her out the door and downstairs to the foyer of the mansion. There were sounds of activity from the kitchen already, but no one came out to check when Maggie opened the front entrance.

They faced each other, silent for a long moment before she rose on tiptoes and danced a kiss across his lips.

"See you tonight," she said.

"Tonight," he replied and left.

She watched him as he slipped through a break in the privet hedges lining the property boundaries. Chill morning air spilled through the open door, and she hugged herself to ward off the cold. The weather had taken a turn overnight, and misty fog blanketed the ground. *Definitely not a beach day*, she thought, closed the door, and turned.

Connie and Emma stood there, stunned expressions on their faces.

Chapter 11

"JUST HOW MUCH DID YOU SEE?" SHE ASKED.

"Enough," Connie said, accusation icing the single word.

Emma elbowed Connie and said, "Ease up. We suspected something was going on last night after you bolted to your room."

Maggie breezed by them and into the kitchen, but her friends were quickly on her heels and peppering her with questions.

"Spill, Mags. Did you do it?" Connie asked, blunt as always.

"You can't possibly think this makes sense," Emma pointed out, ever the relationship pessimist.

Maggie whirled and faced them, anxious to end the inquisition. She held up her index finger to count down and said, "One, I didn't do him, but he sure knows how to rock my world."

That statement had Connie's mouth flapping open and closed like a sea bass pulled from the ocean, fighting for breath.

She popped up another finger. "Two, I'm not sure if this makes sense, but I like spending time with him."

"Because he rocks your world," Connie interrupted.

"Because I have fun with him and because he's sexy and handsome, and I need to find out if this is something that can become more."

"More complicated, you mean," Emma said and dragged a hand through the long strands of her hair in a sure sign of frustration. She plowed on. "I mean when it was just smoochies, I thought, it's just a thing, you know, and not *a thing* as in a *serious* thing."

Maggie rubbed the back of her neck and sighed, almost as frustrated as her friend. "I don't know what *it* is, but I want to figure it out. I'd like the two of you to support me because you're my BFFs and your opinions matter to me."

Connie and Emma shared a brief look that communicated a great deal, Maggie could tell.

Connie was the first one to step forward and give her a hug. "We're not just your BFFs—we're your BFFFs, best fuckin' friends forever, and we'll do whatever you need."

Emma joined in, hugging the two of them hard. "Whatever," she said.

When they finally separated, sniffling, Maggie wiped at a tear and said, "Well, for starters, we're going to have dinner tonight with the Pierce brothers."

"What?" Connie shouted at the same time Emma said, "Wait, really?"

"Dinner. Tonight. Owen will call with a time later. And because my grandmother and Mrs. Patrick taught me never to go anywhere empty-handed, I want to make dessert to take over," she said and walked to hug the older woman, who had just entered the kitchen. "Right, Mrs. Patrick? A good guest always brings something for the dinner host," she said, which prompted a pat on the arm she had wrapped around the older woman.

"Normally, it does, my girl. Unfortunately, you're not known for your prowess in the kitchen."

"Don't you remember those cookies you made that

one time? We could have used them as skeet pucks, they were so hard," Connie said with a grin.

"And the spaghetti dinner? Globs of pasta all glued together in... What was that? Ketchup?" Emma teased.

Mrs. Patrick patted Maggie's hand again in sympathy, but Maggie wasn't going to be dissuaded. Ignoring the assorted tales of her cooking woe, she said, "Owen has a sweet tooth."

Wiggling her eyebrows like Groucho, Connie said, "If you're the sweet, I bet he does."

"You guys can help me, right?" she said, glancing back and forth between her two friends, who shared another conspiratorial look.

"If by help she means we can bake it for her, I guess we can," Emma said.

Maggie pursed her lips and angrily shot back, "I really do mean you'll help and not make it for me. It's time I learned."

"Since when did you decide to get all domestic? Or do rich girls really get tired of eating out all the time?" Connie said with a below-the-belt shot.

Although they had clicked when they'd first met, the issue of the haves and have-nots had always simmered beneath the surface of their friendship. Every now and then, it would break through and cause upset, usually on Maggie's part.

Connie was a Cuban hothouse flower transported from her ethnic enclave in Union City to the mostly lily-white university thanks to a full scholarship. Emma was a suburban girl from Edison whose parents' divorce had upended her family life and finances, forcing her to work her way through school.

"Low blow, Connie. If you don't want to help a friend, I'm fine with that."

Connie winced and looked away, shamefaced. Emma laid a hand on Connie's shoulder and said, "We'll help, only... You're not even having a real thing with this guy, and already, you want to change. I see it happen over and over. Girl meets guy. Girl suddenly becomes someone else."

While Emma hadn't said it, Maggie knew what else they were thinking. Hell, she'd thought it more than once herself as she'd seen one acquaintance after another get married. Those women suddenly had more important things to do than to hang out with their girlfriends.

She walked over to them for a group hug, embracing them tightly. "I will never, ever stop being BFFFs with you guys. And besides, this thing with Owen—we all know how impossible it would be."

"More impossible things have been known to happen," Connie mumbled.

"Yeah, you're right. But all I'm asking is a little help in making a cheesecake," she said.

Emma eyed her carefully. "A cheesecake? Where did that come from?"

She shrugged. "It's sweet and tasty. We all love cheesecake. It's not really baking, just some cream cheese and stuff, right?"

Emma rolled her eyes and huffed out a complaint. "And cookies are just butter and flour. You really do have a lot to learn, my friend."

"Great, so teach me. Show me how to make a cheesecake."

"Coffee first," Connie grumbled and slipped away from the group hug to pour herself a big mug of java.

"And eggs. I'm starving," Emma said.

"I'll help," Maggie said, but both her friends immediately held their hands up like cops stopping traffic.

"No, you sit. Mrs. Patrick and I can make breakfast. You're going to need all your strength for the cheesecake," Emma warned.

Her housekeeper chimed in with her agreement. Maggie looked at the older woman, who said, "Sit, and if you can't sit, you and Connie can set the table."

She helped Connie do just that, made herself a giant cup of coffee, and sat to wait for breakfast. It didn't take long for the two women to dish out perfectly fluffy and tasty scrambled eggs and crisp, smoky bacon.

Which just made her think that if breakfast could happen so easily, how much harder could it be to make a cheesecake?

―⁓―

Owen crept in through the french doors in the back, hoping not to wake Jonathan. As he entered stealthily, however, he realized his brother was in the same position he'd left him the night before, sprawled out on the couch with his laptop.

He was busily typing away until he caught sight of Owen sneaking in.

"Yo, Bro. I guess you're glad I dared you to go over last night," Jonathan said, a smug smile on his face.

Owen walked over and sat on the coffee table in front of his brother. His brother's sun-streaked light-brown hair stood up in weird spikes. It looked like Jonathan had dragged his hand through it more than once in frustration. Dark smudges of fatigue sat above the strong suntanned lines of his cheekbones.

"Don't tell me you've been up all night." While his father thought Jonathan had no work ethic, Owen knew that Jonathan's businesses demanded hours that weren't necessarily nine to five.

His brother shrugged broad, powerful shoulders. "When the muse hits, you don't ignore her. I just finished some basic specs for this new fuel cell, and my brain feels like I emptied it all out on the page. I should go get some shut-eye," he said and powered down his laptop. He glanced in Owen's direction, his observant inventor's eyes not missing a thing. "You, on the other hand, look like you got plenty of sleep, which is downright disappointing. I was hoping you'd nailed Maggie last night."

Annoyance flared at Jonathan's crudeness. "I don't want to 'nail' Maggie. I want to make love to her."

Jonathan burst out laughing. "Look at you, all Mr. Sensitive Guy. I get it. Maggie has grown up really nice, but it's too soon for love."

On that point, his brother might be right. While he had feelings for Maggie and had had them for some time, he wasn't quite sure it was love...yet. He knew she had similar feelings, or he could be deluding himself and it was just the allure of being with her because he shouldn't. Because doing so would royally piss off his father, and in some deep, dark part of himself, he wanted some kind of payback for the years of being told he wasn't good enough. Ruthless enough. Or maybe it was that he'd lacked a woman's touch in his life for so long. Since his mother had walked out on them decades earlier, there hadn't been the tenderness and sense of home that he felt whenever he was with Maggie.

"Whatever it is, it's mutual and it's…"

He searched for the words to describe the peace he felt when he was with her. What it felt like when passion rose as he kissed her. Touched her and heard the exciting little sounds she made. How his gut twisted when she called out his name as she came and the very Neanderthal satisfaction at knowing he'd been the one to bring her that pleasure.

At his prolonged silence, Jonathan leaned closer and darted his gaze all across his face. "Fuck, Bro. I take it back. You've got it bad for Maggie. She's the one."

Owen pushed off the table and came to his feet, discomfited by the inspection and his brother's perceptiveness. "I don't know if she's the one, but I intend to find out. I invited her and her friends to come over for dinner tonight."

"No way. Please tell me you didn't," his brother said as he rocketed to his feet and raked his fingers through his disheveled hair again.

Owen smiled and clapped his brother on the back. "I did. Seemed to me like you and Connie could talk about old times," he kidded.

Jonathan shook his head furiously. "Fuck no. That chick is like sand in my shorts, rubbing me the wrong way all the time."

Despite his brother's words, Owen recalled many a night when Jonathan had snuck out and risked himself on the Sinclairs' wisteria vine in order to see Maggie's friend. After doing it once, he had no desire to do it ever again.

He threw his arm around Jonathan's shoulders for a bro-hug. "I guess you'll just have to man up for your big bro. Make sure it's a nice night for the ladies."

Jonathan elbowed him playfully and shoved him away. "Because to get into Maggie's pants, you have to make nice with her friends."

To shut up his brother, he said, "I've already been in Maggie's pants, Jon." He sauntered away, feeling perversely satisfied at the stunned look on Jonathan's face. But that pleasure faded quickly as he climbed the stairs and thought about Maggie. He wasn't the kind to kiss and tell, but he trusted Jonathan not to repeat what he'd said. Not that Maggie and he being together was a secret, given the fact that she'd kissed him in full view of her friends.

She'd kissed *him*, he thought with a smile and headed to his bedroom to plan.

If tonight was going to be the night, he wanted everything to be perfect.

Chapter 12

Maggie wiped away the bead of sweat running down the side of her face and piped the last of the whipped cream onto the top of the cheesecake. She had no sooner put down the plastic bag with the remnants of the whipped cream than Emma handed her a bar of dark chocolate and a peeler. She eyed her friend dubiously.

"Chocolate needs to be peeled?"

Emma rolled her eyes and grabbed the items from her. "So sad," she teased and proceeded to show her how to use the peeler to create delicate curls of chocolate that she artfully placed on top of the whipped cream. After, she grabbed a small grater and added a dusting of chocolate all across the top.

When her friend was done, all three of them and Mrs. Patrick examined the cheesecake.

The older woman clapped her hands together and grinned. "Brava, Maggie. It looks wonderful."

Connie said, "I have to say, it actually looks edible."

"You might not be as hopeless in the kitchen as I imagined," Emma added.

"Well, thanks for the vote of confidence," Maggie said, pride and humor in her tones.

Connie glanced at her watch and said with a grimace, "I guess it's time to go over."

"Don't look so overjoyed," Emma replied and nudged her friend.

In one way or another, Connie had been dropping hints all day about how much she didn't want to do dinner that night, but Maggie wasn't about to let her off the hook. Especially given Owen's comments from the night before about her friend and Jonathan.

Connie's ongoing displeasure was a sure sign that whatever had happened with Owen's brother wasn't resolved. Being forced to face him again might just provide the impetus needed to set that relationship to rights again.

"Time to go," Maggie said, grabbed the plate with the cake, and waited for her friends to go ahead of her to open the door.

Outside, they walked down to the sidewalk and up to the front door of the Pierce home. Unlike her house, there were no planters filled with fragrant and colorful flowers. The beds all along the perfectly manicured lawn contained only pachysandra, ivy, or boxwoods trimmed to within an inch of their lives. Many years earlier, the flower boxes on all the windows that used to overflow with an assortment of blooms had been taken down and never replaced. While the house was well maintained, the life that had once been there had seemed to be sucked away, and the dark scheme of the paint colors on the home only added to the gloom.

It lacks love, Maggie thought and wondered if it had anything to do with their mother leaving the boys and taking away any hope of happiness with her. Even though she'd lost her mother also, her mom's vibrant spirit kept the house alive and full of life.

They had no sooner set foot on the front porch than Owen yanked open the door, smiling broadly.

He stepped aside and swept his arm wide. "Welcome. Please come in."

"Said the spider to the fly," Connie mumbled beneath her breath, but if Owen heard her comment, he ignored it.

As Maggie walked in, she held out the plate to him. "I made dessert. It needs to go in the fridge."

He nodded and accepted the cheesecake, some surprise on his features. "Thank you. I didn't know you liked to cook, but it looks wonderful. Why don't you all follow me to the kitchen? We thought we'd do informal tonight."

As they walked through the foyer and living room and back to the kitchen area, Maggie looked around, trying to get a feel for the place where Owen had spent so much of his life. When they had spent time together as kids, they had usually been running around outside on the beach. They'd never spent time inside together, since Owen's father wouldn't have tolerated having Maggie inside. As long as he hadn't seen her, it was fine for her and the boys to play together. But then the boys had stopped coming down, and when they'd returned, the fight between the families had kept them apart.

There were big, comfortable leather couches in the living room and an immense flat-screen television. The rest of the furniture had a very contemporary feel, so someone had clearly remodeled recently, unlike her home with its period antiques. Here and there was some artwork, mostly landscapes with a beach feel. The shore. Lighthouses. It all came together to have a decidedly masculine feel, but there was another thing she noticed: no family pictures.

Jonathan was in the kitchen, an apron over his jeans and T-shirt. There was some kind of saying on the shirt, and she recalled that Owen's brother often wore shirts that said something outrageous or funny. The apron covered whatever this one said.

As they walked into the kitchen, Jonathan moved away from the stove, and with a broad smile on his face, he sauntered over and hugged her. "Nice to see you again, Maggie." He embraced Emma next, bantering with her as he did so. "How's the world's best wedding planner doing?"

Emma grinned back at him. "Busy making the world less safe for confirmed bachelors like you."

His demeanor totally changed when it came time to greet Connie. He kept his distance and provided her with only a quick nod. "Connie."

"Jonathan. I almost didn't recognize you. It's been so long since I've seen your face in the news," Connie replied, firing the first salvo after his abrupt greeting.

Jonathan grinned again, but there was nothing friendly about it. "I should have known you were around when all the sharks migrated to safer waters."

"Professional courtesy," she shot back quickly, downplaying any upset his comment might have caused.

"Now, now, children. It's time to play nice," Emma said, pulling out her smoothest and most calming wedding planner voice to control the situation.

"Of course. Sorry. Let me get back to the sauce," Jonathan said. He returned to the stove where he stirred whatever was in the pot as capably as he had stirred up Connie's emotions, Maggie thought.

"Make yourselves at home. I'll open up some wine,"

Owen said and motioned to the big oak table that had been set for five.

"Let me help," she said and followed Owen back out to the living room and a dry bar at one side of the room.

As he deftly opened a bottle, he whispered to her, "I thought this was a Pierce-Sinclair family feud."

Maggie chuckled and glanced back toward the kitchen, where Connie and Emma had taken seats side by side at the table and his brother was still at the stove, working at another pot as it boiled over. "Connie is family, so maybe she's part of the feud by extension," she quipped.

"Or maybe there was more to those climbs up the vine than any of us knew," Owen said, confirming what she had been suspecting all day.

"Maybe," she acknowledged and followed him back to the table. As Owen poured the wine for all of them, she grabbed one glass and walked over to Jonathan. When she handed him the wine, he smiled and glanced back toward her friends and his brother.

"Sorry for starting off the night so badly, Maggie," he said in tones low enough that only she could hear.

"Never too late to set things right," she responded and was surprised by the sad, almost wistful glance he shot her friend.

"Some things just can't be fixed," he said dejectedly, and as the pan with the hot water began spitting and spilling over again, he took off the cover and started stirring it.

"Anything I can do to help?"

He jerked his chin in the direction of a large colander sitting on the counter.

"Put that in the sink for me."

It wasn't really what she'd been asking, but she did as he requested, prompting hoots and claps from her friends.

"Maggie's getting domestic again," Connie kidded.

"Is that not her thing? She made the cheesecake, right?" Owen asked.

Maggie tried to tune out the assorted tales with which her friends—maybe soon to be ex-friends—regaled Owen. He laughed out loud at one incident involving an egg in the microwave, but she had no time to defend herself, since Jonathan recruited her into the role of sous chef. He instructed her on how to drain the pasta he dumped into the colander so he could finish off the sauce. Once she was done with that, he thrust a bowl full of salad at her and asked her to take it to the table.

"We're eating family style," he explained.

She walked around the island separating the work area from the kitchen table and placed the bowl in a spot directly in front of Owen.

"Having fun?" she challenged with a quirk of her eyebrow.

His dimpled grin was her only answer before he said, "Sit down and let me help Jon finish up. After all, I did invite you."

She took a spot at Owen's right and across from Emma, who was in the chair closest to where Owen's brother would sit, providing a buffer between him and Connie.

A second later, Jonathan came over with a big bowl of pasta covered with a rich meat sauce. Owen followed and placed a large gravy bowl with more sauce beside it as well as a plate with a hunk of Parmesan and a grater.

"Smells delicious," Emma said, and Connie grudgingly agreed with a reluctant grunt.

Maggie eyeballed Owen as he sat beside her and waited as Jonathan took each person's plate to spoon out some pasta. Afterward, he dolloped on more of the sauce and, with an expert's ease, garnished the pasta with freshly grated Parmesan.

While he did that, Owen served everyone salad and then went back to the work area before returning with a basket filled with warm Italian bread. He sat and raised his glass in a toast, and Maggie held her breath, not sure what might be an appropriate topic.

"To friendships renewed," he said, creating an obvious maelstrom of emotions around the table with those simple words.

She clinked her glass against his, thinking that they were far more than friends and yet not. As his gaze met hers steadily, it occurred to her that building their friendship might be a better way to move along their relationship, since sex could only complicate matters.

With a smile and subtle dip of her head, she acknowledged his toast and turned to scrutinize the others at the table. Emma and Connie merrily tapped glasses, as did Emma and Jonathan. But Jonathan and Connie were slow to move, obviously uneasy, until Jonathan's gaze briefly met hers and he finally, reluctantly, touched his glass to Connie's and repeated the toast. "To friendships renewed," he said, clearly having taken their earlier discussion to heart.

Maggie hoped whatever had happened between them could be fixed in time.

"*Mangia*," Jonathan shouted, and in a flurry of activity, everyone dug into the meal he'd prepared.

The pasta was deliciously al dente while creamy at the same time. The freshly grated Parmesan was sharp against the sweetness of a Bolognese sauce packed with bits of pancetta, onion, and tender veal.

"Amazing," Maggie said at the same time Emma said, "I need this recipe. Where did you learn to cook like this?"

Seemingly self-conscious about the praise, Jonathan shrugged and said, "I had to work with some Italian designers and spent about six weeks in Bologna. While I was there, I decided to take some cooking classes in my free time."

—◦◦◦—

Owen smiled as his brother went on to delight them with tales of that trip and then another business excursion as Maggie asked what he had just worked on. It pleased him to see the respect and admiration the women had for his little brother and how comfortable Jonathan quickly got with them and their praise. It was something they had both sorely lacked from their father. He'd always thought Jonathan's daring experiments were a negative way of getting the attention he'd repeatedly lacked.

Attention like he was getting from Maggie and her friends. It made him wonder if he, like his brother, wasn't looking for attention in a wrong way.

She must have sensed the change in his mood, since she laid her hand over his. The subtle gesture garnered awareness from every person at the table that made her quickly rip her hand away and deftly ask Jonathan another question that brought everyone's focus back to his brother.

The meal passed quickly, and before long, they were slicing up pieces of Maggie's cheesecake. Owen took the first bite, and the flavors came alive in his mouth. The slightly tart but smooth sweetness of the cream cheese had just the right hint of vanilla. The tasty whipped cream melded well with the earthiness of the dark chocolate.

"Not too shabby for someone who isn't domestic," he teased but with a big grin to let her know it was more than all right.

"I think this is the first thing I've made that didn't require having the poison control number handy," she replied and dug into her own piece.

He liked her self-deprecating humor. Liked the easy way she had around her friends and his brother. More than liked the sexy half glance she tossed his way and the little twist of her mouth promising laughter was on its way.

Her eyes glimmered with crystal-blue light, a sure sign she was happy, which made him happy and created a nice, warm feeling in his heart.

Dessert finished way too quickly, but it was still early, and he didn't want the night to end just yet. Possibly not for a long time, since they all seemed to be having such a nice time. Even Connie had mellowed and appeared to be enjoying herself after the initial dustup with his brother.

He glanced outside to where the low-lying fog from earlier that morning had dissipated. Even though there had been a brisk feel to the late-summer air all day, they could start up the fire pit he'd prepped earlier to stay warm.

"If you ladies would like, I could get a fire started,

and we could sit out on the lawn and have some after-dinner drinks."

"Or s'mores. We have all the fixin's," Jonathan said, earning immediate agreement from the three women.

Obviously, his brother was more in tune with what these ladies liked, but Owen was fine with that. "I'll go get the fire going," he said but detoured to a nearby mudroom to snag some of the blankets they used on the beach just in case the fire couldn't warm the night air enough. Outside, he tossed the blankets on the wooden Adirondack chairs and some chaise longues they'd hauled out of a storage area earlier in the day. He hoped that the paper he'd tucked in between the logs in the fire pit hadn't gotten too damp in the couple of hours while they'd eaten. He struck a match and guarded it against the slight ocean breeze that had kicked up. Touched it to the newspaper, which immediately caught fire. Seconds later, the first little pop from the wood and glow along the edge of the log confirmed the fire had taken hold. He waited a few more minutes, and as the flames grew stronger, he tossed on a couple more pieces of wood.

The rest of the crew—and he liked to think that they were a crew now—spilled out of the house, laughing and carrying the ingredients for s'mores. They placed the trays with the chocolate, graham crackers, marsh-mallows, and the long barbecue skewers on tables by the fire. Emma and Connie grabbed the Adirondack chairs. His brother plopped down onto the chaise longue next to them, leaving him and Maggie to sit side by side on the second.

Maggie grabbed a skewer and two marshmallows and handed them to him.

He tapped his chest and said, "Me hunt. Make fire. You cook."

"Neanderthal," she teased back, grinning.

She took back the skewer, shoved the marshmallows on, and set the skewer over the fire, but he took hold of her hand and drew the skewer back a little to the edges of the flames.

"You want to melt them, not incinerate them," he kidded.

"Not domestic, remember?"

He shook his head and chided her. "It's a wonder you've survived this long," he said but helped her cook the marshmallows and then assemble the treats.

She took a bite, and squishy, gooey marshmallow and softened chocolate oozed from the sides of the graham cracker. She licked all around the edges, and his gut twisted as he imagined her licking him with as much gusto. As her gaze met his briefly, it was obvious she knew just where his thoughts were, since her blue eyes darkened to the color of the ocean at night, and she did a very deliberate lick all along one edge.

His dick jumped to life in his jeans, and he leaned forward and took a bite from her s'more, making sure to brush his lips against her hand as he did so.

"Very tasty," he said and was extremely satisfied with the way her hand trembled as she popped the last bit of the treat into her mouth.

"If you two are done with your foreplay over there, maybe you want to take a walk on the beach," Jonathan called out, earning a forceful elbow from Connie that made him grunt with pain.

"I think that's a great idea," Maggie said, flying to her feet and holding her hand out to him.

Not quite how he had expected to get her alone on the beach, but he'd take it and kill his brother later. Hopefully much later.

Popping to his feet, he grabbed the blanket off the longue, tucked it beneath his arm, and slipped his hand into Maggie's.

"Let's go," he said.

Chapter 13

NOTHING ABOUT THE NIGHT HAD GONE QUITE THE WAY Maggie had pictured it.

Not Connie and Jonathan. Or how all of them had gotten along like a group of long-time friends, maybe because they were friends on some level, considering how many years they'd all known each other. Or how she and Owen were now strolling along the sand at the water's edge, hand in hand. Silent. Tucked close to ward off the unseasonable chill of the night, their hips and shoulders brushing together as they moved. His presence was comforting, the night peaceful with no need to fill the silence.

After a few minutes and a sharper gust of wind that bit into them with a chill made worse by the damp fog blanketing the shoreline, Owen led them back up toward the dunes that provided some protection from the breeze and from prying eyes. He spread out the blanket and sat. Urged her to rest between his outstretched legs, her back to his chest to protect her from what was left of the wind. He wrapped his arms around her and tucked his face against her cheek, creating delicious warmth from the contact.

They were virtually alone, with only the muted shadows of a few distant beachgoers far down the beach at the water's edge.

Long moments passed until he said, "You know what they expect us to be doing, don't you?"

She peered at him from the corner of her eye. His features were neutral, giving away nothing of what he was thinking.

"I do," she said, but then plunged onward. "So do we do what they expect because they're expecting it?"

"In which case are we doing it because of that expectation, or do we really want to do it?" he finished for her, so in sync with her thoughts that it was almost downright scary.

She turned in his arms because she wanted to see every aspect of his face for this discussion. Possibly a mistake. The kiss of moonlight made his hair seem almost impossibly black and brightened the shards of silver in his amazing eyes. The ephemeral light cast shadows on his features but chiseled the sharp edges of that very masculine and handsome face. Gilded the strong line of his lips, so irresistible. She ran her index finger across his upper lip and then down to the spot where she knew that damn irresistible dimple lurked.

Meeting his gaze, she saw how his pupils had dilated with her caress and were now pools of a gunmetal hue. "Do you want to do it?"

He cupped her jaw and skimmed his thumb across the ridge of her cheekbone. "What do you think?"

If he had asked her last night or even earlier that night, before his toast, the answer would have been a resounding yes.

Now, she wasn't so sure it made sense, although she had no doubts that she wanted him physically. All the signs were there as he scraped his thumb across her cheek again. The little twist of desire between her legs. The heat racing across her body and the tightening of her nipples beneath the sexy lace bra she'd worn in anticipation of tonight. But wanting more than that?

"I think we both want..." she began but faltered.

"I want to touch you. Kiss you. I thought about it a lot since last night and this morning, but I think we need to take it slow, Mags," he said.

"Slow is always good," she kidded, although she knew where he was going, and she was actually surprisingly on board with it.

He grinned, and that enticing dimple emerged, prompting her to lean forward and drop a kiss there before shifting to lightly brush her lips all along the edges of his lips.

"What is this?" he asked.

She chuckled and repeated what he'd said to her that morning, which now seemed like ages ago. "If you can't tell, I must not be doing it right."

He barked out a laugh so loud, she feared the others up on the lawn might hear. She covered his mouth with her hand and felt his smile there. Saw his amusement in the silvery glitter alive in his gaze.

"You always surprise me, Mags," he whispered.

"Maybe because we don't know each other well enough yet to take this to the next step."

One dark eyebrow quirked upward. "Which is?"

She rolled her eyes and gave a rueful shake of her head. "I don't think I need to spell it out for you, Owen."

"S-e-x," he spelled out, and disappointment slammed into her because deep down, in some part of her, she'd been hoping it would be more than s-e-x. More like l-o-v-e.

But maybe s-e-x was a first step to more. To the happily ever after that Tracy was always chasing,

Connie didn't have time for, and Emma just didn't believe in. She was like none of her friends that way. She'd always thought it would happen if the right man came along. But for lots of reasons, she wasn't sure Owen was Mr. Right.

He must have sensed the change in her mood. He stroked his thumb across her cheek again, his touch both reassuring and sensual.

"Let's get to know each other better, Mags," he said, and before she could agree, his lips were on hers again, coaxing a response. Gentle but demanding. Exploring the edges of her lips with quick little kisses and her bottom lip with a sexy nip that he soothed with his tongue.

She huffed out a breath as her nipples tightened even more, and deep in her center, that intimate bite had her insides pulsing with need.

"Owen," she whispered and dug her hands into his thick hair, urging him close.

Owen opened his mouth as she licked the seam of his mouth with her tongue. Groaned as she darted and withdrew in a sexy tease.

He ran his hands down her back to her buttocks and cupped them. Pulled her tight to him so that her center was poised right over the long, hard ridge of his erection.

Her sharp gasp as she felt him against her had him swelling even more beneath his jeans. When she rocked her hips against him, he grasped her hips to hold her still.

"Slow," he whispered and kissed her again. He took his time learning the shape and feel of her lips. The way her warm breath spilled against his as she sighed with pleasure. He moved away from her lips to the corner of her mouth for another kiss. A sample of her. He dropped a trail of kisses along the line of her jaw until he reached the sensitive spot just behind her ear. With a nibble and another kiss, he shifted to her earlobe and nipped and tugged, drawing another soft moan from her and a slow shift of her hips along his erection.

"God, that feels so good," he whispered and let out his own deep moan when she drew back over him.

"They say anticipation just makes the wait worthwhile," she said and mimicked his actions, dragging her mouth along his jaw and to a spot just below his ear.

When she opened her mouth on him and sucked, he nearly jumped out of his skin. Each pull of her mouth had his dick pulsing in expectation, but he dampened that need, because tonight was not about sex.

"If you keep that up, I may not be able to wait," he confessed.

Her husky laugh nearly undid him. With a quick love bite at that spot, she shifted back onto her buttocks and met his gaze. "I like you, Owen. I like that you can be honest with me," she said, which made him feel like a total dick since, in some ways, he wasn't being totally honest with her about lots of things. Like the lie he'd told his father. A lie that directly involved her. A lie that he'd told to save his own dreams as well.

"I like you too, Mags. I'd like to see you again when we get back to the city," he said, vowing to himself that he would not let that lie get in the way of what was happening between them.

"I'd like that too, Owen," she said and snuggled against him trustingly.

His heart did a little jump of contentment with her action. He hugged her close and settled in to enjoy the peace in her embrace and the quiet of the late-summer evening. It wasn't quite how he had pictured their night together would end, and yet somehow, it felt more right than he had ever expected.

Chapter 14

THE PAPERS THAT CONNIE SPREAD OUT ACROSS THE BOARDROOM table on Tuesday morning told a story of a life interrupted and hopes and dreams that would never be fulfilled. By the end of the meeting, one thing was irrevocably clear. Maggie's only choice was to put her big-girl panties on and stand up to her dad to save their Sea Kiss home, her town house, and the stores.

All were a big part of her heart, she thought. Especially the stores. There were so many memories of visiting as a child. Her mother had taken her to the Fifth Avenue location regularly to walk the floors and speak to the staff. It wasn't unusual for them to spend a few hours in the office her mother had had before her marriage had merged the Sinclair's and Maxwell's business interests. After that, she'd moved to the office in the Chrysler Building but had still spent time in the flagship store office when she visited.

At Christmastime, one of the floors would become a Winter Wonderland for the children, complete with Santa and his elves. She remembered sitting on Santa's lap and giving him her wish list of toys. She also recalled sitting there the year after her mother had died and asking for just one thing: to have her mommy back and meet the new little brother who had died as well.

Forcing away the sadness, she vowed to try to make things right. But if this was going to be the very last

Christmas for the stores, she intended for it to be the best Christmas ever. That would take months of hurried planning, because they were already late for the holiday season thanks to her father's refusal to change. But she was up to the challenge both for herself and for her store's employees.

———∿∿∿———

To text or not to text. That was the question.

Owen had always found texting to be too impersonal, much like voicemail.

He hadn't left one earlier when he'd called Maggie. She'd been out of the office, so her assistant had routed him to her voicemail, but after he'd recorded a stilted message, he'd deleted it and hung up.

He didn't dare to just show up on her doorstep. First, there was getting by building security. That meant someone from Maggie's office had to clear him. By the time he took the elevator up the fifty-some floors, he worried that there'd be talk about why he was there and lots and lots of gossip. Maggie's employees had to have seen the earlier photos in the paper. And of course, it wouldn't be any kind of surprise for Maggie, because he'd have to have been cleared to come up.

Just way too complicated, he thought as he leaned back in his chair and considered his options, hating his indecisiveness until he finally put together a plan of action. With one quick call, he had a bouquet of flowers headed her way with a very simple note.

He set a reminder on his phone and turned his attention back to the drawings one of their architects had dropped off earlier that morning. He'd been in meetings all day but had been eagerly awaiting the plans. He unrolled the drawings and weighted down two of the sides so he could examine them.

They'd purchased a building in the high Nineties on the East Side, not far from their new condo complex on what real estate agents were selling as Central Park North. It would always be Harlem as far as he was concerned.

Since not even a facelift could fix the issues with their newly acquired building, they had moved out what few tenants were left to some of their nicer rental properties so they could demolish the structure and construct high-end apartments. With the building's views of the East River, easy access to the FDR, and a nearby subway station, he didn't think they'd have any trouble getting more than decent rents once it was done. They were also setting aside some units for lower-income families.

As he pored over the drawings, he smiled. The architect had done a good job, providing a variety of units on the assorted floors, luxury condos on the higher levels, and a stunning penthouse along with easily accessed common areas, like a fitness room and a recreation hall that tenants could reserve when they needed more space for an event.

He did have some additional ideas about the mix of units in the building. The demolition and new construction would be costly, and they needed a certain number of apartments to quickly recoup those costs as well as the original investment in the building itself.

Those ideas prompted a load of new thoughts about how to restore some of the smaller Sea Kiss summer cottages that were still suffering Sandy damage. Issues with insurance and battles between FEMA and the local authorities had left them uninhabitable even years later. He could run those ideas past Maggie to see what she thought before he raised the concept with their committee in Sea Kiss.

He sat down at his computer to draft a memo with his ideas when his phone beeped to remind him that he had to call Maggie.

Walking to the entrance to his office, he closed the door and, for good measure, drew the blinds along the glass that made up one wall of his office, wanting total privacy for this moment. He strolled back toward his desk, sat on its edge, and engaged the video call app on his smartphone.

It rang and rang and rang.

He worried that either the flowers hadn't gotten there in time or that she was busy or that maybe, worst of all, she'd just reconsidered and had no desire to see him. Disheartened by that possibility, he was about to disconnect when she breathlessly answered.

It took a few seconds for her pixelated image to come together. She was smiling, her crystal-blue eyes bright and glittering.

"Thank you so much for the flowers. They're lovely," she said and shifted the camera so he could see them.

He grinned when he saw that the florist had gotten the order perfectly. A riot of off-white and pink cabbage roses were mixed with deep-blue hydrangea and stargazer lilies, just like the summer flowers he'd noticed that weekend at Maggie's Shore home.

"You didn't have to," she said as the camera did a dizzying whirl before settling on her face again. "And while this is nice, you could have called or texted me a message."

"I hate texting," he said.

Her smile broadened, and she said, "I do too, plus there's one thing I hate even more."

"Voicemails," they said at the same time, drawing laughter from both of them.

After the humor had quieted down a little, he really took the time to examine her. She seemed more peaceful than she had the other day. Maybe even downright happy. Her eyes, the windows to her soul, were free of the shadows and darkness he had seen just days earlier.

"I can tell things seem to be going better."

While that might please him to no end, he knew his father would not be at all happy if Maggie had suddenly found a way out of the mess her company was in.

"They are, but why don't we save that discussion for tonight? Dinner? Somewhere neutral?"

He huffed out a laugh before he said, "Do we need to establish a DMZ?"

Her full lips quirked in a way he couldn't quite read. "More like a DFZ?" At his questioning look, she clarified. "Dad Free Zone."

He grinned and nodded. "How about the Mesa Grill? I'd like to run some ideas by you for fixing up the Sea Kiss summer cottages."

Maggie considered his choice and smiled. "Sounds great. Tex-Mex and spicy is definitely not something either of our dads would like. Eight o'clock? I don't know about your dad, but mine is usually in front of the television by then."

"Mine too. See you then, and, Maggie…"

She waited, expectant. It was clear she was unable to read him, so he flashed her a megawatt grin to dispel any doubt.

As she smiled back, he said, "I like seeing you happy."

Chapter 15

MAGGIE SAW OWEN WAITING FOR HER BY THE DOOR TO THE restaurant despite a late-summer heat wave that was toasting the city. Luckily, a thunderstorm was on its way to provide needed rain and cooling. The impending storm was sending gusts of wind whipping down the avenue, ruffling the thick strands of his black hair into disarray.

As she approached, he held his hand out, and she slipped her hand into his, following his lead as he pulled her close and hugged her. She told herself not to read too much into how right it felt. How she knew that he'd had a smile on his face right before he'd brushed a kiss across her cheek. How her deep inhale of satisfaction filled her senses with the smell of Owen.

"Hello, Maggie," he whispered against her ear.

"Hello, Owen," she said and shivered as the first fat drop of rain landed on her sun-warmed skin and more quickly followed.

"Let's get inside," he said, and hand in hand, they rushed into the restaurant.

There was a good crowd in the place even on a Tuesday night, thanks to the popularity of the celebrity chef and the food, which was always excellent.

Owen had made a reservation, and with barely a pause to check off his name, the hostess was soon guiding them to an intimate table in a quiet corner.

He held the chair out for her gallantly and then took the spot to her right, surprising her. It put him much closer to her, so close that their knees bumped under the table.

A waiter immediately arrived with menus and asked if they wanted any drinks.

"How about some margaritas on the rocks?" Owen said.

She nodded and, after the waiter left, quickly perused the menu. The drinks arrived in minutes, they placed their orders, and once the waiter had departed again, Owen held up his drink and said, "To Maggie's happy day."

It was impossible not to smile at the toast and at the day she'd had, so she touched her glass to his and took a sip. Sweet and sour lime blended perfectly with the Cointreau and Jose Cuervo.

"Dare I ask what made your day so great?" Owen said and set his glass on the table.

"You may," she said and took another sip. Her gaze skimmed briefly across his, and it was impossible to miss the gleam in his eyes that said he might dare to do more. She ignored the flutter of desire inside her and pushed ahead with her story. "For starters, I had it out with my dad. Not an easy thing to do, but I told him we were going to start making changes, including canceling a contract we'd argued about last week."

Owen grimaced, obviously understanding how hard the whole working-with-dad dynamic could be. "How'd he take it?"

Maggie started to speak but then slapped a hand over her mouth. "I'm sorry. Our truce clearly said no talk about family or business."

One corner of Owen's mouth quirked up in a half grin. "We could make an exception tonight. After all, friends talk about all kinds of things."

Friends, she thought, only they both wanted to be more than friends. If only for tonight, she was willing to expand the terms of the truce, because for the first time in a long time, she felt both happy and optimistic about the stores. That also meant she might be able to have enough to save the shore home and pay off the loan on her town house.

"My dad dug in his heels at first, but then surprisingly, amazingly actually, he gave in."

She recalled that moment when her father had seemed to have an epiphany and how his whole demeanor had changed in what seemed like the blink of an eye. Her throat tightened with emotion, and her voice was husky as she told Owen, "He said I had never reminded him more of my mother than at that moment. That when she'd been passionate about something, she wouldn't let go. He said that if I truly believed this was what needed to be done, he wouldn't stand in my way anymore."

She knew it was obvious to Owen how much her father's words had affected her. Tears shimmered in her eyes, and her voice was thick with feeling.

As one tear escaped and ran down her face, he cradled her cheek and swiped away the moisture with his thumb. "I'm glad he finally relented. And I know these are happy tears, right?" he said, gallantly trying to restore the joy she'd been feeling earlier.

With a sniffle and a nod, she said, "Yes, they are. Happy tears. Thank you."

She covered his hand with hers and stroked it.

Bestowed a watery smile on him that brightened little by little as they brought their joined hands to the table, and she provided a brief rundown of how the rest of her day had gone. How she had prepared to start some of the changes she'd been planning for so long.

"It sounds like you're going to be very busy," he said.

She detected the regret in his voice that it might mean he'd see less of her in the coming months. "It'll be crazy, but I've got good people working for me. I know we'll get it done."

As the waiter came over with their meals and placed them on the table, he asked, "And maybe have some time to sneak in another weekend or two down at Sea Kiss?"

Maggie narrowed her gaze and searched his features, trying to get a sense of how serious he was about what he was proposing, since she was suddenly having a major attack of doubt about how much she could trust him. Truth be told, she really was contemplating sleeping with the enemy, much as her friends had kidded her. Plus, in some deep part of her, there was still the fear he'd leave her the way he had so many years earlier.

"Maybe, only… What we say here is between the two of us, right?"

That he got what she was intimating was immediately evident. His lips, those lips capable of that sexy, boyish grin, firmed into a knife-sharp line that cut into her with his displeasure, and his beautiful gray eyes became as lifeless as those on a shark.

"There are probably a million reasons why you shouldn't trust me," he said.

"Hundreds of millions if you're referring to the

stores," she said, trying to lighten the mood, because she didn't want to let her fears ruin what could possibly be something really good between them.

The slight upward tilt of his lips was tempered by a tired exhale. "You can trust me, Maggie. I'm not my father's son, even though he wishes that I were."

"I know I can trust you. I'm sorry about your dad and about the way he treats you and Jon," she said, but it was painfully obvious that her words had caused hurt that couldn't be brushed away with just a few words.

"We deal, don't we? We both lost our moms. We both have difficult fathers. Maybe we get lucky and they change. Just look at you. You managed to finally get your dad to see the light."

He attacked the last of his steak with short, jerky movements, and she opted to remain silent and let time ease some of the upset. As wonderfully prepared as the meal was, the flavors were dull thanks to the unhappiness still simmering in Owen.

When the waiter arrived to clear the table and asked about dessert, they both demurred. Clearly, their time together would be over quickly tonight.

After Owen paid for the meal, since this time it was a date, they hurried outside.

The rain had come and gone during dinner, bringing a bit of chill to the night, but it was nothing compared to the frostiness between them.

She faced him just as he said, "I'll walk you home."

"You don't have to. I can just grab a cab."

A small gust sent her hair across her face, and he reached out and tucked it back behind her ear. "I insist. I like to make sure my dates get home okay, remember?"

She was about to protest when a powerful gust of wind blasted down the avenue and sent her reeling against him.

—~~—

Owen cuddled her close, and the feel of her, the easy way she slipped an arm around his waist, melted some of the ice that had surrounded his heart during their dinner discussion. She looked up at him, question in her gaze, and he smiled, bent his head, and answered her with a kiss. A sweet, undemanding skim of his lips along hers. A kiss meant to reassure and also rebuild the happy mood with which they'd started the night. As the kiss ended and she pulled away, the relaxed grin on her face signaled his success and broadened his own smile.

As they had the other night, they walked the few blocks to her home, strolling through Union Square and down to her town house directly across from Gramercy Park. He ambled with her up her stoop, waited until she had opened her door, but paused there as she entered. She turned, faced him with puzzlement on her features, and stepped outside again.

"Don't you want to come in?"

Inside him, expectation and doubt tangled together like roses and weeds in a struggling garden. He grazed her cheek with the back of his hand, a hesitant touch. "I do, but we both know what might happen if I do."

"And that would be wrong because?" she asked, unmistakably questioning his reluctance.

"Because you need to *really* trust me. So even though I want to come inside and be with you, I'm going to hold back my baser instincts."

"Baser, huh?" she said with a wicked grin.

He chuckled and cradled her cheek. "*Way* baser, Mags. But not yet. Not until I know that *you* know I'm trustworthy."

She narrowed her gaze and examined his features. "You surprise me at times, Owen."

He grinned and rushed in for a quick, demanding kiss. At her sigh of acceptance, he resisted the temptation and pulled back.

"You surprise me *all* the time, Mags."

Before she could say anything else or seduce him with another kiss, he backed away and skipped down the stairs. He paused at her front gate and nearly changed his mind when she covered her mouth with her hand, as if reliving their kiss.

Trust, he reminded himself. She had to trust that he would not betray her to curry favor with his father. He had to trust that, unlike the mother who had left him and Jonathan and never looked back, Maggie could never be that callous.

With a brisk wave, he hurried home to take the world's most frigid shower.

Chapter 16

TEACHING MAGGIE THAT SHE COULD TRUST HIM MIGHT RUIN him for life, Owen thought a week later as he turned the dial on the gym shower as cold as it could go. He washed quickly so he could be on his way to the office and stop thinking about Maggie's sexy muscles as she worked out in the weight room and the subtle but enticing touches and smiles as they passed each other in the gym.

Fuck, he thought. Even the icy blast of water wasn't enough to quell the desire shooting through him.

He gritted his teeth against both the cold water and the heat of passion and finished before anyone else in the shower noticed his predicament. Speedily wrapping the towel around himself, he rushed out to the locker room, sopping wet, grateful that between his wet state and the cool air in the gym, the last of his erection subsided.

Toweling down, he dressed, and a short time later, he was on his way to the office. With every block and avenue that passed, dread grew in his belly. Not with the thought of the work that awaited him, because he liked what he did, but with the thought of facing his father and having to deal with his questions about Maggie and their relationship.

It had been nearly three weeks since that first dinner. In that time, they'd shared several meals and regularly run into each other at the gym. They'd gone for a jog along Sea Kiss Beach, and he'd discovered that despite Maggie's athleticism, she was somewhat klutzy. He'd had to grab her to keep her from doing a header as they'd raced up the steps of the Sea Kiss lighthouse.

Not that he would complain about having Maggie close to him. All those luscious curves and toned muscle. The way she tucked her head just beneath his chin and how the soft silk of her hair grazed the underside of his jaw. The smell of her, so fresh and flowery, despite the miles they'd jogged.

"Pardon me, mister. We're here," the driver said from behind the glass security partition.

He mumbled an apology for keeping the driver waiting and handed him the fare and a tip. Exiting the taxi, he walked around the corner and changed up his usual breakfast, getting an egg sandwich and supersize latte. He lamented yet again that New York delis rarely had pork roll and told himself he would just have to wait until this weekend in Sea Kiss to satisfy that itch. Maybe another itch if things with Maggie kept moving in the right direction.

In his office, he ripped open the deli bag and used it as a place mat for his sandwich and coffee. He ate while he perused the *Wall Street Journal* his assistant had left on his desk. Sipping his coffee, he checked more news sites on the internet and logged in to see how his personal investments were doing. Satisfied with what he saw, he turned his attention to a memo on another possible real estate acquisition and, after that, reviewed the status of the project on the Upper East Side. He smiled, immensely satisfied. Everything was going well with that redevelopment. Demolition was moving along nicely, and it looked like construction would start right on time. Barring any issues with delays in the necessary permits or inspections, they would be able to start renting the units as planned.

Life is good, he thought, but then he looked up and saw his father heading down the rows between the cubicles toward his office. His features were set in unforgiving lines, and the expression on his face couldn't have been more sour. If his father had been a cartoon, he could picture little, black storm clouds circling around his head and following him along. Add a couple of lightning bolts and torrential rain to match the darkness that swirled around him, and the picture would have been perfect.

He feigned interest in another report as his father came to his door and stood there, waiting to be acknowledged. That game went on for a few more minutes before his father finally grew tired of waiting, slammed the door shut, and stomped into his office. Literally stomped, his feet loudly thumping against the thick carpet.

Owen raised his head tardily and dipped his head in greeting. "Father. What brings you here this fine day?"

With a glower and a huff, his father dropped into the chair in front of Owen's desk, signaling that this wasn't going to be a quick discussion.

"How are things going, Owen?"

Owen motioned to the papers in neat piles on his desk. "Everything is going well. The Sunnyside location seems like a good acquisition to consider. The Upper East Side project is on time and—"

"That's not what I'm talking about, Owen," his father said, every syllable filled with contempt.

Owen wouldn't take the bait. "What do you want to talk about?"

"Goddamn it, that Sinclair woman of course," his father nearly hissed and skewered him with his direct gaze. His father's eyes were so much like his own, it was downright scary. He didn't want to imagine himself thirty years from now, staring at a bitter, old man in the mirror with those same exact eyes.

"What's happening with Maggie is...complicated." *And personal*, he wanted to add, but that would be sure to inspire anger and nothing else.

"Complicated? You don't know the meaning of complicated," his father said, voice rough with emotion, and looked away, as if suddenly uncomfortable with the discussion.

It was almost too much to hope that his father might finally be softening his stance. That he might share something more about what had happened between himself and Bryce Sinclair.

"Please explain it to me, Father. Please tell me why it's this way. Why it can't change."

His father gripped the arms of the chair, his knuckles white from the pressure. His gaze was downturned, averted, but Owen could still detect the gleam of moisture there. He wouldn't call it tears because, well...he'd never seen his father cry. Not ever. Not when his wife had left. Not when Jonathan had hit the road. Not ever.

"Father? Please tell me why it's so complicated," he said, experiencing sudden sympathy for him.

In the blink of an eye, his father's demeanor did a one-eighty. A blank stare and features hard as stone replaced the softness he'd seen barely moments earlier.

"It's not complicated at all, Owen. You fuck the girl. You marry her. You get the properties. Sounds pretty simple to me." To emphasize his point, his father slapped his hands on the arms of the chair.

He couldn't deny that he wanted to sleep with Maggie, but hearing it said so crudely and with such venom made his stomach revolt. As for marrying her... he hadn't thought about it, although the idea wasn't displeasing. After all, when you loved someone...

Whoa, whoa, whoa, the little voice in his head shouted to control that runaway thought.

He didn't love Maggie. Not yet, he didn't think. If he did, he needed to be honest with her and with himself about the situation they were in. He needed to tell her the truth about the lie he had told his father and about the reasons why he'd even considered such a preposterous and hurtful idea.

Not to mention that he had to have an exit plan for what he would do once his father tossed him out of the company. His stomach twisted at the thought of that happening, since he had always imagined being part of the company's future. He told himself that he could handle it if he was forced to leave. He had money and connections. He would find something to do with himself. Maybe he'd even start up his own real estate development company.

Avoiding his father's too condemning gaze, he said, "It is not as simple as you'd like to think, Father. Unlike you, I find it harder to fake love."

A rough harrumph greeted his statement, and his father's features softened once again. "Is that what you think I did with your mother?"

Interesting, he didn't said "my wife," Owen thought before responding. "I don't think you ever loved her."

He didn't need to say that he didn't think his father had ever loved anyone, but his father knew and shot to his feet with unexpected agility.

Jerking a shaky finger in Owen's direction, he said, "You have no idea what it means to love someone. To lose them." He jabbed his gut with that unsteady finger, and the sheen of tears came to his eyes once more. "It sticks with you here, no matter what you do. It *never* leaves you, no matter how hard you try to forget," he said, his voice tight with the emotion he strangled into submission.

Unlike whoever left him, Owen thought. It hadn't been his mother, he realized in a moment of blinding clarity. It made it a little easier to understand why she'd left his father but not any easier to understand why she'd left her two sons behind.

"I'll keep that in mind, Father."

With another angry poke of his finger in Owen's direction, his father said, "Fuck her. Marry her, but *don't* fall in love with her." In a softer tone, he said, "Don't ever fall in love."

He stalked out of Owen's office, stomping down the hall, leaving behind a host of questions whose answers might explain the hate eating at his father's soul.

━━∿∿∿━━

Maggie listened patiently to the presentation from her advertising department, although she was anything but patient inside. She had laid out what she wanted for their holiday campaign—something that created the feel of old-time New York. The elegance of shopping in a store instead of online. The memories created by spending time with your family in the winter playground they would be building on the vacant floor adjacent to the now-shuttered restaurant in the flagship location. Her plans even included restoring that restaurant to its former glory and hosting high teas and brunches for their shoppers in addition to a smaller kiosk where they could buy treats to munch on while waiting for a visit with Santa.

Her team wasn't quite getting the message she wanted to get across for some reason. Maybe because they were all part of Generation X or millennials and their real-time lives were intertwined with their online personas. She was part of the same group but had never gotten all caught up in being online. She'd been too busy with work to spend much time on social media, but she understood the allure of it. As the presenter finished, she said, "You've got a good start, but something's missing. How about we all take a walk downstairs to the restaurant floor? See what's happening there so you can picture it better?"

The four members of the team exchanged worried looks, but then each one nodded their agreement.

She stood, and they followed her out of the meeting room on one of the business floors of the store and down the stairs to the employee's lunchroom that was adjacent to the restaurant. There were a few people there, taking advantage of the calm space for their break time, enjoying the food the kitchen staff still prepared for the employees even though the restaurant hadn't been in business for several years. She had that going for her at least—a good staff and a kitchen that, while underutilized, was still in tip-top shape. It made it easier to put that part of her plan into place.

Pushing through the doors to the kitchen, she greeted the workers and kept walking through to the other set of doors into the restaurant, where she already had carpenters and painters renovating the space. Outside the restaurant, on the opposite side of the floor, other laborers were busy creating where Santa, his elves, and his workshop would be along with an expansion of their toy department and the kiosk for the quick treats.

She moved into the center of the space, held out her arms, and did a slow pivot as she said, "I remember coming here to the Savannah Courtyard with my mom for high tea when I was a kid. I couldn't wait to get all dressed up, and it was so exciting to think that I was grown-up enough for the fancy finger foods. Afterward, I would sit on Santa's lap and ask him for the gifts I wanted for Christmas. I loved spending time here with my mom."

She choked up as she recalled those moments and how in a child's naïveté, it had never occurred to her that those moments might be way too few in number.

"I didn't realize just how special those times were, but I know now. I want others to have moments like that to remember. To cherish."

She gestured to the murals on the walls that stretched to high ceilings where a painted sky was always blazingly blue and eternally sunny. Painters were already at work, giving the dulled paint new color and sparkle.

"Imagine all this full of life again. Imagine something better than a bunch of boxes on your front porch—time with your family, a relaxing afternoon combined with a visit with Santa."

Santa being Mr. Mitchell, one of the retired floor

managers who had always played the role when Maggie had been a child. Not that she'd recognized him at the time. Of course, there would be other Santas hired to give Mr. Mitchell a break, as well as elves and additional temporary staff to entertain customers as they shopped.

"I want a visit to this store to be a magical experience. To be about more than pushing a button and getting the cheapest price. That's not to say we won't offer competitive pricing on quality merchandise. We need to get that across as well."

"Not asking too much," one of the advertising team grumbled beneath his breath.

She understood. It was a tough mountain to climb, but the only other option was giving up. That was something she wouldn't do. For her mother. For herself. And for the many employees who would lose their jobs if the stores closed.

"Go back to the drawing board. Think about all this," she said and gestured to the room once more. "Think about what we want the store to be for the people who walk in through our doors. How we can make it special for them. How this experience will be far better than placing an order on their computer or smartphone."

The head of the advertising department peered at each of his team members before indicating his acceptance with a slow nod. "When would you like the new mock-ups?"

It was already Tuesday afternoon, and she would be asking a lot of them, but they didn't have much time left to put their plans into place. They'd need to do some buys for ad space in the local papers and on the area television stations. Plus, they'd have to work up a social media campaign to boost their traditional efforts. To do that, they'd have to act quickly.

"Can you have something for me by Friday afternoon? I'll look at it over the weekend, and then we can meet on Monday morning to discuss it."

If the team members were dismayed by her request, they hid it well. The department head didn't hesitate when he said, "We know how important this is for all of us, Maggie. We'll have it ready."

Chapter 17

MAGGIE HATED THE THOUGHT OF CANCELING ON OWEN, BUT her people had delivered as promised, and she wouldn't disappoint them by not having her comments ready on Monday morning. Granted, it probably wouldn't take all weekend to review their revamped campaign, the drafts for the print ads, and the storyboards for the television commercials, but she had a lot of other things to do as well for Monday morning. Not to mention that a weekend away with Owen at the Shore…

Even though it was well over four weeks since that game-changing night and they'd had what you could call dates on multiple occasions, a weekend alone carried all kinds of implications, namely that it was time to take the next step: having sex.

She wouldn't call it "making love" just yet, because she wasn't sure she was in love with Owen. She liked being with him. He could be funny and sensitive. Occasionally broody, but rarely. Intuitive. Understanding.

Incredibly sexy.

Dear Lord, when he kissed her, touched her, the desire he kindled made her insides burn hotter than a habanero pepper. That heat and need could only lead to one thing, and despite her bravado of the other night on her stoop, she wasn't quite sure she was ready for that next step.

She picked up her phone, and because she was

feeling cowardly, she dialed him instead of using the video app. She didn't like lying and wasn't particularly good at it. He'd read her like a book and know she was just searching for a reason to delay what was happening in their relationship.

He answered after the first ring, his voice sounding all chipper, which only made her feel more incredibly guilty.

"Hey, Mags. Are you as excited as I am about getting away for the weekend? I was thinking we could get a head start and leave later tonight instead of in the morning."

She grimaced and stammered as she began her excuse. "Owen, I'm so sorry, but something's come up. I'm not going to be able to make it this weekend. You understand, right?"

Silence filled the air for long moments before his tired sigh broke the condemning quiet. "Sure, Mags. I get it. Work always comes first with people like us. Maybe we can get together for dinner sometime next week."

Despite his words, the hurt and disappointment were obvious, and even without the video to see him, it was obvious he was pulling back and giving her space because he understood her well enough to know she needed it.

"That sounds lovely. Maybe we can even get away next weekend?" she offered, ignoring all her doubts about whether she'd be ready to sleep with him in just another week.

"Sure. Have an easy weekend. Don't work too hard," he said.

Before she could utter another word, he hung up, leaving her more confused than when they'd started the conversation. He'd given up too easily, and a part of her was a little disappointed that he had. Another part of her was annoyed with herself, because as hesitant as she was about having sex with him, she liked spending time with Owen.

Now that wasn't going to happen this weekend. Maybe never if he took her reticence to mean that she didn't want to move the relationship forward.

Cursing her indecisiveness, a trait of which she'd never been accused, she packed up the papers for the campaign her advertising team had developed, determined to review them that night. She also stuffed into her bag the notes on the financing she'd need to complete the plans for the holiday overhaul and an agreement with a top Italian knit designer for an exclusive clothing line that would launch in midfall for an added boost of publicity and hopefully sales.

Maybe she could even get Connie to come over during the weekend and take a look at the contract. She dialed her friend, and like Owen, she answered on the first ring. But unlike Owen, her voice was far from chipper.

"Everything okay?" Maggie asked.

"A little crazy since one of our clients just got sued, but I won't be involved in this one."

"I guess that's good, right?" she said.

But Connie's answer was an exasperated, "They only want the big boys working this case."

To ease her friend's upset, she said, "I was hoping you could look at a contract for me over the weekend."

A long pause followed, not unlike the one during her conversation with Owen. Much like that discussion, her friend responded with, "You're blowing him off, aren't you?"

She sucked in a deep breath and then expelled the words like a rapid-fire semiautomatic. "Yes, I canceled with Owen. I have a lot of work to catch up on and need to make up a lot of time over the weekend."

Connie's response this time was immediate. "You were never a good liar, Mags. I sense regret has already set in, which is why this call is about Owen and not about some contract you need me to see."

"Did I do the right thing, Connie?" she wondered aloud, definitely sorry about skipping out on what had promised to be a very nice weekend with a very sexy, handsome, and understanding man. While she wanted to save the stores for herself, her mother, and her employees, she wanted more in her life. She needed more.

Silence greeted her again, but this time when it was broken, the concern in her friend's voice was impossible to miss. "How about dinner tonight? Bryant Park Grill?"

Maggie glanced at her watch. It was only four o'clock, but she was already dog tired, both physically and emotionally. She needed out of the office sooner rather than later.

"Can you do five? And by the way, there really is a contract to be vetted."

"I'll meet you in your lobby at five. Email me the contract. I'll have something for you by tomorrow afternoon."

While the day had dragged, the hour until dinner flew by like a supersonic jet.

Maggie hurried down to the lobby and arrived a few minutes early. It gave her a moment to appreciate the beauty of the building in which she worked when she wasn't at the office in the Fifth Avenue store.

The art deco style was apparent in every little detail from the elevator doors with their geometric inlaid designs to the polished stainless-steel mailbox. Above the entire lobby, a painted canvas on the ceiling depicted the workers who had labored on the structure while muscular male figures celebrated the technological achievements of that era.

"Playing tourist?" Connie asked as she walked up to Maggie and peered up to investigate whatever Maggie was busy viewing.

"Stopping to smell the roses," she admitted.

"I'm sure there are plenty of roses in Bryant Park at this time of year. Let's go smell them while we appreciate the meal and the company," Connie said and urged her around one crowd of sightseers standing in the lobby and to the revolving doors, where another group of tourists was creating a bottleneck as they fumbled to get the door moving. They detoured to the second revolving door and circled through it and onto Forty-Second Street.

The sidewalks were teeming with visitors to the city and commuters racing home on a Friday night. They navigated through the crowds, shooting through gaps and breaking apart to get past the packed Grand Central area and up to Fifth Avenue and the huge public library with its famous lions. Walking past the library, they entered Bryant Park and strolled over to the restaurant.

There were a few people already waiting for an early dinner, but the host recognized them as they came in and greeted them warmly. "It won't be long, ladies. Why don't you enjoy a cocktail while you wait?" he said and motioned toward the bar off to one section of the building.

"I don't know about you, but I could use a drink," Connie said.

Maggie followed her into the bar, where they sat on some stools and efficiently ordered cosmos to keep them busy until a table was ready.

"To friends," Connie toasted.

"To my BFFFs," she said with a big smile and took a sip of the smooth, bright cocktail.

"Totally. Bottoms up," Connie replied and urged Maggie to chug her drink rather than sipping it slowly like a teetotaler experimenting with their first taste of alcohol.

"Trying to get me drunk?" Maggie teased as she stared at the bottom of the glass.

"For sure," she said and, with a wave of her hand, instructed the bartender to bring another round. The young man was just setting the glasses before them when the host came over to tell them their table was ready.

"May I?" he asked, and at Connie's nod, he swept up the glasses and walked with them to the table for two close to the windows.

It was still bright out, and all around them, the colors of the lawn, trees, and flower beds were vibrant and alive. With the arrival of dusk in a few hours, the lights of the buildings all around the park would spark to life with the arrival of dusk.

In a couple of months, the lawn would be covered with a skating rink to kick off the holiday season, and small kiosks would pop up all around the park so visitors could shop and eat while they enjoyed a New York Christmas. Maggie wanted those same holiday revelers to enjoy time at her family's store.

At the table, Connie gave her a drink-up gesture

and scooped up her own cocktail glass for a sip. As Maggie watched her friend quickly consume the cosmopolitan, it occurred to her that even though she'd initiated the call for help, Connie apparently needed to vent as well. She eyed her friend over the edge of her glass.

"Everything okay at work?"

"Just feeling a little stressed. Rumor has it they've been discussing who they'll make partners, and I'd like to be in the running. But with them leaving me out of this big case…"

A lot of Connie's identity was wrapped up with being a successful lawyer, so Maggie understood how important it was for her friend to become a partner. Despite that, she sensed there was more to Connie's mood.

"Is that the only thing that's bothering you?" An indecisive shrug answered her. "Want to talk about it?" she said.

"Not really," Connie replied, and as the waiter came over, she quickly perused the menu, placed her order, and added another round of cosmopolitans for them.

Prying anything from Connie was as hard as hacking into the Pentagon, unless of course you created an overload of the system with something like the cocktails. Maggie gave the waiter her order and was careful to control how she drank her liquor while plying Connie with yet another cocktail as she discussed what she was doing with her staff in preparation for the holiday season.

By the time dinner was finished, she was feeling a little buzz, but Connie was well lubricated. So much so that Maggie said, "Why not stay the night?"

Connie hiccupped and teased, "Are you trying to take advantage of me?"

She smiled. "Totally. Come on. We can have more girl talk. Maybe have another drink."

"Only if you spill about why you bailed on Owen," Connie said, still sharp despite the many cosmos.

Maggie made an *X* across her chest with her index finger. "Cross my heart, I'll spill," she said, but she intended to get her friend to divulge what else was bothering her.

They walked back toward the library and Fifth Avenue and flagged a cab to head downtown to Maggie's brownstone. Friday night traffic was rough, as was the ride in the taxi. By the time they got to Maggie's, they were both ready for fresh air and something else to drink.

Since it was a beautiful late-summer night and in New York, you had to take advantage of them before the colder and wetter weather set in, she directed her friend out to the small courtyard behind her kitchen.

"Get comfy. I'll be out in a second."

Connie motioned upstairs with her index finger. "I'm going to change and get totally comfy."

Maggie smiled and nodded. "You know which room." She had two extra bedrooms that Emma and Connie used to crash if they were staying in the city, and each of her buddies kept clothes and other necessities in the rooms and the nearby Jack and Jill bathroom. Connie only did overnights every now and then, since her place in Jersey City was a short ferry ride away. Emma stayed pretty often, since the trip back to Sea Kiss, where she lived and worked, was a longer trip.

"I do," Connie said with a wobbly, still a little drunk

smile, and as she went up the stairs, Maggie followed. She might as well get comfortable also.

Her bedroom took up the entire floor above the two guest bedrooms and was an open-concept space that included a library and sitting area with a fireplace. A little tingle went through her at the thought of lying in front of that fireplace, naked, making love with Owen. It had been a recurring dream that she couldn't shake out of her head despite her concerns about taking the relationship to that level.

Inside her room, she quickly exchanged her bespoke suit for yoga pants and a loose T-shirt with a fanciful cartoon of a crab that read *Don't bother me. I'm crabby*. Corny, but it had caught her eye while at a convention in Baltimore, and she'd broken down and bought it.

As she skipped down the stairs, she met Connie on the landing, and together they went to the kitchen, mixed up a batch of strawberry margaritas, and prepped a tray with glasses and some chips and salsa to take outside.

The small courtyard behind her brownstone consisted of a ten-by-ten brick patio flanked on the sides with raised beds loaded with flowers. Waves of pink and purple petunias cascaded over the edges of the beds made from antique bricks saved by her contractor from the demolition of a home on Long Island's Gold Coast. Hydrangea, lavender, delphiniums, hollyhocks, and an assortment of other taller plants and bushes provided height in the beds and rested against the brick wall that surrounded the entire space, softening the roughness of the bricks.

Beyond the patio was another ten-by-ten square

of perfectly manicured lawn and more flower beds. There were still lots of blooms, but once they had a killing frost in a couple of months, it would be time to clean up all the beds and prep them for the winter and next year.

"I love it out here," Connie said with a sigh as she sank into the white, wooden Adirondack chairs Maggie had chosen, eschewing the more traditional wrought-iron set her designer had wanted to place there. The chairs reminded her of the ones they kept on the lawn at her Sea Kiss home, and that recollection brought thoughts of Owen and how perceptive he'd been in realizing the reason for the design of her town house.

"I see that smile," Connie said with a smirk. "You're thinking about Owen."

"I am," she said without hesitation and added, "And your mood has little to do with work."

The smirk deadened to a flat line like a heart monitor on a dying patient. "Yes and no. I mean, it is about work and feeling like I'm about to hit a glass ceiling. But it's also about other stuff, namely Jon. I really wasn't ready to spend time with him anytime soon, so the dinner was kind of tough for me."

She took the time to examine her friend as Connie chugged down a few big gulps of the frozen margarita.

"And I guess I've been brain-dead not to notice before now that something was up with you and Jon."

Grimacing, from both icy liquor and the discussion, Connie said, "Nothing is up."

Maggie sensed her friend was holding back but decided not to pry about what might be going on between her friend and Jonathan. "I see that you're not denying there was before. At least that's what Owen told me after he climbed up the wisteria vine and I worried he'd break his neck."

"Which he might have, because don't get me wrong, Owen is prime, but he's not Jon," Connie said, confirming that, despite all her denials, Jonathan still held a spot in her brain and possibly her heart.

As for the two brothers, Connie was right. Owen was all man, lean and strong, but Jonathan was all man with a capital M-A-N. He had the kind of body that wasn't built in a gym, all hard muscle with the occasional nick or scar to prove he'd earned that body by challenging himself in dangerous and extreme ways.

"He'll break your heart," Maggie blurted out before she could restrain herself. "I'm sorry, it's the liquor," she said and covered her mouth with her hand to hold back her alcohol-aided lack of discretion.

Connie chuckled and gave a sad little wag of her head. "Don't you think I know that? Why do you think I keep away from him?"

"Which is why I decided to blow off Owen. He'll give me nothing but heartache," she said with a determined nod and finally took a sip of her drink, which was starting to melt around the edges of the glass.

"Bullshit and you know it. Owen would never intentionally hurt you. He's not like his SOB father."

Maggie was surprised by the vehemence in her friend's voice. "You really believe that?"

Connie did a little bobble with her head and took another sip before responding. "I have to confess I was worried when you first mentioned him. Even way back in college, I could see the sparks between you two, but I knew there was history there."

"*Family* history," she clarified and earned the stink eye from her friend, so she relented and confessed. Holding up her index finger, she said, "The only history back in college was one kiss on the beach when we were eighteen. No biggie."

Connie snorted. "*Way* biggie. It's obvious he's got the hots for you. For real. No game there. Nothing to do with the family BS or the stores or the property."

Maggie took a long moment to think about her friend's assertion, but doubt had sunk its claws deep and was holding on tightly. "How do you know?" she asked, almost timidly.

Connie tried to tap her temple, but it took her a few tries before she got the right spot. "I can read people. It's what I've been trained to do," she said, her words slightly more slurred than they had been before thanks to the addition of the margarita.

Maggie took another little taste of her drink and hoped that mixing the vodka and tequila wasn't going to be something they'd both regret in the morning. Which made her think about what she was going to regret more with Owen: giving in to the temptation or putting a stop to whatever was going on between them. There was no in-between option, as far as she was concerned, because it wasn't in her nature to vacillate.

Although with Owen, she'd done a lot of questioning and delaying. *Unfortunately, no seizing,* she thought.

"You're doing it again," Connie teased and pointed a finger at her face.

She felt her smile broaden and chastised her friend.

"You know, if I can stop being afraid of what's happening with Owen, maybe it's time you faced up to what you feel for Jon."

With a very unsteady back and forth of her head, Connie said, "No way. Absolutely no fucking way."

But as Maggie sat back and sipped her drink while her friend continued the no-Jonathan rant, she thought, *Methinks she doth protest too much.*

Chapter 18

SINCE OWEN HAD PLANNED ON GOING DOWN TO SEA KISS FOR the weekend, he decided to go despite Maggie bailing on him. Besides, Sea Kiss was the place he escaped to when he sought peace or a place to think things through, and right now, he needed both.

As he walked in, he was surprised to find Jonathan there again, rolling around on the floor with a new puppy.

"I didn't expect you to be here," Owen said as his brother rose, came over, and hugged him.

"Dad never comes down here, and I figured you'd be at work. Again. So why not take advantage of an empty house?" he said with a casual shrug. "I'm surprised you're down this early," Jonathan said and, for emphasis, looked at the nonexistent watch on his wrist.

Owen had never known his brother to wear one for a variety of reasons. First, he just seemed to have a natural body clock that woke him at the same time every day. Second, and more importantly, Jonathan just didn't give a shit about keeping to any kind of schedule. He did what he did when he wanted to.

"Didn't feel like working this weekend. Besides, what if I just wanted to get away for a change and relax?" Owen said and dropped his overnight bag by the couch.

"You? Away? Relaxing?" Jonathan said, but then as he peered at Owen's face, he seemed a little taken aback.

"You were supposed to come down here this weekend with Maggie, and she blew you off."

He nodded. "She said she had to work this weekend. We were supposed to stay at her place."

"And?" Jonathan said and made a suggestive gesture with his eyes.

Because he didn't want to discuss it, he pointed to the tiny ball of white-and-cream fur happily wagging its tail on the floor beside his brother. "Not quite what I expected you to choose for a dog."

The elfin terrier mix cocked his head, examining Owen, and then did a little bark that wouldn't even scare away the proverbial fly.

Jonathan laughed, bent, and scratched behind the dog's ears, earning yet more happy wagging and yips of joy. "He kind of chose me when I went to the shelter. Walked right up to the window of his holding pen and started jumping up and down. Barking like a madman. When they took him out, he sat at my side, patiently waiting. I knew he was the one."

At that comment, the dog jumped onto Jonathan's bent knees, splayed his paws on Jonathan's chest, and started licking his face, prompting more laughter from his brother.

"You two really are a pair," he said, grinning. He liked seeing Jonathan happy, and if the pup was going to do it, so be it.

Jonathan set the dog back down on the ground with a "Sit" command that lacked any real control, but the dog listened anyway. "Smart too, aren't you, Dudley?" he said, as proud as any parent of their new baby.

"Dudley?"

Jonathan grinned and said, "Like in Dudley Do Right, 'cause at least one of us has to do the right thing."

"And I don't doubt that you do that when you need to."

Jonathan clapped him on the back. "Come with me. I was going for a walk up to Fireman's Park. Lots of dogs there on a Saturday."

Owen nodded, and they strolled the few blocks through the heart of Sea Kiss.

Main Street was already in full swing on a late-summer Saturday. Beachgoers ambled up and down through the assortment of shops all along the street before heading to the beach. Later in the day, like the tides along the shore, they'd return after their time in the sun for lunch, dinner, or more shopping. After Labor Day in a couple of weeks, the crowds would virtually disappear until the next summer season.

"How about I make you dinner?" Jonathan said as they strolled from one quaint shop to another, checking out the offerings while Dudley obediently kept close and waited patiently on his leash when they stepped inside some of the shops.

Owen hated to disappoint his brother, but he wasn't really in the mood for company. He just wanted to hole up and lick his wounds, but Jonathan would have none of that.

"I'll make dinner," he said, and as they went from one store to the next, he gathered an assortment of foods and handed the bags to Owen to carry. When he shot his brother a glare as he added another package to the load, Jonathan just shrugged and said, "I buy; you carry."

"Then let me get these," he said and paid the butcher for two immense grass-fed, organic rib eye steaks his brother had selected. As his brother grinned wickedly, he knew he'd been conned, since the steaks had been the most expensive items on their impromptu menu.

"Why do I always fall for whatever it is that you want?" he said as Jonathan grabbed the bag from the merchant.

With an easy shrug of his broad shoulders, Jonathan said, "Because you love me, Big Bro."

Which he couldn't deny. Through all the turmoil in their early family life and the bitter loneliness after the departure of their mother, the two brothers had always stuck together. He wrapped an arm around Jonathan's shoulders, hugged him hard, and gave him a brotherly noogie, earning a protective bark and growl from Dudley.

"Back off, Bro, unless you want to lose an ankle," his brother teased, dragging laughter from both of them.

Jonathan walked into the surf and skate shop and greeted the young woman who was the owner with a big smile and a hug. She seemed to know just what he wanted, since she grabbed a bar of wax from the shelf and quickly rang it up.

"Waves are supposed to be great today," she said as she handed the bag to Jonathan.

"I'll let you know after I catch a few rides, Sammie," he said with a wave as they walked out of the shop.

They strolled to Fireman's Park, where a number of dogs were already off leash, running around and playing with each other. The dogs were larger than Dudley for the most part, obviously making Jonathan hesitate to release him.

"Come on, Dad. You can let him go," Owen kidded, although he intended to keep a close eye in case one of the bigger dogs got too rough with the petite terrier.

Jonathan rolled his eyes, bent, and unclipped the leash from Dudley's collar. In a blur of speed, the mutt shot off to join a group of dogs that were busy chasing each other all around the statue in the center of the park. Seeing that everything was copacetic, they sauntered over to a bench and sat.

Owen watched the dogs play for a bit before he said, "So what's up with you? New design in the works?"

Jonathan did a halfhearted shrug. "Just did the initial specs for one. Now it's off to my engineers and design team to see how they can incorporate my ideas in the new vehicles and fuel cells, so I thought I'd take a little time off."

"You going to take the pooch with you on whatever adventure is next on the list?"

The terrier was busy jumping up and over the back of a much larger Labrador, and as soon as Dudley landed, the Lab playfully chased him.

"I was thinking of taking a little staycation. Maybe even setting up shop down here," Jonathan said, surprising him.

He examined his brother's features just to make sure it wasn't a joke. Clearly, it wasn't. He pondered it for a moment before saying anything out loud. "You get yourself a dog. The cooking thing is way domestic. Now your next adventure is staying home? What's up? You sick or something?"

With a bark of a laugh and a wag of his head that sent the longish strands of his sun-streaked hair into motion, his brother said, "I'm feeling like way too sensitive a guy as I say this, but I'm worried about you. I want to be here for you if this all goes to shit."

A sideways glance at Jonathan confirmed that he was being deadly serious, but it also told him that there was more to the change of heart that had his wanderlust brother suddenly deciding to stick around. But he appreciated the concern and let his brother know.

"Thanks for worrying, but I can handle it," he said, rather unconvincingly.

His brother turned slightly on the bench, and his keen gaze swept over Owen. "You said that when Mother abandoned us, and you've been handling it for both of us for some time. Maybe it's time I helped *you* deal. Made *your* life a little easier."

He couldn't deny that not having to worry about how his father would rant and carry on about another of his brother's escapades would certainly be a welcome change. Especially now, when he had so many other things to handle, like the situation with Maggie. But then again, with Jonathan out of the news, his father's attention would be focused solely on him. Possibly not a good situation.

"The one thing that would make my life easier is to have Father out of my face about Maggie, but if anything, he's more fixated than ever on the Sinclairs," he confessed.

Jonathan was silent for several minutes, staring away into space before he said, "Do you ever wonder if there's more to the story about the reason for the fight?"

He thought about it often, especially since his father's reaction the other day. There was just too much anger there—and possibly pain—for it to be just about a business deal gone bad or a friend's betrayal.

"I do," he admitted. "I always wondered if all that

hate and bitterness wasn't a big part of the reason that Mother left. He made her so unhappy."

"He makes *everyone* unhappy, but that was no reason for her to leave and never look back. We were her boys," Jonathan said, lashing out at the mother who had deserted them so many years earlier. A mother who, in all that time, had never even bothered to find out what was happening in her sons' lives.

He felt his brother's pain more acutely than he did his own. He'd been the one to shoulder the bulk of the fallout from that desertion. He had been the one to try to keep things steady for his little brother. To absorb the misery heaped on them by their father after their mother's departure. He'd been too busy to allow the pain to register and had gone numb to it. But Jonathan hadn't.

Wrapping an arm around his brother's shoulders, he hugged him hard and said, "We were her boys, but we can't let that hurt hold us back now. We can't keep on running away from relationships because of it."

Like his brother had been running away for years with his assorted escapades. He understood it now, for the first time in his life. And he questioned if maybe, just maybe, it was part of his commitment problem as well.

"I'm not running anymore, Big Bro. There's a nice empty warehouse on the other side of the tracks. I'm going to talk to someone about buying it. Maybe get some light manufacturing going besides the design work. The Sea Kiss area could use some new jobs, don't you think?"

He considered Jonathan again and realized that he was totally serious. Way more serious than he'd ever seen his little brother, but since he was, Owen wanted to help. "It could. I can give you the names of some people to contact for real estate in the area."

"I'd appreciate that. And what about you and your life? What about Maggie?" Jonathan said.

"Maggie is still a work in progress," he confessed, unsure of just what to do to move that relationship to another level.

Jonathan poked him in the ribs and grinned. "Don't wait too long, Bro. Maggie doesn't strike me as the type to wait forever."

Chapter 19

MAGGIE WAS BLASTED AWAKE BY HER ALARM. SHE GLARED at the phone and silenced it with a swipe. Sinking back into the comfort of her mattress, she stared at the ceiling, considering all that still had to get done before Monday morning.

Too much, she thought. While the Friday overnight with Connie had been both relaxing and eye opening, they had both had a touch of regret on Saturday morning about how much they had imbibed. They'd had way too many, not something they did regularly, and the excess of alcohol was exacting punishment.

They woke up late, sluggish, and with headaches. A nice brunch with lots of lattes had been restorative, and after, they'd tackled the contract with the Italian designer over yet more lattes, thanks to her new espresso machine.

Connie had a wealth of ideas about changes to make the agreement more balanced, and together, they'd hammered out an email to the designer's lawyers in Milan so that they would be able to review it first thing Monday morning. She hoped they wouldn't make too much of a stink about the proposed amendments, because she was already late in getting the merchandise for the fall season. It should have been ordered months earlier—would have been ordered, if her father had been more reasonable. With his change of heart, however, she had to try to do things at a breakneck pace, and if she could get the deal done, it would be good exposure and revenue for the designer.

Connie had gone home the night before, and as Maggie lay in bed, she thought about what she had to do that morning. A review of the papers in the quiet of her home and what she would do next, both about the stores and about Owen.

Owen, she thought, and a tornado of emotions swirled around in her head just as they had all night long, keeping her awake.

Guilt, predominantly. He had obviously been disappointed that she'd canceled, and he had clearly not bought her excuse. But she *had* worked that weekend and still had to review the drafts of the ads and television spots for the holiday campaign once again. They needed something more, only she wasn't quite sure what despite looking at them multiple times.

As the snooze period on her phone ended and the alarm blared to life again, she shut it off and crawled out of bed. A shower followed by some coffee and breakfast might be just the thing to get her going so she could finish everything on her to-do list.

Maybe she could even call Owen later and apologize for canceling. Possibly even propose another weekend together. One that might lead to the next step in their relationship, if that's what you could call the on-again, off-again roller coaster they seemed to be riding.

She was tired of her own indecision, because she normally wasn't someone who wavered like that. Except possibly with her father, where she tended to show more restraint because she knew that standing up to him could lead to upset on both personal and professional levels.

And yet, standing up to her father hadn't created as much of an issue as she had expected. In fact, now that she thought about it, he'd seemed almost relieved that she'd finally taken the bull by the horns and decided to implement some of her ideas. Relieved and proud.

That realization propelled her through her shower and a megadose of coffee. By the time she finished that first latte, she felt awake enough for the challenge and reached for her phone, intent on making things right with Owen. But just as she was about to call him, the familiar beep of the video app rang out, and the avatar with his smiling face filled her screen.

She swiped to accept his video call, and just the sight of him had her heart pumping a trifle faster and heat coming alive in parts down south. It wasn't right that he looked so handsome and put together that early in the morning. Which only made her wonder how he'd look in bed right next to her at the break of day, just as the sun was rising. Hopefully, he'd be rising as well.

"Hi, Owen," she said, her voice a little husky from disuse and her sexy thoughts.

"Hi to you too. You look a little tired," he said and winced, well aware it wasn't what most women would like to hear.

Still, she appreciated his perceptiveness. "I am a little wiped," she said and got right to what she had earlier planned to say. "I'm sorry I canceled our weekend. I was really looking forward to it."

He squinted just a little, considering her, and then blurted out, "I'd like to say that I was looking forward to it too, but that's not completely true, because I was also wondering if it wouldn't have been a big mistake."

"Not holding anything back, are you?" she said with a chuckle.

"Being honest, Mags. It's the right thing to do if two people are in a relationship."

And there was that word again, just as it had been rattling around in her brain all morning. She wanted to gesture between the two of them like he had the other day in the gym, but he wasn't going to be able to see with the limitations of the phone, so she just said, "Is that what *this* is? A relationship?"

"If that's what you want it to be," he immediately said, the lack of hesitation on his part confirming that he was game for it to be just that.

Take charge, Maggie, the little voice in her head commanded, and she said, "That's what I want it to be."

He smiled broadly, bringing alive those delicious dimples, and the happy gleam in his dark gaze was visible even through the smartphone camera.

"I'm glad. So I think this would be the part where I say we should meet for a late breakfast. Brunch maybe?"

She bit her bottom lip and glanced at the pile of papers on her dining room table. There had been too many of them to lay out on her home office desk.

"Maggie?" he questioned at her silence and diverted attention.

"I really do have work to do," she said and shifted the phone to let him see the papers on the table before turning it back to her face.

He nodded. "How about I bring something in? Give you a break before you go back to those papers."

"I'd love that," she said, jumping all over his idea,

because she wanted to see him and put to right some of the hurt she'd caused by abandoning him for the weekend.

"I'll be there in about an hour," he said, and before she could utter a goodbye or change her mind, he ended the call.

She stared at her T-shirt and shorts for only a second before bolting up the stairs to change. While she wasn't a dress-up Barbie kind of woman, she wanted to look more presentable when he arrived.

She hurried through a shower and blow-dried her hair. Dashing into her closet, she rummaged through assorted pants, blouses, and dresses, discarding each and every one for a different reason. Too fancy. Too boring. Too fuck me. She wanted to be subtle after all.

Casual, casual, casual, she reminded herself, and with time evaporating like morning dew under the rising sun, she jerked her favorite pair of jeans off a hanger and paired them with a crop top that would just graze the low waistband of the jeans, inviting him to touch and inch up. A flush of heat bathed her body at the thought of that and what might follow.

Wanting to be prepared in case it did happen, she opened her lingerie drawer and picked out a matching La Perla bra and bikini panties in barely there pink trimmed with lace in a slightly rosier hue. The colors complemented what little summer tan she had and the slight touch of chestnut in her dark hair.

She speedily slipped into the jeans and top, brushed out her hair, and kept her makeup to a minimum. A little blush, mascara, and a swipe of lip gloss had her looking like the au naturel girl next door, and she was fine with that. Except for maybe the darkish circles under her eyes, a testament to their late Friday escapade and a restless Saturday night spent thinking about Owen.

Skipping down the stairs, the doorbell rang just as she set foot on the landing in the foyer. She inhaled deeply and laid a hand across her midsection to stop the nervous flutters there, worse than thousands of butterflies flitting around a summer garden. With another breath, she stepped to the door and slowly opened it, not wanting to appear as jumpy and eager as she was.

He stood there, his hair slightly damp and brushed back from his sculpted features. He was in preppy mode in casual khakis and a pressed button-down Oxford shirt in a pale blue that brought out the lighter streaks of color in his eyes.

"Morning, Mags," he said with that dimpled grin that started up those restless flutters again and kicked her heartbeat up a notch. His voice was smooth, the tone low, making her imagine again what it would be like to hear that voice beside her in the quiet of morning. Or as a whisper in the dark of night as he made love to her.

"G'morning, Owen. It's good to see you and—" She pointed to the bag he held. A typical brown paper deli bag with a few grease spots here and there.

He raised the bag and jiggled it. "Got you something I know you'll like."

She motioned him in and over to the breakfast bar by the kitchen. She hadn't had a chance to move all her papers off the dining room table.

"I hope you don't mind if we eat here. I wasn't quite ready for company."

"I'm cool," he said and sat at one of the stools while

she grabbed some plates, napkins, and cutlery and set them on the quartz counter of the breakfast bar.

"Juice?" she asked.

He shook his head. "Just coffee."

"Sweet and no foam," she said, remembering how he liked it because it was just how she liked it. Yet another thing they had in common.

She made the coffees and took them over to the breakfast bar. He had pulled two sandwiches from the bags and placed them on the plates. As she handed him the latte and sat, she realized he'd brought egg sandwiches, but not just any egg sandwiches, she could tell from the smell. As she unwrapped the white deli paper off the one half, she said, "Pork roll. My favs."

He grinned. "Mine too. I bribed my local deli guy last week to order some to have handy for me." He wasted no time in ripping off the paper on his sandwich and devoured the first half in a few quick bites while she lingered over hers, enjoying the meld of salty meat, fried egg, cheese, and a perfect kaiser roll.

"Delicious," she said and washed down part of the sandwich with some coffee while he finished the other half of his breakfast, slightly slower but way faster than her, which gave him time to sit there, sipping his latte and watching her.

"You've been working hard," he said, his tone filled with concern and not condemnation.

She shrugged, guilt rearing up again. She knew there was only one way to get past that emotion. "I am beat, and while I have been working, I think we both know that wasn't the reason I canceled on you."

"I know," he said matter-of-factly and with no trace of

anger. But he quickly added, "I confess that I was pissed at first. It was a beautiful weekend down the Shore, and I was looking forward to doing some surfing."

She smirked, rolled her eyes, and said, "Surfing? That's all? You're such a guy."

One side of his mouth quirked up in a teasing grin. "If I said I was disappointed that we didn't spend some time together, would you believe me?"

"Or would I think that you're just playing me?" she retorted, but her words lacked any sting.

"I can see how you could think that," he said, shrugged his broad shoulders, and polished off the rest of his coffee just as she finished her breakfast sandwich. He motioned toward the pile of papers on the dining room table. "Is that your work for the weekend?"

"Part of it. Connie and I spent a good chunk of yesterday going over an exclusive distribution agreement."

He twined together his index and middle fingers and said, "Connie and you are like this?"

She nodded. "And Emma, although it's a little tough with her being in Sea Kiss. Still, they're like my sisters. Tracy too, but in a different way."

"She's high maintenance."

Maggie confirmed it with a quick bob of her head. "Totally, but we still love her."

Obviously intrigued by the scattered papers on her table, her excuse for dumping him for the weekend, he said, "Mind if I take a look?"

It was hard for her to mask her reluctance, so he crossed his heart with his index finger and said, "Promise not to spill any big secrets."

"It's just that…it's there, almost. But something is

missing," she said as, in a whirl of motion, she walked over to the papers and began straightening them out on the tabletop.

He followed her and stood at her side as she explained the two different print campaigns and then skimmed her hand over the storyboard for the television commercial that incorporated the messages from the print versions into one.

"I can totally see this, almost like a spoof. Boxes just being tossed up on a porch, all beat up," he said and pointed to that ad.

"Definitely. That's exactly what I wanted, with a voice-over about Christmas being more than just that. But this…" Her voice trailed off as she picked up the second ad and laid it on top of the storyboard where the two ads were supposed to merge to complete the message she wanted to convey.

Owen scrutinized the papers, understanding what she was feeling, deliberating about what was lacking, when it came to him like a thunderbolt from the heavens. He hurried out to her living room and the side table that held a collection of photos. Snagging one, he returned to the table and placed the photo over the draft of the print ad.

"*You're* what's missing. You and your mom. The memories that will never leave you," he said, because that was what she was clearly trying to get across with the campaign: boxes were just boxes, but memories were forever, especially good memories.

She danced her fingertips across the surface of the photo, her touch tender.

As he glanced at her from the corner of his eye, the longing was obvious. The pain, but also the love. He had his brother's love, but he'd never experienced that kind of love from his father. As for his mother, they'd had some fun times before she'd just up and left. Since then, he'd never sought it out from a woman either, maybe because of his mother's abandonment.

Now, standing there with her, the thought of it both thrilled and scared him. It made him contemplate what it would be like to be loved like that by her.

When she spoke, her voice was husky with emotion and the threat of tears. "I remember when this was taken. We'd come to the store for the holidays, and after we went to see Santa, my mom took me for high tea in the Savannah Courtyard. I felt so grown-up, and my mom… I so wanted to grow up and be like her. So beautiful and smart and special."

He wanted to tell her that she was all of those things and more but held back. It was maybe too soon for that.

"*This* is your story, Maggie. You should be the one to tell it in these ads. No one else will be as effective."

She stood there without moving, without breathing possibly, for an unnerving second. Then she inhaled shakily and held her breath before facing him.

"Thank you. I was too close to see it."

Tears shimmered in her eyes. One errant tear leaked out and slowly trailed down her face. Another soon followed.

The tears tore at his gut.

He cupped her cheeks and gently swiped the tears away. At her brave half smile, he leaned in and kissed the corners of her eyes, tasting the saltiness of her pain against his lips and the quiver of her lashes as her eyes drifted closed.

He couldn't hold back anymore. He needed to help her heal. Wanted to feel her sorrow vanish with his love. His love, he finally admitted to himself. Despite everything that said this was insane and could bring nothing but more heartache, he was in love with her.

The first kiss was gentle, urging peace to her soul. She answered in kind, accepting his solace. The second kiss demanded more. Demanded that she engage. Give more of herself.

As she pressed into him, she dug her fingers into his hair and cradled his head in her hands. Opened her mouth to invite him to enter. Taste. Savor.

God, but she was so sweet and responsive.

When he danced his tongue across perfect white teeth, she playfully chased it and then lightly bit his lower lip, jerking a groan from him.

He was hard, so hard, that he had to bring a stop to this or there would be no turning back. And as soon as he thought that, she shifted away slightly and met his gaze.

"I want you, Owen. I want this," she said, laying her hand on his chest directly over his beating heart.

"I want it too, Maggie." He'd wanted this since they were eighteen and he'd kissed her on that moonlit beach. Maybe even since they were children, playing on the beach together happily. Being with her back then had always seemed to make any day special.

Maggie smiled and pointed an index finger heavenward. "My bedroom is two flights up."

"Good thing I work out," he teased, bent, and scooped her up in his arms.

Maggie grabbed hold of his shoulders and laughed out a halfhearted protest. "You don't have to carry me."

Owen grinned. "I know what you spent all your summers reading in the gazebo," he said as he hurried to the stairs and began the climb to her bedroom. Without any strain or hitch in his breath, he said, "I know what the heroes in those books do."

She chuckled, pulled herself close to nip his earlobe, and whispered, "Bet you can't guess what the heroines do."

"Sweet Lord, I can't wait to find out," he said and quickened his pace up the stairs.

He entered her room and, with a muttered "Wow," marched straight to her antique four-poster bed, with its artfully draped canopy of gossamer-light fabric.

Her body skimmed along his as he released her, and she slowly sank to her feet. As soon as she touched the ground, he rested his hands just above where the jeans ended, his palms slightly rough against that sensitive skin—and hot. So, so hot.

With a gentle sweep upward, he bracketed her body beneath her breasts and urged her close, her hips grazing against his erection, trapped beneath the khaki he wore. The tips of her breasts, tight and hard with her need, just brushed the starched cotton of his shirt.

She inched her hands up to the first button of that shirt and half glanced at him as she deliberately, leisurely, slipped each button free until his shirt hung open.

"You're killing me, Mags." He didn't need to say what he wanted, because it was obvious she wanted it too.

Maggie laid her hands on his chest, cupping his nicely defined pecs, brushing her thumbs across the hard paps as he eased his hands upward and mimicked her actions, cradling her breasts. Teasing the hard tips between his thumb and forefinger, each little tug blasting straight to her center, creating a sympathetic twist of need.

He grabbed the hem of her crop top and drew it up and over her head. Stopped to gaze at her in the sexy lingerie she was glad she'd worn.

He idly traced the swell of her breasts with the tips of his fingers and said, "You're so beautiful, Maggie."

She felt more than beautiful with him gazing at her like that. She felt…cherished.

Reaching behind, she undid the bra and slipped it off, baring herself to him, delighting in the swift inhale of his breath and the jump of his arousal against her belly.

He cradled her breasts again, his touch slow and unhurried. Patient as he learned just what she liked. A little tweak of her nipple followed by his sweet kiss. The long pull into his mouth and a crazy swirl of his tongue that made her knees buckle.

She grabbed hold of his shoulders, encountering the soft cotton, but she wanted to feel him. Only him.

She swept away his shirt, and he broke away from her only long enough to let it drop to the floor and then met her lips in a kiss.

Unhurried. Searching. Over and over, their mouths met as he hauled her close, her breasts crushed against the hard wall of his chest.

She opened her mouth and accepted the slide of his tongue. Danced hers along his until they were both breathing hard and there was no holding back.

Faster than a New York minute, they finished undressing, shoes, socks, khaki, and denim flying free until she stood before him in just the tiny bikini bottoms.

His touch was restrained, almost reverent, as he cradled her breast and then tenderly skimmed his hand down her body to the lacy edge of the panty. He dragged the back of his hand back and forth across the flatness of her belly, just above the low waistband. Then he dipped his hand lower, eased the fabric down her legs, and helped her step out of them.

"So, so lovely," he said, and before she could say another word, he urged her to the edge of the bed and covered her body with his.

His weight on her was pleasant as he kissed her again, his firm lips inviting her to join him. She raised her hips, butting them against his erection, and his body shook with need.

He broke away from the kiss and licked his way down her neck to her breasts, where he nipped and sucked at her tight nipples. Each little drag of his lips sent a beat of desire between her legs. She threaded her fingers through his thick hair and held him close, urging him on with soft keening sounds and the press of her body to his.

Owen nearly came undone at her response, and it was all he could do not to plunge deep into her and take her. He shuddered as he wrestled his need, wanting to bring her pleasure first. Wanting to learn every inch of her gorgeous body.

He teethed the tip of her breast and skimmed his hands down her body to her center. Parting the silken curls there, he found her core and caressed the swollen nub, building desire. Her body tensed beneath him, and she arched her back, pressing into his touch.

She trailed her hands down and dug her fingers into his shoulders, inciting him with the sharp bite of her nails into his skin and her needy moan.

Slipping one finger into her, he stroked her and barely kept from losing it at the wet heat of her and imagining how she would feel surrounding him.

He licked and sucked at her breasts, loving the taste and feel of them against his lips. Needing more as he continued to play her with his fingers and she moved beneath him, inviting him to join her.

"Maggie," he breathed, almost a plea.

"Now, Owen. Please now," Maggie said, lost in the desire he had created.

She cradled his hips with her legs, opening for him. His hard heat teased her nether lips, but he found restraint and broke away from her to cover himself with a condom he whipped from his pants pocket. He returned quickly, poised at her center, and locked his gaze with hers.

"Owen," she said, fighting back worry that he'd reconsidered.

"I want to see your face when we make love. I want to see you go over with me."

She nearly came with his words but held back. "I want that too."

He thrust inside, and she gasped at the fullness and heat of him. At the feeling of perfection at being joined with him.

He didn't move for long seconds, and she shifted her hips, deepening his possession. Compelling him to move and take them over.

He drew back and thrust forward, his thighs hard and powerful against the sensitive skin of her inner thighs. His arousal stiff and insistent within her, building passion. Dragging her up ever higher.

She joined him in the dance, undulating her hips. Her gaze focused on his, watching those amazing charcoal eyes darken to almost black. Watching the silver become molten with heat.

His lips, those full, generous lips that had brought her such pleasure moments earlier, had a slight hint of a smile as he met her gaze.

"God, Maggie. This is so good. So good," he said.

"Yes-s-s-s," she nearly keened as another plunge of his hips drove her higher, and it was all she could do not to close her eyes against the desire growing inside her.

She bucked up, meeting his thrusts. Dug her fingers into his buttocks, feeling the power in his body as he moved. Relishing his hardness along her body as her blood hummed in her veins, driving satisfaction through every cell in her being.

Her climax hit her, as fast and powerful as a speeding freight train.

She cried out his name but never shifted her gaze away from his face as his features tightened for a moment and a long, sibilant breath escaped him as he uttered her name and joined her with his release.

He stilled, his body taut except for the quivering of his muscles as he held his weight off her.

She wrapped her arms around his back and dragged him close. Kissed the side of his face and whispered, "That was amazing."

"Yeah, it was," he said as he returned her embrace, hugging her tight.

Stroking her hands up and down his sweat-damp back, she restored calm and peace with her touch until he roused and pushed up on one arm to look at her.

"Are you okay?"

She nodded. "Yes, I am. And you?"

He grinned, revealing that enticing, boyish dimple on the right side of his face. "I'm good. Better than good actually."

"Definitely better than good," she replied with a chuckle and traced her finger along the indentation on his face as she had wanted to do for so long.

His dimple deepened as his smile broadened with her words. "Does that mean you might want—"

"A repeat? What do you think?"

"I think that great minds think alike."

Chapter 20

WAKING UP BESIDE HIM HAD BEEN JUST AS GOOD AS SHE had imagined. Actually, it had been way better than she had imagined.

Heat roared over her like a brush fire as she recalled their early morning lovemaking and the kiss they'd shared at her front door before they'd gone their separate ways. The promise they'd made to see each other again tonight only kept those flames banked and ready to burst to life again.

As she entered the conference room just outside her office, she fanned her cheeks to dispel some of the warmth and laid out her team's campaign materials on the table. When her brain and body hadn't been occupied with Owen, ideas had been whirring around in her head, set loose in part by Owen's comments about who should be in the commercials. She added color prints of the photo of her mother and her in the Savannah Courtyard to each team member's papers. She had snapped a photo with her smartphone before coming to work.

As her team trudged into the room, she smiled and said, "Thank you for all your hard work. I really think we're close on this one, and with just a few more tweaks, we can think about getting the print and TV ads in place and develop the social media campaigns to get the word out."

There were some grumbles from the team, but they

each dutifully sat and picked up the photo and the notes that she'd had Sheila prepare earlier that morning.

"The first ad with the boxes on the porch is spot-on. I even think we should make it more of a spoof, maybe with the boxes flying wildly against the door and porch. Spilling open or maybe a crash like glass breaking."

"Told you so," one of her team members said and jabbed the colleague next to him with a quick elbow.

"Funny is always good. We can work on that," said Tim, the head of the team.

"Wonderful. I think that as good as funny is, awakening emotions is also great. Think the Budweiser Clydesdales kneeling across from the New York City skyline after 9/11. Think John Lewis and their amazing annual Christmas messages."

"Yeah, one year, I tried to get my friend in the UK to get me one of those damn penguins, but it was impossible," said Sarah, another young member of the team.

Maggie pointed at her and said, "Right. So picture this." She waved her hands like a sorceress conjuring a spirit. "A black-and-white photo of a mom and daughter sharing high tea. Slowly, the people in the photo come to life and join together to say, 'We are Maxwell's on Fifth. We're here to help you make memories that will last a lifetime. We're here to make you part of the Maxwell family.'"

Silence followed, and she didn't dare look at them just yet. She was too lost in her memories and the vision she'd had for the commercial. She pressed on.

"The woman serving tea behind my mother and me is Mildred Evans. She runs the kitchen now, and her granddaughter is with us for the summer. The security guard off to the far left is Jim Matthews. He's getting ready to retire, but his son just left the U.S. Marines and is joining us soon. All of *you* are part of the Maxwell's family, and I want people to see us. Know that we are here for them and to make their dreams come true."

Inhaling deeply, she finally faced the half dozen young men and women who made up the team, unsure of what their reactions would be. Judging from the combination of thoughtful glances and smiles, it looked like the campaign might fly with them.

"I know my idea needs tweaking."

"It's a great idea. We could even work up videos for social media with stories from our employees, telling us about their experiences at Maxwell's. Have a contest where people can share pictures of the new memories they're making or their old photos of fun times at the stores."

A flurry of ideas soon turned into a blizzard of creative plays on her words and the concept. Looking over at her team head, Tim, she said, "It looks like you don't need me anymore. If you can have something for me in the next few days and work up a budget for it, we can move on this."

Worry clouded Tim's face. "This may be costly, Maggie. All those videos—"

She laid a reassuring hand on Tim's shoulder, as much to bolster herself as him. "You worry about the creative. I'll worry about the money."

With a reluctant nod, Tim said, "We'll have everything ready in a few days."

"Perfect."

Which meant she only had a few days to try to find

the financing to continue the renovations, order inventory, and pay for the advertising she hoped would start the turnaround for the stores.

—~~~—

Owen had never imagined how nice it would be to wake up next to a woman day after day after day. He'd never been in that kind of relationship and had never really wanted to be. But a week later, after spending the night with Maggie at her home in Sea Kiss, he began to see the appeal. Or maybe it was that somewhere deep inside, he'd known that he'd loved her forever, and every meeting with her had only confirmed that she was the one for him. Maybe that was the reason that no other women he'd dated in the years since then had measured up enough for him to commit to a long-term relationship.

Not that you could call the last seven days since their first lovemaking long term. But they'd spent so much time together as kids, and they'd had that magical summer-night kiss at eighteen. They'd worked together for years on various Sea Kiss committees and had seen each other at assorted business functions.

This morning, she was tucked against his side, her thigh thrown carelessly over his, her arm and hand resting along his torso while she used his shoulder as a pillow.

He breathed deep, inhaling the scent of her. Flowers. Citrus. Sex.

Even now as he lay there, half-awake, savoring the quiet of a Saturday morning in Sea Kiss, memories of the last few days together roused passion. Made him want to forget sleeping in so he could wake her.

But she beat him to it as she raised her head, skimmed a kiss along his jaw, and murmured a drowsy, "Good morning."

He trailed his hand up and down her back and kissed her forehead. "You wanted to sleep in, remember?"

"Hmm," she replied and moved her hand down to encircle him. Sucking in a rough breath, he held back a groan as she stroked him and said, "Still want to sleep in?"

"Hell no," he said and reached for her, but she moved down his body and took him into her mouth, blasting away any thoughts he might have had. All he could think about was the way her mouth moved on him and her hands caressed him, urging him on. Dragging a rough groan from him as she did something wickedly delicious with her tongue that had him bucking up off the bed and nearly coming undone.

"Maggie, please," he said, reaching for her, wanting to be buried deep inside her when he came.

"I want that too, Owen," she said and climbed up into his lap and positioned herself over his erection. He scrambled to cover himself with a condom he grabbed from the nightstand drawer, and she guided him to her center and then slowly sank down on him, a long sigh escaping her as he filled her.

It felt so good. Almost too good. It had never been this good before, and he suspected it would never be as good with anyone else.

He loved her, and maybe he always had. That just made this situation way more complicated and danger-ous for both of them.

She met his gaze when she started to move, riding him. Drawing them higher and higher with the roll of her hips until she tired and he effortlessly shifted her onto her back. He hiked her legs up to deepen his penetration and, with a few strong strokes, vaulted them over the edge.

The quiet after the storm was broken only by their rough breaths that returned to normal little by little and the slight sighs of complaint as they eased apart only to tuck tight into each other again.

He must have dozed off, since it took her gentle nudge and the smell of maple syrup and bacon to revive him.

"Wake up, sleepyhead," she said, smiling. A silky peach-and-cream robe was wrapped around her enticing body.

He sat up and grinned at her as she placed a breakfast tray over his lap and he found the source of the heavenly aromas.

"It smells great," he said, admiring the perfectly made waffles swimming in butter and maple syrup that sat beside slices of crisp bacon.

"I hope it tastes great too, since Mrs. Patrick gave me lessons on how to make them. I actually think I'm getting the hang of this cooking thing."

"I'm sure it will be tasty." He dug in, and with a loud hum of appreciation, he confirmed just how good the food was.

Maggie ate hers with gusto, and he appreciated that she wasn't afraid to eat what she liked. He'd never been a fan of stick-figure fashion types and much preferred Maggie's womanly curves. Especially now that he'd had firsthand experience with just how wonderful they were.

Beneath the protection of the breakfast tray, blood

rushed into his privates, but he strangled that desire because he wanted her to know it was about more than sex.

"Want to do some surfing later?" he asked, because thinking about sports was one way to dim his desire.

Maggie laughed and shook her head. "Klutz, remember? But I'll join you on my bodyboard."

Which he'd settle for, because it meant getting to see her in a bikini, which was almost as good as seeing her naked. Maybe better, because while other guys might catch a glimpse and ponder what was beneath the strategically placed fabric bits, he was lucky enough to know. Lucky to be able to touch and taste all that amazing femininity.

It didn't take long for them to finish breakfast, dress, and take the tray back down to the kitchen where Mrs. Patrick was sitting and reading the paper.

"Don't you two look happy," she said with a wink.

"Yeah, we are," he said, wrapped an arm around Maggie's waist, and drew her even tighter against him.

On the way out to the patio through a back mudroom, Maggie grabbed a beach bag sitting in a cubby and a bodyboard from a nearby storage area. Together, they walked over to his family's garage, where he took down his surfboard from its holder on the wall. It was just a short stroll across the mansion's great lawn and down the private boardwalk to the beach.

There were already a number of people out and about, enjoying the pleasant day. The lifeguards had marked off the areas for swimmers, and they trudged over to the red-flagged area where surfers and anglers could compete for positions.

Luckily, there weren't any fishermen out and only a few surfers, since the waves were a little choppy and not all that big. Only two or three feet, with an occasional larger swell. Not ideal, but you had to take them when you got them on the Jersey Shore.

They spread a blanket and towels out on the sand and strode into the water together. For late summer, the water had a bit of a chill thanks to a westerly wind, but it was refreshing.

"I'll float and watch you for a while," he offered, not wanting to take any risks since the lifeguards weren't protecting this part of the beach.

She rose up on tiptoes and kissed him. "I'll be fine."

He eyed her dubiously. "Klutz, remember?" he said, repeating her earlier words.

"Not on my bodyboard," she teased.

Before he could react, she pushed off and dove into the waves, paddling out to where she could catch a wave and ride it in. He stood there for her first ride, impressed with how she perfectly timed the wave and rode it all the way back to shore, throwing in a neat barrel roll in the middle of the ride as if to show him she knew just what she was doing.

Tossing his board into the water, he climbed on and paddled out. Floated on the ocean's surface with the board as he gauged the waves and how they were breaking.

Maggie took another ride in, executing a 360 on the crest of one wave before wiping out close to shore. She popped up, dripping and laughing, her board back under her arm.

As she threw it back into the water and swam out for another ride, he realized he could stop worrying about her. She was a happy mermaid in the water.

He wasn't able to catch a lot of waves thanks to their

choppiness, but those that he did surf provided nice rides and allowed him to show off a little of his own expertise to Maggie, who took some time off from her bodyboarding to float in the water and watch him. When the cold of the water finally started robbing too much of his body heat, he waved at Maggie and pointed to the beach.

She nodded, and they snared the next wave in to shore. They hauled their boards up to the blanket and lay side by side under the rays of the midafternoon sun, warming themselves and chasing away the chill of ocean.

After long minutes, she rolled onto her side to look at him. "That was fun, but I know what else might be fun," she said and wiggled her eyebrows.

He leaned up on an elbow and liked seeing the playfulness and joy on her features. "I can tell that I'm going to like your idea of fun."

"Definitely." She jumped to her feet, pulled on a cover-up, and held her hand out to him.

He stood and delayed only to gather up their towels, boards, and the blanket before taking hold of her hand. They strolled up the sand and across the short stretch of boardwalk. Walked up the great lawn and into the mudroom to drop off their things. As she grabbed her cell phone from her bag, it started to ring. She glanced down at the number and lost all trace of the happiness that had been on her face just seconds earlier.

"Everything okay?" he asked at the obvious concern on her face.

"I hope so," she said and swiped to answer the call. She stepped out into the kitchen as she listened to the caller.

He followed her, trying not to eavesdrop, but it was impossible not to hear the letdown in her voice or see the way her shoulders fell in obvious disappointment as she ended the call with, "Thank you. I understand."

He came up behind her and laid a hand on her shoulder. "I won't ask if everything's okay because it's obviously not."

She shrugged and wagged her head dejectedly. "Just business."

Even though they'd gotten past their truce not to discuss family or business, he knew better than to push. If she wanted to talk about it, she would when the time was right.

"How about we get cleaned up? Decide what to do about dinner?"

Her back still to him, she nodded and didn't wait for him to head up the stairs and into her bedroom. He followed a few paces behind, giving her the space that he thought she might need.

In the room, she dispiritedly yanked off her cover-up and dropped it to the floor on the way to the bathroom. He picked it up, folded it, and placed it on the bed.

Ambling into the bathroom, he stood behind her as she kneeled by the large, two-person Jacuzzi she had started filling. He laid his hands on her shoulders and massaged them gently. "It'll be okay," he said, offering comfort, wanting to ease her distress, but she said nothing and rose.

She faced him and laid her hands on his chest. "I appreciate it, Owen, but I really don't want to talk about it right now," Maggie said, her mind obviously still in that numbed state that takes over when something bad happens. "Let's get clean," she said, reached behind her, and unhooked her bikini top.

"Let's," he said.

Chapter 21

THE PLEASANT WARMTH OF THE WATER ENVELOPED MAGGIE, but it was nothing compared to the heat of Owen's body surrounding her. The hard wall of his chest was a perfect pillow along her back as she rested against him. His thighs and arms hugged her, keeping her close while he trailed a soapy washcloth across the swells of her breasts.

"That feels so good," she said, wanting to purr like a cat at the gentle and sure stroke of his hand. He had nice hands, strong with long, blunt fingers that had the delicate but sure touch of an artist.

"You feel good, and I have to say, I like your idea of fun," he teased, clearly wanting to restore the lighthearted mood they'd been sharing before the call.

"Mmm" was all she said, appreciating what he was trying to do. Aware that at some point or another, they'd have to talk about it.

She should have expected what the answer would be. She had known it was a long shot that the hedge fund on her list of white knights would lend her the capital she needed to go ahead with her plans. That left just two names on her list. Ryder Pemberton and Owen. Or maybe it was better to say just Ryder, because she'd never believed in mixing business and pleasure. Owen definitely fell into the pleasure category and maybe more. The maybe more was scarier than she had imagined, because the thought of losing him…

Owen hadn't pressed after the call, appreciating that it wasn't the right time. Maggie wasn't sure that there would ever be a right time, so maybe now was as good a time as any.

"The call was from Gold Shore Asset Funds. I had reached out to them for financing, but they're worried that if we keep on burning through money like we've done the last year, the value of the store locations won't be enough to cover the losses. I guess they thought I wasn't a sure enough risk."

———

Owen didn't know whether she'd really heard what she'd said. That *she* wasn't a sure enough risk. Not Maxwell's, but her, because *she* was the heart and soul of the stores. But she was a sure enough risk as far as he was concerned.

"How much do you need?"

She shook her head. "More than you can manage."

"Bullshit. If I were you, I'd have me on your list. Don't deny it."

"Of course you're on my list. The *very last name* on the list," she admitted with a reluctant shrug. In a flurry of motion, she eased from the tub, grabbed a towel, and wrapped it around herself like armor against him.

He surged out of the water, tugged a towel off a nearby rack, and swathed himself in it. He followed her out to the bedroom, where she had picked up her clothes and sat on the edge of the bed, holding them in her hands like someone sleepwalking and unsure of what they were doing.

Hurrying to her side, he kneeled before her and took

the clothes from her. He set them aside and tenderly took hold of her hands. "I wasn't kidding, Maggie. I want to help."

"Really? And what will your father have to say about that?"

He shook his head and fought back unease about the lie he'd told his father and, in a way, the lie he was telling her. "I don't care what he'll have to say. This is between the two of us."

"And what will other people think, Owen? The ones who know we're seeing each other? What will they say about you giving me money?" she shot back, angry color riding high on her cheeks.

He shrugged. "They'd say it was about time that you and I explored our attraction. As for the giving you money part, we can figure out what would be the appropriate thing to say."

She arched a brow at that, and it occurred to him what she'd meant. With a stammer, he said, "We're business people, Maggie. People will understand it's just a business loan and nothing more."

She motioned between the two of them and said, "And this? What's happening between us? Do you really think people will be able to separate the two?"

Sadly, she was right. People could be cruel and petty. Even downright nasty, and their relationship was already causing talk. Anything more, like an exchange of money, would clearly bring out the worst in certain people.

"We're two logical and responsible people. We should be able to think of something," he said, wanting to find a way to help her but aware that by doing so, he'd be creating even more issues for himself. Thanks to his lie, his father was waiting for a move like this from him and expecting him to betray Maggie. If he found out otherwise, Owen would find himself tossed out of the company. He told himself he could survive that financially, but losing his identity and his place in the business...

That thought was driven away as Maggie mumbled something he didn't quite hear, especially since it sounded a lot like, "We could get married."

"Huh? Can you repeat that? A little louder. I think I may have gone deaf or something," he kidded and dragged a hesitant smile from her.

"I said, 'Maybe we should get married.'"

Well, hell, he had heard it right, and while it sounded crazy at first, it made sense in a weird but logical way.

"I could lend you the money as your wedding gift," he said, quickly catching on to what she intended.

"And I could give you whatever collateral we agree on as your wedding gift," she confirmed, but then quickly added, "But not the Fifth Avenue store."

He understood all too well. She was the soul of the business, but the flagship store was part of her heart. He hoped that at some point he'd be part of her heart and soul as well.

"Not quite how I had pictured this happening, but it makes sense," he confessed, trying not to be disappointed that the discussion of their marriage was businesslike and rational. But then again, that's the kind of people they were, and anything else would be out of character and totally irrational.

—⁓—

"You pictured this happening?" Maggie asked, not really sure what he meant by the offhand comment. She was scared to believe that he meant what she hoped he did, namely that he had pictured their relationship getting to the marriage stage.

A slight dip of his head and half shrug answered her. "Well, I'd kind of thought about it. You and me. Where this was going, if it was going anywhere."

"Which you hoped it would?" she asked, the pitch of her voice rising in encouragement.

The first hint of a smile brightened his features, and his eyes glittered with growing amusement. "Fishing, Mags?"

She looked away from him, snatched her shirt from beside her, and nervously plucked at the fabric. "I'm usually more direct, Owen, but yes, I am fishing. I know my proposal wasn't very romantic—"

"Your proposal was decidedly unromantic," he said and cupped her cheek. He urged her face up to meet his, so handsome and full of life. "I care for you, Maggie. I have for some time. My gut tells me this is the right thing to do. If you agree, let's sit down and discuss what we need to do to finalize this plan."

A business plan. Not a marriage commitment. Not a love affair, she thought, but as she locked her gaze on his, maybe what she needed—what she wanted more than anything—was there in the depths of his eyes. Maybe.

He'd said he cared for her, and that was a good start. In time, maybe it could be more. Maybe it could be what she'd always pictured for her marriage. A real marriage filled with the kind of love her parents had shared before Fate had taken her mother away.

She stuck her hand out to seal the deal, afraid to

delay for fear they'd both reconsider. That common sense would rear its ugly head and logic them out of this crazy-ass arrangement.

"Agreed. Let's sit down and work this out."

Chapter 22

OWEN OFFERED THEIR APOLOGIES TO MRS. PATRICK, WHO had wanted to make them a celebratory dinner to commemorate their engagement. They cut short their Sunday to visit Maggie's father and tell him the news. As a precaution, Maggie phoned her father on the way, so when they arrived, he quickly ushered them into his study and sat them down for the discussion.

Owen shook her father's hand with purpose, trying not to seem as anxious as he really was. He took a seat beside Maggie on the big leather couch opposite the wing chair where her father ensconced himself. With his slightly wrinkled button-down shirt, open at the collar, and the oversize sweater he wore, he had a Mr. Rogers look about him, but the gaze he fixed on Owen was direct and determined. He might look cuddly, but there was nothing soft about him, Owen realized. His face was stern with nothing to give away what he might be thinking about the two of them and the reason they were there.

"I'm sorry I didn't do this in the traditional way, sir," he said as he took hold of Maggie's ice-cold hand and twined his fingers with hers in a show of unity.

"And what way would that be, Owen?" Maggie's father asked, his voice surprisingly neutral.

Owen risked a quick glance at Maggie's pale face, well aware of how difficult it was for her to defy her father with this engagement, because he knew how his father had reacted when he'd first found out about their dating.

"I'm sorry I didn't call and ask your permission for Maggie's hand in marriage."

Her father blew out a breath and waved an exasperated hand in his direction. "My daughter is her own woman. She doesn't need my permission, but I think she would like my blessing on this engagement, and I have to confess, I'm worried about the suddenness of this decision."

"But will you give us your blessing, Dad?" Maggie asked, a tremble in her voice as she squeezed his hand so tightly, he worried she might break a bone.

Her father looked between the two of them and down to their joined hands before facing them again.

"I remember how the two of you used to play together on the beach. I always wondered if it could become more, but the enmity between your father and me spilled onto you kids... I never expected you might find each other again." He paused and inhaled deeply, reached into his sweater pocket, and withdrew a small black box, like one that might hold a ring.

"Since this is so sudden, I know you haven't had a chance to look for a ring, and you probably wanted to pick one out together, but..." He stopped again, emotion nearly strangling his words as with a choked voice he plunged on. "It would make me very happy if you used this ring. It's been in our family for generations, and it was Maggie's mom's ring." He leaned forward and held the box out to Owen.

With a half glance at Maggie, who had tears streaming down her face, Owen took the box and opened it.

The engagement ring inside was a stunning

table-cut sapphire, the blue so dark, it almost looked black. Surrounding the ring were a dozen or so glittering diamonds.

"This is beautiful, sir. I'd be honored if Maggie wore this to commit to me."

Turning on the couch, he slipped the ring from the box and took hold of Maggie's hand. While they had worked out the terms of their supposed marriage bargain hours before, as he gazed at her face, he knew they couldn't delude themselves anymore about the step they were about to take. About the commitment that went far beyond the terms of any kind of business deal.

"Maggie, will you marry me?"

With a sniffle and a tear-filled "I'd love to," he slipped the ring on her finger.

It fit perfectly. Looked right at home on her slender finger, and as he leaned over and kissed her, nothing had ever felt more right.

———⁓———

Since Owen knew that the announcement with his dad would not go as well as the meeting with Maggie's father, he opted to go it alone to reveal the engagement the following morning. Especially since he needed to tell his father that his plans to get to Maggie in order to obtain the Sinclair properties had been nothing but a great big lie. But as his father glared at him, his gray eyes cold as stone, telling him the truth became an impossibility. Somewhere inside of Owen, he still wanted his father's approval, and his father would never approve of a marriage with Maggie based on love. Worse yet, he feared losing his position at Pierce Holdings, since he loved what he did and he'd known nothing else for far too long.

"I didn't think you had it in you, Owen," his father said, his gaze searching Owen's features as if to gauge if Owen was being truthful.

"Maybe I'm more like you than you think," he said, the words bitter on his tongue.

His father continued the stare-down, but then something slipped into his gaze. Something softer and almost like concern.

"Being more like me... Are you sure about this, Owen?" his father asked, giving Owen hope that things could change. Making him think that he could finally tell his father the truth.

"Am I sure? Are you saying that maybe it's time to end this fight with the Sinclairs?" he pressed.

His father hesitated and fisted and unfisted his hands in obvious agitation. "I can't ever forgive Bryce Sinclair. What he did... I can't."

Despite his father's words, Owen sensed that change was possible. Maybe not today, but soon. "Nothing is forever, Father."

"Nothing except death," he said, possibly revealing too much, since he immediately jumped to this feet, slashed his hand sharply through the air and added, "Enough. You did just as I asked, but this prenup agreement... It seems to me that it will only make it harder to get our hands on the store locations."

With disappointment alive in his gut and the deception weighing on his conscience, Owen said, "As I told you before, Maggie is a smart woman. She wouldn't go into this deal without guarantees. The prenup was something I had to agree to so I could seal the deal."

His father paced back and forth as he considered Owen's words, then he stopped and faced him. "What if she turns the stores around? What if she repays you the monies you're lending her?"

Which Owen hoped she would, because he believed in her and her vision for the stores. But if she didn't… Offhandedly and without meeting his father's gaze, he said, "There was always that possibility, Father. At least now we have first crack to buy the properties if it doesn't work out."

"And if the losses are more than the value of the properties? There may be other creditors wanting their piece of the locations and inventory to repay them."

He'd known that based on the earnings report and what Maggie had told him about Gold Shore's concerns, but he hadn't cared, since he wanted to help her fulfill her dreams. With a shrug, he said, "At least we have an in now. It's more than we had before."

He felt the force of his father's stare, but Owen kept his face averted, hoping his father wouldn't discern the truth on his features.

"We'll see" was all his father said, too easily. It created worry that his father had seen through his ruse.

"Will you come to the wedding?" Owen asked, even though he was fairly certain of what the answer would be.

"And see Bryce Sinclair? Have him think that everything is fine between us? Hell no." As his father left Owen's office, he shouted out, "But I'll be delighted to attend the divorce proceedings."

Chapter 23

CONNIE SHOOK HER HEAD SO HARD, MAGGIE WORRIED HER friend might need a neck brace to keep it from twisting off.

"I cannot believe what I'm hearing. It's a joke, right?"

"No joke, my friend," she replied calmly to make it clear to Connie that she wasn't kidding.

Connie continued wagging her head from side to side, forcing Maggie to reach out and cup her friend's face.

"No kidding," she repeated, even more seriously.

Her friend shied away from her touch and stared at her hard. "I'm your BFFF, and that's why I'm saying, this is insane. You can't treat marriage like a business deal."

Maggie arched a brow in what she hoped was an imperious look. "Are you telling me you don't write prenups for your clients?"

Connie finally settled down and glared at her with the kind of look that Maggie supposed her friend used for adversaries in court. "You know I do, Margaret Ann Sinclair. But I know you want more than a business arrangement between you and Owen. I know that inside, you want the whole ball of wax. The happily ever after."

"What if I do? It doesn't make how we're doing this wrong," she parried.

Connie's stance loosened a bit. "You know he's the one. The *only one* and if you start it like this, it's almost like giving up before you even get started."

She hadn't been ready for Connie's reaction. Certainly not her friend's concern that Maggie was "giving up" as she'd put it.

"Funny, but I thought you'd be more worried about the possibility I'd have to give Owen the properties." If she lost the properties, she wouldn't be able to make the balloon payment on her family's mansion, and the bank would assume ownership of the property. With the town house also leveraged, it would only be a matter of time before she lost that as well.

"I know losing all those things that were your family's would break your heart, but you'd heal in time. Losing Owen after you fell in love with him…"

"I *care* for him a great deal, but we're both still working on the love thing," she countered, denying what she feared was deep in her heart. Fear like her friend Tracy had challenged weeks earlier.

A long, almost painful silence followed until Connie yanked a legal pad from the side of her desk and picked up her pen.

"I'll do whatever you want, Mags. Whatever. Tracy and Emma and I will be here for you no matter what."

"I know you will, Connie. But you don't have to worry. Owen and I know what we're doing."

It was evident from the look on her friend's face that Connie wasn't quite as sure but wasn't about to argue with her anymore.

"Tell me the terms again," Connie said and started writing as Maggie repeated the details of the deal she'd made with Owen.

His brother was quiet for several long minutes after Owen told him about his engagement.

"Wow. Just wow," spilled out of Jonathan's mouth. But then he immediately held up his hand to silence Owen and said, "Sorry. Don't get me wrong. I think you and Maggie will be great together."

Owen narrowed his gaze and peered at his brother, trying to gauge his sincerity, and while he didn't detect any guile, something wasn't sitting well with Jonathan.

"Why do I get the feeling you're not being one hundred percent truthful?" Owen said.

Jonathan blew out a rough breath and looked away, shaking his head. With a sharp shrug, he said, "It's not going to be easy for you. You'll have to deal with Father."

"Done. Hers too. He gave us her mother's engagement ring as a gift," he said.

"Wow. Okay. I have to confess I wasn't expecting that camp to give in so easily," Jonathan said and raked the longish strands of his hair back with his hand.

"What else?" Owen asked, not wanting anything left unsaid between them.

"There's the stores and her friends. Not sure how they're going to react, especially Connie."

"Who I expect you to escort as my best man," he said and clapped his brother on the back.

"You're a cruel, cruel man, Owen," he said but with a grin. "So how did they react?" he tacked on.

Owen wagged his head and shrugged. "I'm not sure. Maggie was going to talk to them today. Luckily, Emma is up from Sea Kiss for some kind of bridal show in the city."

"And Connie lives in her office, so *no problema*," Jonathan said with decided bite.

"If she really bothers you that much, I can get someone else to escort her," he said, thinking of at least two other friends who he wanted to be groomsmen at the wedding.

Jonathan waved his hand in a not-needed gesture. "It's okay, Big Bro. Besides, I wouldn't want to turn that woman loose on any other unsuspecting male. I can handle her."

As the discussion turned to who else would be standing up beside him at the wedding, it occurred to Owen that Jonathan could totally handle Connie and in more ways than one. He hoped that the time they'd have to spend together during wedding events would help settle whatever had happened between them. He wanted his brother to be happy. He suspected that for that to happen, Jonathan had to settle any unresolved issues that lingered with Maggie's best friend.

Emma glanced between Connie and Maggie, her features a mask of disbelief.

"You're joking, right?" Emma said, her words an eerie echo of Connie's lament earlier that day.

"No joke, and as the world's best wedding planner, I need your help to pull this off. Two to three weeks. A month at the most. We want to get married as soon as possible."

"Even if I didn't think you were crazy, no one can plan a full-scale wedding that fast. No one," Emma said.

Maggie reached out and laid her hand over Emma's. "You can. And of course, I expect you, Connie, and Tracy to be my maids of honor."

Emma directed her gaze to Connie. "You tried to talk her out of this, right?"

Connie nodded. "I did, but she's dead-set on this, so I figure it's up to us to help her in any way we can."

"Including picking up the pieces when this all goes south?" Emma said with a pointed lift of her brow.

Maggie slammed her hands on the tabletop. "Enough. Seriously, enough. In the last day or so, I've had to deal with my dad and the two of you, and I'm tired of it. Owen and I want to get married. We'd like for all of you to be supportive. If you can't be…"

She left it out there, wanting to give them the option of refusing but hoping it wouldn't come to that. They were her best friends forever, and she wanted them there on what she hoped would be the happiest day of her life.

"I want you there. I *need* you there. I can't imagine not having you at my side when I marry Owen."

Emma and Connie shared a hesitant look, but then, like the ripple after a stone was tossed in a pond, acceptance flowed over them.

"Okay. Whatever you need, Mags. It'll take a lot of hard work and planning—" Emma began, but Maggie cut her off by reaching over and hugging her hard.

"I know you will do it up perfectly, Emma. Just tell me what you need to get started."

Chapter 24

"IS THAT WHAT I THINK IT IS?" TRACY SAID AND REACHED for Maggie's hand as she sat down at the table they'd reserved for lunch the following day. "You're engaged to Owen. Amazing," Tracy said before Maggie could utter a single word.

"How did you know? The gossip column?" Pictures of them had been plastered in various newspapers along with an inset picture of her mother's sapphire engagement ring.

Tracy waved her off with a flip of her hand. "Who reads that crap? I've known for a while that Owen was the one for you. It was just a matter of time before it happened."

Maggie felt like she had just dropped into some kind of Tracy Twilight Zone. Flagging down the waitress, she ordered two margaritas. For herself.

"Would you like anything?" the young woman asked Tracy.

"Cancel her margaritas. Bring us a bottle of Cristal. We're celebrating my best friend's engagement," she said.

Maggie was having a tough time squaring away this Tracy with the one who'd been so unhappy in her marriage. She squinted at her friend, trying to decide if she was actually some kind of pod person, when the waitress brought over the champagne, an ice bucket, and tall flutes. The waitress expertly popped the cork and filled the flutes with the bubbly.

"Color me confused," Maggie said, trying to figure out what was really happening with her friend.

"I get it. A couple of months ago, I was bawling over Bill cheating on me and totally unhappy. We've been working things through in therapy. I've been learning more about not only myself but others. I'm trying to be more aware of what other people are feeling and how to be supportive." Tracy paused, leaned closer, and said, "So the real question is, are you sure about this, Mags? Marriage isn't something to be taken lightly, as I've found out."

Because there was only one answer, she held her glass up and clinked it against Tracy's.

"Here's to marrying Owen," Maggie said.

~~~

The week passed by in a blur of paperwork as she fine-tuned the prenup, exchanged emails with her advertising team and the contractors working on the store renovations, undertook more negotiations with the Italian designer and his prima donna demands, and of course, spent time with Owen.

Owen, she thought with a smile. Long nights of making love and early mornings making love since he'd basically moved into her town house. He'd said that he felt more at home there than in his condo.

As she lay beside him on Friday morning, he woke slowly, his muscles tightening in a stretch, his erection growing as she shifted to rest her thigh across him.

"Good morning," he said without opening his eyes, his voice sleep husky.

"It is a good morning," she said enthusiastically.

He opened one eye in a semiglare. "Chipper this morning, aren't we?"

"Definitely. It's always good to find a hard man in my bed," she teased and caressed him with her thigh.

"That was so, so bad, Mags. Seriously bad," he said with a laugh and rolled to trap her beneath him. "I think that deserves some punishment."

She grew serious as he pinned her arms above her head and heat filled his gaze. "I'm not into that kind of kink."

He arched a dark brow and smirked. "Does that mean you're into some other kind of kink?"

She considered his question for a moment, then leaned close and whispered, "I'm into you, Owen. I want you. In me. Now."

He chuckled and nudged her thighs open. He poised at her center and said, "I wouldn't want to disappoint."

He drove in with one sure stroke and yanked a sharp breath out of her from the force of his possession. But he didn't move, allowing her to adjust to the fullness of him inside her. To the feel of being one with him as he held his weight off her and smoothed her hair, his touch tender.

"This feels so right," he said.

"It feels perfect," she said and cradled his back with her hands. Stroked her hands up and down the length of it with slow, leisurely movements.

—∿∿—

Inside Owen, the pressure grew to move but also to tell her the truth about the lie he'd told his father. The lie he was telling her as he remained silent while they sped toward marriage.

But much like he needed to breathe, he needed Maggie.

He didn't want to lose her, so he kept his silence as he finally drew out of her and started a dance that was both familiar and yet new. Every time they came together, he learned something different about her. About what she liked and how he could bring her ever-greater pleasure. About how much joy and satisfaction being with her brought him.

As she met him in a kiss that nearly had him losing it, the words burst free.

"I love you, Maggie."

She froze for the longest second, tightening his gut with fear until she smiled up at him and combed her fingers through his hair with gentleness and great care.

"I love you too, Owen. I think I have since we were kids building sand castles on the beach. Or maybe it was since we were eighteen and you kissed me that first time. Or when you carried me home from the frat party. I could keep on going, so maybe I should just say, I think I've loved you forever."

It was a relief to hear her say it but also a burden, because he knew how much hurt he could cause if he didn't come clean. But he couldn't right then and there. Maybe after they were married and she understood why he had done it. Or possibly when they were old and gray together and it no longer mattered. But not now. Not when it was all so good. Not when it was so much better than he had ever dreamed.

He didn't want to lose her. He knew what it was to have someone you loved walk out thanks to his mother. He didn't want that to happen with Maggie.

He kissed her again, sealing the deal between them in ways no piece of paper could. Giving her his heart and soul. Hoping as they rose together toward passion that it would be enough to sustain them until the day he could be totally honest with her.

She'd had assorted stints as a bridesmaid and had heard her share of horror stories from Emma about bridezillas and all the things that could and did go wrong at weddings. But staring at the pile of folders, brochures, and samples spread out across the kitchen table in her Sea Kiss home not only had Maggie's mind whirling, but also brought new perspective on why some brides went crazy. She was close to tucking tail and hiding away in a corner, whimpering like a whipped puppy dog, when Owen laid a reassuring hand on her shoulder and squeezed it soothingly.

"We can do this, Mags. We handle multimillion-dollar companies every day. One little wedding won't break us," he said, his tones smooth and without any hint of the panic she was feeling.

"It's just so much," she said, awestruck.

Emma nodded and organized the items on the table into neater stacks. "It's because you've got such a short timetable. Normally, we'd have more time to decide on things like the theme—"

"There has to be a theme?" Maggie asked with a gulp. In all the times she'd pictured getting married, there had never been a "theme," per se.

"No, there doesn't. Right, Emma?" Connie said from across the width of the table as she sat beside Jonathan.

He'd offered to assist his brother with all the wedding prep since there was so much to do in so little time.

"No theme. You said you wanted to keep it intimate. Simple," Emma said and hauled a stack of pamphlets and brochures to a spot directly in front of Maggie and Owen. "These are all the venues for the kind of wedding people expect from people like you, but—"

"I know one venue that is totally available and absolutely perfect," Maggie jumped in and held her hands in a check-it-out gesture. "This home."

Emma grinned. "Great minds think alike. We can do the ceremony at sunset down on the beachfront. Go from there to dinner and dancing on the great lawn. Finish up with a Viennese table on the patio, and then off you go to wherever you'd like for your honeymoon."

"We decided to postpone that until after the Christmas season," Maggie said, earning glares from both her friends.

"A honeymoon night or weekend, then," Emma said.

Maggie glanced at Owen to see what he thought of the idea of using her home as the wedding venue. He was smiling and lifted her hand, brushed a kiss along her knuckles. "It's where we've spent so much time together and where we had our first kiss. Seems perfect to me."

"What about the weather? What if it rains? Or we have a hurricane?" Connie said, ever the pragmatist.

"If the weather is bad, the first-floor landing could be set up for the minister and bridal party. The foyer and areas off it are spacious enough to fit most of the guests. The tents will deal with even heavy rains, and if we have a hurricane, no one would be coming anyway," Emma supplied.

Maggie glanced around the kitchen and then out to the patio and great lawn. She closed her eyes for a moment, picturing what her family's summer home would look like all decked out for a wedding, like it had been months earlier for Tracy's. She smiled as she pictured walking down the great lawn and boardwalk and onto the sand for the ceremony, much like her mother and father had done thirty years earlier.

"That sounds perfect, Emma. This is home, and it is special to all of us," she said and fought back thoughts that it might be the last celebration her family had there if she failed to turn things around with the stores. She looked around the room to everyone gathered there and nodded to confirm that's what she wanted.

Tracy had also come in from her home in Princeton to offer moral support, and she was the one who piped up next. "This home is very Victorian, and I know the word 'theme' wants to send you running, but a Victorian-style wedding would be wonderful."

"Another great idea," Emma said and pulled out a book with party favors and a second with table linens. "We go simple with lots of antique ivory, silver, flowers, lace, and pearls. Antique birdcages, teapots, and candles. Plus, after the men leave, I'll show you even one more reason to go with that theme."

Emma glanced past the bridal party to Carlo, her caterer extraordinaire and possible Prince Charming, who had been sitting silently, patiently, at the end of the table. "If we go with that theme, can you work up a menu for us?" she asked.

Carlo nodded, the movement almost regal, it was so precise. "Lots of courses. Sorbet or ices between the tastings. French in nature. Make a signature cocktail for Maggie and Owen. Offer other cocktails from the era as well as wine, soda, and more modern beverages. We can do something similar for the rehearsal dinner."

"That sounds wonderful. Thank you, Carlo," Maggie said before returning her attention to Emma. "I hate to sound like a bridezilla, but I'm not sure I'll have the time to look through all this with everything else I have going on."

Emma chuckled and rolled her eyes playfully. "And that's why you're going to pay me the big bucks. Although I will give you a BFF discount." Emma faced the men and said, "While we'd love for you to stay, you know it's bad luck for the groom to see the bride's gown before the wedding. Carlo has graciously offered to fix dinner for everyone over at the Pierce house, so please go. *Now*."

"Yes, ma'am," Jonathan teased with a mock salute as he shot to his feet.

Owen nuzzled Maggie's cheek and whispered, "I don't want to leave you alone for a second, but I don't want any bad luck either."

Grinning, she kissed him and swept her hand across his cheek. "I'll make it up to you later."

"You better," he said, then stood and followed the other two men out the door.

She tracked his passage across the patio and to the side of the yard, then turned back to her friends. "Okay, so how is it possible you've already picked the gown you think I'd want to wear?"

Emma tapped her forehead. "Not just *think* you're going to wear. That you *will* wear. Just give me a moment."

Her friend walked to the side door that led into Mrs. Patrick's private quarters and knocked. The door immediately flew open, and together with her housekeeper, Emma wheeled out a mannequin swathed in a big white sheet.

She shook her head. "I don't get it."

"Don't be in such a rush," Connie chided.

Tracy added, "Show some patience, woman."

"Mrs. Patrick. Would you do the honors?" Emma said and gestured to the mannequin.

"It would be my pleasure." As she unwrapped the sheet from whatever was beneath, she revealed yards and yards of satin and lace aged to a lovely ivory hue. "When Emma came over midweek to talk about the wedding, I took her upstairs to the attic to show her this." With another few tugs, she pulled away the last of the sheet to reveal the antique wedding gown beneath.

A beaded bodice that would hug her breasts led to satin that seemed to wrap in disarray across the midsection and then down to ever-fuller sweeps of fabric that created a short train in the back. More beadwork flowed down diagonally from the bodice to the hip and then graced each point where the satin was gathered to form the skirt of the dress.

It was stunning, Maggie thought as she slowly rose and approached the gown. She feathered her hand gently across the beadwork, admiring the delicate work.

"Your mother wore this when she got married. So did your grandmother. It was her mother's gown. Your great-grandmother's gown," Mrs. Patrick explained.

"Well?" Emma asked at her prolonged silence.

Maggie grinned, wrapped her arms around both women, and hauled them close for an immense hug.

"I love it. Can I try it on?"

"We hoped you'd say that. Come with me," the housekeeper said, took hold of her hand, and urged her toward her private quarters.

Emma, Tracy, and Connie followed, Emma wheeling the mannequin back into the living room of the space.

While Maggie shucked her clothes, tossing them onto the couch where Mrs. Patrick patiently folded them, her friends carefully removed the wedding gown from the mannequin and held it up so she could step into it.

As she eased in one foot and then the other and her friends carefully inched the dress up and into place, it was like stepping into the embrace of all the women in her family who had come before her.

Her mother.

Grandmother.

Great-grandmother.

All of them had worn this garment on what they'd all hoped would be the happiest days of their lives.

Like she hoped.

Connie buttoned up the back of the dress, and Emma smoothed the fabric of the bodice into place. Tracy straightened out the train to let it flow behind her, a short river of ivory satin.

"It's a little tight since you're not wearing a corset, but we can let it out a little. What do you think?" Emma said and gestured in the direction of a cheval mirror at one side of the room.

Maggie took hold of the soft, smooth fabric of the skirt and lifted it slightly to walk to the mirror. Standing there, holding her breath, she was unable to believe just how right it felt. How amazing she looked.

The four other women came to stand behind her.

"You look just like your mother on her wedding day," Mrs. Patrick murmured and covered her mouth with her hand, tears glimmering in her eyes.

Maggie's gaze in the mirror skipped from Tracy to Emma to Connie. "What do you think?"

"Perfect," they all said in unison.

"Perfect," she repeated, hoping the rest of the wedding preparations would go as smoothly.

Chapter 25

"Bro, please tell me I don't have to wear this," Jonathan said and swatted at the ruffles on the shirt that spilled over the collar of the vest.

Owen scrutinized the elaborate frock coat with the even more ostentatious shirt, vest, and pants they had been forced into trying on. Wincing from the sight of it, he glanced in Emma's direction.

"Seriously, Em. I know we're going Victorian, but can't we find something a little less..." His voice trailed off, since he couldn't even find a word to describe the outlandish costumes they'd had to put on. "Just less," he finally repeated and started unbuttoning the vest and shirt, eager to be out of the frippery.

Emma nodded, walked over to her colleague, and whispered something in the man's ear.

"Certainly. That sounds like a marvelous suggestion," the man replied.

He raced out of the dressing room and, barely a minute later, scurried back in with different outfits for the men to try on.

Owen and Jonathan went in and exchanged the over-the-top Victorian suits with cutaway tuxedos in slate gray, brilliant-white shirts with gunmetal-colored ascots, silvery-gray vests with delicate embroidered scrolls, and black pants with a subtle gray stripe. As Owen glanced at himself in the mirror in the dressing room, he thought he looked rather dapper.

He stepped outside to where Jonathan was already modelling the outfit for Emma.

She clapped her hands, grinned, and said, "You look fabulous. Like Hugh Grant in *Four Weddings and a Funeral*."

"Chick flick," he said at the same exact time as his brother, and they both rolled their eyes and laughed.

Emma walked over to straighten the ascot and vest. "A nice diamond or pearl stickpin here," she said and pointed at a spot in the middle of the fabric. Skimming her hand across the vest with its hand-stitched swirls, she said, "I love this design and the color. The subtle shades of blue in the fabric will be great with the flowers and the navy we chose for the bridesmaids' dresses."

"Jon, what do you think?" His brother had been unusually silent as he stared at the mirror.

"I'm liking this vibe, Owen. It's different, and I don't feel like I'm dressing up for Halloween."

Owen turned to Emma. "I guess you have a winner," he said, and as he met her shrewd gaze, it occurred to him that he'd been played. "You did this on purpose, right? Showed us the most outrageous outfit so you could sneak this one in instead of the everyday tuxes we'd want to wear."

She grinned and flipped her hands up in a you-got-me pose. "You know the deal, Owen. Show the buyer the houses they won't want and then smack them with a dream home that is decidedly over their budget. Besides, you guys are going to look great."

"Ladies will be all over us," Jonathan said, but then quickly added, "Well, over me anyway, since you'll be a married man. Shit, I can't get over it. You're getting married."

As Owen turned to look in the mirror once again, he almost couldn't believe it either. In a little over three weeks, he'd be married to Maggie.

He smiled so broadly, he thought his face might crack, and Jonathan clapped him hard on the back.

"That's the look of a man in love," his brother said.

Emma had been standing beside him, eyeing him carefully. At Jonathan's declaration, she met Owen's gaze, hers slightly more relieved.

"Yes, it is," she said.

He felt like he had passed some test with Maggie's friend. It surprised him, since, based on what Maggie had told him, Emma was a diehard cynic when it came to love and marriage. But somehow, as their gazes connected, it seemed as if she was willing to relax that cynicism on behalf of her friend. Just to make sure, he said, "I do love her, Emma. I won't ever hurt her."

"We'll see" was all she said and stepped away to finalize the details with the shopkeeper.

―⁓―

"I'm sorry your father couldn't make it to the rehearsal dinner, Owen. I was hoping the two of us could put things to rights," Maggie's father said and squeezed his shoulder, the gesture more paternal than anything his own father had ever done.

"I'm sorry also, Mr. Sinclair," he said and meant it more than the other man could know. Like an inmate on death row waiting for the governor's pardon, Owen had prayed his father would reconsider and end the feud, allowing him to forget about the whopper of a lie he had told. Like that death-row inmate, he was still hoping that his father would arrive in time for tomorrow's sunset wedding.

In the month since announcing his plans to marry Maggie, he'd only seen his father a few times at the office, and they'd barely talked. Part of it was that he was incredibly busy at work with a new project, but Maggie and he had also been run ragged with all the wedding details. In addition, Maggie had been juggling all the changes at the store.

"Bryce. Please call me Bryce. We're going to be family after all," her father said.

"Bryce. Thank you for everything. Maggie has told me that you've been very helpful with all the planning."

Bryce peered at him intently, the look calculating. "I have to say it was a shock when Maggie told me. I wasn't quite sure it was a wise thing to do, all things considered, but I can see that you're good for her. I want her to be happy."

"I will make her happy," Owen confirmed and held out his hand to the other man. For a second, he considered raising the feud and asking Bryce to tell him the entire story behind it, but he held back. This rehearsal dinner was to begin the celebrations and share their happiness. Raising such sorrow at this time just didn't seem right.

Bryce took Owen's hand in both of his and provided a warm and openhearted handshake. His voice was shaky as he said, "Welcome to the family, Owen. I need to see to a few things, so if you'll excuse me."

Owen watched him walk over to Maggie, where the

old man wrapped an arm around her waist, drew her into a tight hug, and dropped a kiss on her temple.

"I can't believe Father didn't come," Jonathan whispered as he strode up to Owen and leaned toward him.

"He said he wouldn't," Owen reminded his brother, who handed him another glass of champagne.

"Fuck him, then. Here's to my big bro on his last night as a bachelor," he said and held up his glass for the toast.

Owen forced a smile, trying not to show just how much his father's absence at the rehearsal dinner was bothering him, and tapped his glass with his brother's. His brother, who he knew he could always count on to be there, despite his crazy antics and wanderlust.

Owen knew that if Jonathan had been in Timbuktu when Owen called for help, Jonathan would find a way to get to his side. He held up his glass for another toast. "To you, my very best friend and amazing best man."

Jonathan actually blushed and did an "aw shucks" shrug before touching his glass to Owen's. "Thanks." Then, as if remembering something, he reached into his pocket and handed him a key. "Before I forget, here it is. Do you need me to do anything else?"

"Not sure. Come with me to talk to Carlo. He'll have a better idea about what's necessary," he said, laid a hand on his brother's shoulder, and steered him in the direction of Emma's caterer, who was giving final instructions to the staff as the event wound down. Only the bridal party was left in the ballroom of the large Sea Kiss inn where they had chosen to hold the event.

As they approached, Carlo turned away from his staff and faced them, a broad smile on his face. "Gentlemen. Are you ready for tomorrow?"

"About as ready as any man can be to lose his free-dom," Jonathan kidded and elbowed his brother.

Carlo laughed and bent close to them. "Don't let the ladies hear that. Especially Emma. I have a hard enough time trying to convince her that marriage is not as bad as she thinks."

"She's a hard nut, but someone will eventually crack that shell," Jonathan said, earning a sharp poke in the ribs from Owen. With surprise, Jonathan looked at Carlo and said, "Sorry, dude. I didn't realize."

"It's okay. I'm a patient man," Carlo said without anger, but the fleeting glance he shot in Emma's direc-tion was filled with disappointment and yearning.

"Do you need help with the surprise?" Jonathan said, obviously trying to draw the other man's attention away from the ever-pessimistic wedding planner.

Carlo nodded. "I have the address and plans for what you requested."

"And I have the key," Owen said and passed it to Carlo.

"You haven't had a bachelor party, have you?" Carlo asked.

Owen shook his head, and Jonathan said, "We haven't had time with all the wedding planning."

Carlo gave a Gallic kind of shrug. "And after this event, you and Maggie—"

"Won't see each other until the wedding," Owen said and looked in Maggie's direction, already missing her even though they had both agreed to be apart for this one night. She was standing with her father and friends, chat-ting and smiling. She looked beautiful in a wine-colored cocktail dress that bared one shoulder, tempting him with a view of her lightly tanned skin and toned arm.

"Then tonight, while we prep your surprise, we'll have an impromptu bachelor party," Carlo said in a voice that left no room for disagreement.

Owen turned his attention back to his brother, seeking confirmation, but his brother's attention was focused on the women across the way. Or rather, one woman across the way: Connie.

He wrapped his arm around his brother's shoulders and hugged him hard, drawing him back into the conversation. "Come on, Jon. It's time for the men to have some fun."

"For sure," his brother said and finished off the last of his champagne.

As he and Jonathan waited for Carlo, it occurred to him that of the three of them, he was the luckiest. He'd found the perfect woman to share his life, while the other two men...

Well, if they were waiting for Connie and Emma, they might find themselves waiting a very long time.

Chapter 26

MAGGIE STARED OUT THE FRENCH DOORS TO GAZE AT THE line of guests making their way down the short boardwalk and onto the beach where rows of chairs awaited.

They had just finished up the cocktail hour on the patio. They had opted to have it before the ceremony so guests could relax a little while they waited for sunset and so Emma's staff could prepare the patio for the Viennese hour later that night. Emma's people were expertly moving everyone down to the beach, and then they would finalize the details in the area around the great lawn, where tables had been set for the five-course meal Carlo had dreamed up for the wedding fare.

"Just a few more minutes, Mags," Emma said, offering her a reassuring pat on the arm before hurrying outside to assist her people.

Waitstaff scurried about, picking up dirty plates and glasses while another group hauled out a long roll of fabric. With impeccable teamwork, they unfurled a long sheath of white fabric decorated with the same silver scrollwork that adorned the gossamer-like material on the dining tables. It was a perfect match to the design on the vests the men were wearing with their cutaway tuxedos.

When they reached the boardwalk, they tacked down that cloth and returned for another roll. They repeated the process on the boardwalk and then again to provide a walkway to the arbor on the sand where the wedding ceremony would be held. Victorian gingerbread woodwork, white and silver tulle, and flowers decorated the arbor. There were scads more flowers all along the rails of the boardwalk and on the tent poles closest to the walkway.

As soon as Emma's staff was done laying the last of the fabric, Owen took a spot beside the minister by the arbor, and after a quick discussion, which brought a big smile to Owen's face, Emma marched back up the great lawn, careful to avoid the cloth runway.

"It looks gorgeous," Connie said from beside Maggie as they waited for Emma to join the rest of the bridal party.

It really did, Maggie thought. Besides the lovely details for her walk down the aisle, each table held a unique centerpiece that combined antique-looking Victorian items with flowers. Roses, orchids, freesia, hydrangeas, stephanotis, and the ever-important orange blossoms added color and fragrance to the tables and to the tussie-mussie bouquets she and the bridesmaids would carry down the aisle. The flowers were expertly blended in with the teapots, cups, books, birdcages, lace, candles, and other Victoriana on the tables.

Emma had explained that in Victorian times, each of the flowers had special meanings. Orchids for true love and stephanotis for happiness in your marriage. Freesia for innocence while the orange blossoms spoke to chastity and an abundance of children in the union.

"She really did an amazing job," Tracy said, almost wistfully, before quipping, "Almost makes me want to do it again."

Both she and Connie looked at Tracy so abruptly and with so much shock that her friend held up her hands in surrender and laughed out loud. "Come on now, ladies. I know I got off to a rocky start, but I've sworn to make this marriage work."

Emma burst through the french doors, still communicating to someone through the earpiece she wore. Meeting Maggie's gaze, she said, "If you're ready, we're set to go."

Maggie looked down to where Owen waited and then whirled around to the bridal party gathered just inside the exit to the patio. Her father patiently sat on a chair beside the doors. Connie and Jonathan stood stiffly side by side, while behind them, Tracy paired up with one of Owen's old college friends, leaving another of Owen's friends waiting for Emma to take her place.

"Ready as I'll ever be," she replied, anxious to be on her way down the aisle and to Owen's side to exchange vows. Doubly anxious to have the entire event over with so they could share their first night as husband and wife.

Connie and Tracy broke away quickly for a final embrace with her before taking their places in the bridal party.

Emma nodded and did a final approval of the couples and their order, leaving herself next to last. With a quick but intense hug for Maggie, she spoke into her earpiece.

"Alert the minister to ask everyone to be seated. Let me know when you've cued the music so the first couple can come down the aisle."

Maggie laid a trembling hand against her midsection and took a deep breath. Her dad rose from his chair and offered her his arm. He patted her hand in a very paternal gesture, hoping to calm her. "It will be fine, Maggie. Don't worry."

"Owen's dad didn't come," she said softly, and her father shook his head.

"Don't think about his bitterness. Today is about celebrating life," her father said, surprising her yet again.

She nodded and took another shaky breath as the bridal party started their walk down to the beachfront. Emma finally assumed her place and spoke over her shoulder. "Wait for us to reach the arbor and take our places. When I nod, you start your journey, Mags. A wonderful, joyful journey to the man of your dreams," she said with heartfelt emotion, adding yet another surprise to what was already becoming a day filled with unexpected sentiments.

Before Maggie could say anything, her friend and the usher exited onto the great lawn, across that expanse and the boardwalk, until they reached the seaside arbor. They split apart, assuming positions on the bride's and groom's sides.

The chamber orchestra that had been playing Pachelbel's Canon finished, and for a long heartbeat, there was nothing but the susurrus of the ocean drifting up toward the house.

At Emma's nod, the traditional wedding march began.

Maggie shared a tearful look and watery smile with her dad and then stepped over the threshold to begin her journey.

―∽∽―

Robert Pierce had not wanted anyone to see him arrive.

He had succeeded.

He poured himself a scotch and downed it in a few hasty gulps to deaden the ache alive in every cell of his body. Then he poured himself a second drink and walked over to the window in his bedroom that provided a view of the Sinclair property and the beach beyond.

Guests were milling about on the beachfront where his son stood next to a minister before a fanciful bower. A garbled announcement drifted upward, and the guests quickly took their seats. A few seconds later, the muted sound of the music signaled the start of the ceremony.

He gulped down another mouthful of scotch as he watched. Waited as he had over thirty years earlier when Elizabeth Maxwell had marched across that great lawn to marry his then best friend and business partner.

She had been radiant in her grandmother's wedding gown, her tall, slim figure magnificent as she went to take her vows. Vows she should have been taking with him, but he'd waited too long to declare his love. He'd been so busy building his wealth so that she could have the kind of life she'd deserved, only…

Pain as sharp as a knife tore into his gut as Maggie walked out on her father's arm. She looked so much like her mother, it was like seeing a ghost. Maggie wore the same wedding gown, and with her trim figure and coloring, it was easy to imagine that it was Elizabeth again, alive and moving down the aisle to meet him.

He slugged back the rest of his scotch with a few quick swallows, but it did nothing to kill the agony roiling in his heart.

He'd lost the love of his life that day along with his best friend and partner.

He'd thought it couldn't get any worse.

And then eight years later, he'd lost Elizabeth forever.

He swiped at a tear as it escaped and sucked in a deep breath, battling to control the emotions that threatened to swamp him. But as Maggie reached Owen and she stepped to his son's side, he could no longer hold back his grief.

He hadn't cried for Elizabeth that wedding day so long ago. Nor at the funeral he'd refused to attend.

He dropped to his knees, buried his head in his hands, and finally mourned, the sobs racking his body. Threatening to tear his frailness apart from the force of his misery until the fury of his lament was finally spent.

He rose and stumbled back to the window to watch his son be married.

———

Owen felt gobsmacked at his first sight of Maggie on her father's arm as she stepped out of the house and onto the patio.

The dress she wore emphasized her height and slim curves and was clearly vintage, judging from the style and the aged ivory color of the lace and satin. Yards and yards of lace and satin and beads gleamed in the last rays of the early autumn sunset, making her almost glow as she approached, her movements fluid and graceful. Her head was held high, dark curls cascading down to her shoulders while two flower-bedecked combs raked back her thick locks from her face.

Her beautiful face was beaming with joy as her gaze locked with his across the distance that separated them. A distance shrinking with each step that she took toward him and their life together. A long life together, he hoped, shoving aside thoughts of the deception he'd committed to get them here and all that he stood to lose. He furiously locked away the image of the ugliness that had dashed any hope he might have had that his father would relent and come to the wedding.

A dim light and motion in the distance caught his eye, dragging his gaze away from his wife-to-be and to the uppermost floor of his family's home, where his father had his quarters. There, in one of the windows, was the shadow of a man. His father, judging from the silhouette.

What is he thinking? Owen wondered, but only for a second as he pulled himself back to the vision of Maggie coming toward him, a delighted smile on her face and happiness in her gaze despite the shimmer of tears.

Joyful tears, he knew and swallowed past the thick lump in his throat.

Beside him, Jonathan bent and whispered, "She's beautiful, Owen."

"Yes, she is," he said and thought, *And she's all mine. Forever and always, she'll be mine*.

When Maggie reached the foot of the arbor, her father paused and kissed her. He offered her hand to Owen, who held out his arm and accepted her at his side.

Her hand trembled on his arm, and he covered it with his and whispered in her ear, "Together, Mags. We can do this together."

"Together," she replied, and he knew no other vows could bind them as strongly as that simple promise.

Chapter 27

THE WEDDING AND RECEPTION PASSED BY IN A BLUR OF emotions, food, friends, and happiness.

Carlo had outdone himself with the wedding feast, even though Maggie hadn't had much time to eat with all the dancing, greeting guests, and kissing Owen. Not that she'd complain about the latter.

There had been some kind of flavorful consommé to start the five-course meal. A delicious seared duck breast in red wine demi-glace joined by grilled foie gras followed. Next came a succulent filet mignon, roasted fingerling potatoes, and asparagus with hollandaise sauce. After those heavier offerings, the servers brought out a fruit and cheese tray before the traditional cake cutting and a Viennese hour with so many different desserts, she couldn't begin to name them. Between each course, dainty dishes of lemon ice had been served to cleanse the palate.

The champagne flowed liberally. An intricate fountain on the patio burbled with a copious shower of the bubbly while waiters also served glasses of champagne and other drinks to guests. At the bar areas stationed to the sides of the property, fanciful ice sculptures graced punch bowls filled with the signature cocktail Carlo had promised, a delicious mix of vodka, fruit brandy, and assorted citrus juices.

The photographers and videographers did a delicate

dance around the space, capturing the occasion while trying not to be noticeable or interfere with the festivities.

Everyone seemed to be enjoying himself or herself, even Connie and Jonathan, who appeared to have put aside their prickliness for the evening.

"It's all so wonderful," Maggie said, almost in awe, and glanced at Owen. Her husband Owen.

He grinned an impossibly broad grin filled with joy that reached up to his amazing dark-gray eyes. Eyes glittering with happiness and trained solely on her. "It is, Mrs. Pierce."

"Sinclair-Pierce," she reminded him with a playful poke.

"Mrs. Sinclair-Pierce. Are you ready to go?" he asked, and the light in his eyes grew heated, warming her core with the promise of what would happen on their wedding night.

"I'm ready. Time to change and then wish our guests goodbye." She rose and grabbed hold of his hand, leading him from the dais that had been erected parallel to the wall of privet hedges that separated the two properties. Inside, they hurried up the stairs to the two different bedrooms they had used to prepare for the wedding.

At the door to hers, Owen blocked the entrance with his arm and swooped in for a kiss that promised so much.

"Don't take too long," he urged her.

"I won't," she said, until she remembered that her vintage dress had dozens of tiny buttons down the back.

"Would you help me get undressed?" she said, looking over her shoulder to guide his gaze to the problem.

He wiggled his eyebrows and teased, "In a hurry? The guests are still here, and besides, I have something very special planned for our first night as man and wife."

She rolled her eyes, shook her head, and presented him her back. "Please just undo the buttons, because I *am* in a hurry to see what you've planned."

They'd agreed that their honeymoon would wait until the holiday season was over and the stores were hopefully more stable. But for the rest of the weekend, it would be just the two of them before they returned to work on Monday.

Owen chuckled. "Only married a few hours and you're already bossy," he mock griped and quickly slipped the buttons free, baring the long length of her back and the very modern and very sexy lingerie she wore beneath the antique dress.

He skimmed his index finger along the edge of the silk and lace that barely covered her bottom, leaned close to her, and whispered, "I hope I get to see more of this later."

She swatted at his hand as he reached beneath her dress to splay it across the bare skin of her stomach and urge her tight to him and the growing pressure of his erection.

"You'll just have to wait and see," she said and rushed into the room, shutting the door behind her firmly.

—∿∿—

"Tease," Owen said to the wood of the door, but he didn't linger for long, impatient to see his new wife in that lingerie and less. Eager for her to see the care he'd taken for their wedding night and weekend.

Inside the room, he ripped off his clothes and speedily changed into a lightweight linen suit and cotton shirt. He skipped the tie, not wanting to waste the time to tie it and not feeling the need to put on such airs for their big departure.

Emma would probably pitch a fit that their grand exit from the party wasn't going as she'd planned, but all he cared about was making the exit as quickly and gracefully as they could. When he left the room, Emma stood with Maggie in the hallway, barking orders to her staff via the earpiece. As she saw him, she said, "You should have let me know you were getting ready to leave. We'll have your car ready to go in just a few minutes. We've asked the guests to wait for you out front to send you off."

"You've got five minutes and that's it," he said and held his hand out to Maggie.

She had changed into a short, form-fitting red dress that hugged every curve of her luscious body and had a neckline that dipped low to expose the generous swell of her breasts.

"Do you like? I wore red for good luck," she said at his lingering gaze.

"I like. A lot," he said. Since they had five minutes to wait, he hauled her close for a long, passionate kiss that held the promise of what would follow once they were alone.

"For God's sake, Owen. Can't you wait?" Emma groused as she stomped off to one side of the hall to give them some privacy.

Maggie grinned and gestured toward her friend with a nod of her head. "She's not a fan of PDAs."

He looked toward Emma, who was once again communicating with her staff. "Well, she better get used to a lot of displays of affection if she's going to be around us, because I intend on always showing you how much you mean to me."

Emma turned back toward them, a brittle smile gracing her lips, unshed tears glimmering in her gaze.

"You're all set to go," she said, her voice husky with suppressed emotion.

Owen understood the enormity of what had happened today in Emma's world. The shock to Maggie's friend's system that it was one of them getting married and entering a new phase of life.

Maggie walked over to Emma and hugged her hard. "This doesn't change anything, Emma. You're my BFFF and you always will be."

Emma nodded and swiped at a tear as it rolled down her cheek. "I know. I just want you to be happy." She jabbed a finger at Owen and tossed her shoulders back like a bantam rooster about to fight. "If you hurt her, so help me God, you'll regret it."

Owen took it all in stride. He walked over and embraced Emma. "I'm honored to be part of your family now."

His words broke the dam Emma had built against her emotions. The tears flowed freely now, and she dashed them away as she said, "I've got to go and finish things up. You are paying me for this after all."

She hurried away, mumbling yet more instructions to her staff and leaving Maggie and Owen standing there, hesitant.

"Will she be all right?" he asked and slipped his hand into Maggie's.

She nodded. "Connie and Tracy are here. They'll help her deal." With a deep inhalation, she looked up at him and said, "Ready to face the world, my husband?"

He grinned so hard, he thought his face might crack as he said, "Totally ready, Mrs. Sinclair-Pierce."

Together, they walked downstairs and to the front door where Emma and Carlo stood, waiting for them. Carlo had a comforting hand on Emma's shoulder, offering her support. Owen knew that Carlo hoped to offer Emma more and soon.

———————

When they reached the entrance, Maggie walked over to Carlo and gave him a tight hug.

"Thank you for all that you did. It was amazing." She leaned close, and in a whisper only he could hear, she added, "Please take care of her."

A slow smile spread across his handsome features, and as he glanced down at a barely recovered Emma, he said, "Thank you. I'll make sure everything is okay."

She walked back to Owen, and Carlo opened the door so they could step out to greet the waiting crowd of guests. Connie, Tracy, Jonathan, and the other grooms-men were up at the front, and they embraced each of them and said their goodbyes before hurrying past the rest of the guests, who tossed birdseed and blew bubbles to send them off.

Owen's Lightning prototype sat at the base of the circular drive, and for a second, Maggie wondered how she'd climb into the low-slung car with her body-hugging dress, but with Owen's assistance, she managed to sink down onto the passenger seat.

Inside, the car was the height of luxury and just the kind of toy many men would love to have. A sleek, charcoal-gray dashboard had an immense touch pad to control the car, and lots of black leather enveloped her in comfort. Jonathan's company would clearly have a winner on its hands once the car was available for sale to the public.

After Owen settled in, he started the car, or at least she thought he did as the touch pad and assorted lights snapped to life, but the lack of engine noise like that in a standard vehicle was disconcerting.

"Where are we going?" she asked as he pulled out of the drive. Owen had insisted on planning their wedding weekend and keeping it a surprise.

"A place I thought you might like. Sit back and relax. You must be tired."

As he probably was. She'd been up late with her friends, enjoying a last single girls' get-together. She'd had to get up early to be primped and preened by the stylists Emma had hired to help her get ready. Then there had been the photographers, and before she knew it, the morning and afternoon had flown by, and it was time for the wedding.

Now, as the adrenaline that had kept her going all day wore off, tiredness made her limbs feel like lead. She glanced over at Owen...

No, not just Owen. Her husband Owen, and that realization sent a little thrill of excitement through her, chasing away some of her weariness. Reaching out, she laid her hand on his thigh, needing to touch him. As she did so, the lights from the streetlamps made the rings on her finger glitter. The sapphire-and-diamond engagement ring that had been in her family and the diamond eternity band Owen had slipped on her finger during the ceremony.

"I love you," she said, finding the words remarkably comfortable to say.

He peered at her, dark brows knitted together, before returning his attention to the road. "I love you too, but why say it now?"

The answer came surprisingly easy. "Because there's no expectation of it now. No crowd waiting to hear it. No moment of ecstasy—"

"Ecstasy, huh? That's a tough one to live up to," he teased. Even in the dark of the car, she could see his pleased grin.

It was a tough thing to live up to, but she had no doubt that he'd meet that challenge later, so she continued. "I love you, Owen. It feels right saying it."

He cast a quick look at her, and it was impossible to miss his contentment and the broad smile on his face. "This does feel right, Maggie. You and me together. More than I ever could have imagined."

"I'm glad you feel that way too," she said, reached up, and brushed her fingers through his hair. Leaning over in the narrow space of the car, she kissed his cheek. "Are we almost there yet?" she asked playfully.

He arched one brow. "Impatient, are we?"

"Yes," she confessed, eager to see the surprise he'd planned. Even more eager to spend their first night alone as husband and wife.

"Just another twenty minutes or so, thankfully, since I'm just as ready as you are for tonight."

With that, she sat back in her seat, willing away the minutes and barely containing her anticipation.

Owen drove the way he did everything else. Competently. Responsibly. Powerfully as he handled the roadster with smooth moves. As he eased onto the parkway and accelerated, she allowed herself to close her eyes for just a moment, knowing she'd be safe and well cared for.

———∿∿∿———

Owen peeked over at Maggie to ask her if she wanted to listen to any music and realized she was fast asleep. He understood. After the impromptu bachelor/decorating party with Carlo and Jonathan and all the running around both before and during the wedding, he was dog-tired. But he wasn't about to let exhaustion spoil their first night as man and wife.

He stepped on the accelerator, speeding the car on faster so they could reach their destination, a huge private mansion along the Navesink River and directly across from Hartshorne Woods Park and the Twin Lights. The mansion was on a large property and fairly secluded, providing them privacy. They'd been lucky so far in that the security detail he'd hired had managed to keep away the few paparazzi who had wanted to crash the wedding. But as close as they were to the other homes along their neck of the Jersey Shore, he was sure that photos of their ceremony and celebration would be in the papers by the morning.

He wondered what his father would think of that. What his father had been thinking as he stood up in his room, watching. Had he possibly had a change of heart and been too embarrassed to show it by coming to the wedding? More likely, he had been up there wishing for it to all go south so the prenup would help him secure the Sinclair properties. As the ugliness of his father's hate

ate at his happiness, he forced it away, intending to allow only joy for this very special night.

He pulled off the parkway and navigated the side streets until he was on the road that ran by the river and up toward the Oceanic Bridge. As the road veered hard to the left, he slowed the car and, in the dark of night, searched for the entrance to the mansion that Jonathan had borrowed from a friend who was vacationing in Europe for the summer.

Spotting the address and the ornate wrought-iron gate that was familiar from last night's visit to prep the place, he drove up and tapped in the security code. A second later, the gates slid open, and he drove down the long, paved road to the front courtyard of the mansion.

He parked and turned in his seat so he could look at his wife for a moment, wanting to memorize every single thing about her. She was beautiful even in sleep, her heart-shaped face relaxed. A peaceful smile on her full lips. Lips he just couldn't resist.

He leaned over and kissed her. A soft entreaty for her to waken, like a prince in a fairy tale willing the princess to come to life. Beneath his lips, there was a moment of surprise and then acceptance as she opened her mouth and eased a hand up to his head to cradle him close.

He felt her smile against his lips as she said, "I like waking up like this."

"Well, then I promise to wake you up like this every morning," he said, grinning. Loving the easy way they had between them that made everything seem so right. He reluctantly shifted away from her and asked, "Are you ready for our special night, Mrs. Sinclair-Pierce?"

Chapter 28

"I AM, OWEN. I AM SO READY," MAGGIE SAID AND DIDN'T wait for him to come around and open her door.

He rushed out of his side of the car, hurried across to meet her, and eased an arm around her waist. After another kiss, more intense and demanding than before, he led her to the door of an immense contemporary-style mansion and unlocked the door. Throwing open the floor-to-ceiling wooden door, he turned and swept her up into his arms before she could protest.

"What are you doing?" she asked, her voice filled with laughter as she grabbed hold of his shoulders.

He smirked and rolled his eyes. "And again, if you can't tell, I must suck at carrying my new bride over the threshold."

"You're crazy," she said and dropped a kiss on his cheek. She turned her head just a bit to whisper in his ear, "And I love it and you."

"Ditto, Mrs. Sinclair-Pierce."

She bit his earlobe friskily. "Don't you dare ditto me ever again, Owen."

"Bossy," he kidded as he set her down in the middle of the living room.

She came to her feet beside him in a space so large, it could have been an airplane hangar. They had taken open concept to a new level with one entire wall at the back of the house that was nothing but glass. She could understand why.

The home sat on a small inlet off the Navesink River, and beyond the water were acres and acres of woods. In the far distance, the light from one of the towers of the historic Twin Lights lighthouses glimmered, and even farther away, the tips of some of the Manhattan skyscrapers and the glow of the city were visible. Looking southward, she could see the bridge over to the other side of the river, Barley Point, and the start of the Jersey Shore beaches in Monmouth County. Immediately outside the glass was an infinity pool surrounded by a brick patio, manicured lawn, and flower beds in full bloom.

Inside, the home paid homage to its coastal location with the same kind of vibe she had in her Gramercy Park brownstone.

"This is gorgeous. Who owns it?" she asked as she slowly pivoted to take in everything in the space.

"A friend of Jon's who's away for the summer. I was here years ago for a party, and I thought this place would make you feel at home and at ease after the craziness of the last few weeks."

It did.

She faced him and laid a hand on his chest. "You're really very thoughtful, Mr. Pierce. Thank you."

"There's more," he said and wrapped an arm around her waist. He guided her over to the dining table placed next to the wall of windows and off the kitchen area. Fine china, crystal, and cutlery graced the distressed oak tabletop, and a bottle of champagne was nestled in ice in a standing bucket. In the middle of the table sat a centerpiece that matched those that had been at their wedding.

"Lovely," she said and ran her hand along the thick wood of the table.

Owen pulled out a chair and said, "Take a seat and relax."

Since he seemed to be big on her relaxing, she did just that, making herself at home since the place was both inviting and luxurious.

Owen picked up the dinner plates from the settings and headed into the kitchen. The rattle and clank of plates followed, and within a few short minutes, he returned and set a plate piled high with spaghetti and an immense piece of chicken parmigiana. Then he popped open the bottle of champagne and poured them both glasses.

The smell from the meal was heavenly, and her stomach rumbled noisily in response. "I didn't think I was hungry, but I really didn't get to eat much of the delicious meal that Carlo prepared."

"I didn't either, and Carlo was kind enough to make this and have his staff warm it for us. There are cannoli for dessert."

Just like their very first meal together.

She picked up her knife and fork and cut a piece of the chicken. She ate the bite and said, "You're very romantic, and this is very, very good. Dare I say—"

"Better than at our favorite place, and yes, I am romantic."

"*Really* romantic and sexy and handsome and funny. *Really* funny," she teased, recalling that first dinner.

He grinned and shoved a healthy forkful into his mouth. Murmured a pleased, "Mmm. Delicious."

But after that, all conversation ceased while they

satisfied one kind of hunger and another built quickly. They finished eating, and he swept the plates up, but she laid a hand on his and said, "I think dessert can wait for later. Don't you?"

"Much later," he said and dropped the plates back onto the table. He took hold of her hand and urged her up into his arms. He whispered against her lips, "Much, much later."

His kiss was hard and possessive. It demanded surrender, and she melted into his arms with that demand. She held on to his shoulders as her legs grew weak with desire and her core pulsed in anticipation of making love with him.

Her head whirled as he swept her up again, but she didn't break away from his kiss, meeting his lips over and over. Opening her mouth to his while he climbed the stairs and strode to a room on the second floor.

He set her down gently, her body slipping along his until her feet touched the ground. He eased his hands to her waist, kept her close, and laid his forehead against hers. "I love you, Maggie."

"I love you, Owen."

He cupped her cheeks in his hands and locked his dark, hungry gaze on hers. "I want you, Maggie. I need you unlike anything I've ever wanted or needed before."

"I want you too, Owen. I need you," she echoed and, in a flurry of action, undid the buttons on his shirt and yanked it out of his pants.

But as she reached the waistband of his pants, he took hold of her hands and stopped her.

"Slow, Maggie. Nice and slow," he said, his voice as smooth as the fine bourbon he liked.

She smiled and ran the backs of her hands up his body as leisurely as he had asked.

"Is this slow enough?" she asked with a knowing smile.

"It's perfect. You're perfect."

He kissed her tenderly, unhurriedly, making her feel precious. Cherished. Unlike their first impatient and rash lovemaking, this time, they went as slowly as they wanted. Removing each item of clothing with a lingering kiss and caress. They ambled to the bed pressed tight to one another until he urged her down onto the mattress and covered her body with his. He nudged her legs apart and surprised her by sliding down her body to kiss the pulsing nub at her center.

She moaned and rocked her hips against his mouth. Against his gifted mouth and tongue that could bring so much pleasure. Rouse such incredible passion as he was doing now with the press of his mouth. A lick of his tongue and the slide of his fingers deep into her.

"Owen," she pleaded, clutching at his shoulders. She lifted her hips to urge him for more. To provoke his possession.

———

Owen shuddered at her summons, his body more than ready to both receive her passion and give her the pleasure he knew he could.

He eased into her wet warmth, claiming her body and her heart. Gifting her with his heart as he bent and kissed her, giving her all of himself. Losing himself in her.

He moved, pumping his hips and building the passion

between them. Watching as her eyes darkened to the deep blue of the sapphire ring that proclaimed their union. Seeing the glitter of joy as bright as the sparkling band of diamonds that said she was his.

His and his alone.

Maggie cradled his jaw, her hand trembling as she swiped her thumb across his lips. "Come with me, Owen. Be one with me."

"Always, Maggie. Always," he said, and with a few sharp strokes, he made them one.

—∿∿—

The morning view out the wall of windows on the second floor was just as stunning during the day as at night. The deep blue of the river and ocean beyond, glittering with the first rays of sun. The vivid green from the forest across the way in Hartshorne. But nothing was better than the sight of Owen lying beside her, a dimpled smile on his face even in sleep.

She didn't want to wake him, since they'd barely slept all night. Heat filled her face with the memory of what they'd done all night long and what she still wanted to do with him all day long. Somehow, she found the strength to leave the bed, throw on a robe, and go downstairs to make them breakfast.

The dinner remnants were still on the table along with the empty bottle of champagne. She cleaned up, went into the kitchen, and looked in the fridge that someone had stocked with enough food for the weekend and beyond, tempting her to think about taking Monday off as well, only they both had obligations to fulfill.

Yanking coffee, eggs, bacon, and English muffins

from the fridge, she prepped a quick breakfast for them. She loaded it on a tray and took it back up to the bedroom. As she entered, Owen slit open one eye, and his sleepy grin broadened.

"I don't know what looks more delicious. Breakfast or you."

She chuckled, and after he sat up in bed, she placed the tray over his lap.

"That was so not smooth, Owen. I am way better than breakfast."

He smirked and eyed her. "I don't know. This breakfast looks pretty damn good. Probably tastes pretty good, since you've really taken to this whole being domestic thing."

She quirked a brow. "Is it *really* better than me?"

"I may need another taste to find out," he said, set the tray on the floor beside the bed, and took her lips in a fierce kiss.

"Well?" she said as they both came up for air.

"You win hands down," he said and pressed her down onto the mattress.

By the time they were ready for breakfast, the eggs were cold and the bacon limp. Neither one of them complained as they went down to the kitchen together to make lunch.

Chapter 29

His father hadn't made an appearance in Owen's office since their argument weeks before the wedding. All communications between them in the three weeks since his nuptials were done by either voicemail or email. For a man who had been technologically challenged before the wedding, his father had suddenly gotten all twenty-first century.

Part of Owen was glad that he hadn't had to deal with his father's bitterness and hate up close. But the bigger part of him worried that, like a pot filled with water slowly coming to a boil on the stove, it was just a matter of time before the pressure blew the lid off and caused a mess.

Owen didn't want to deal with any kind of mess, especially since the last three weeks with Maggie had been incredible and amazing. Loving and passionate. He honestly didn't have enough words to describe what it was like to be married to her.

Dishonest, the little voice in his head added, sounding way too much like his father.

He hadn't found the courage to tell her yet, and with every day that passed, he prayed that he would never have to tell her. He hoped every day that his father would realize that tossing him out of the company would be like selling their best performing property for a dime. At least he told himself that. The same way he told himself that everything would be fine and that the loan deal they'd made as their prenup would never need to happen.

He'd made the deal in part because he truly hoped Maggie could turn the stores around. The prenup had just been a way for him to help her make it happen. So far, it seemed like a real possibility that Maggie's plans would succeed. The mid-September launch of the Italian designer's knit collection had sold out virtually overnight. The preliminary sales numbers Maggie had received had indicated that the business might actually be in the black for the month, since the rush of people into the stores for that collection had yielded lots of sales in the other departments. Especially since each person buying one of the designer items got a special coupon for additional purchases that day and a second one for a future purchase.

The beep of his smartphone pulled him from his thoughts and reminded him that he had to get over to the Fifth Avenue store for the official opening of the Savannah Courtyard. The press had been invited to the event along with select dignitaries and celebrities in the hopes that the exposure would bring even more attention to the changes Maggie was making.

He bolted from his chair, raced out of his office and the building to where a limo was waiting for him at the curb. As he approached, the driver opened the door, and he stepped in to where his wife sat, perfectly groomed for the special event. Her hair was done up in some fancy little knot that was more formal than usual and yet still not too fussy. In lieu of a suit, she wore a dress that wasn't either black or blue but somewhere in between and made her crystal-blue eyes pop. Smoky eye shadow hinted at something secret in her gaze while her full lips were painted in a cherry red that made him want to lick it all off. He held back from that taste, because she needed to look perfect for today.

He sat beside her, and nervous energy poured from every cell of her body. He feathered a caress along her cheek and enveloped her hand in his, providing reassurance. "It's going to go perfectly."

"I hope so. I don't want to be pessimistic, but everything is going too well so far."

"And you're afraid someone is going to drop the hammer on you soon," he finished for her, because he'd been feeling the same way. Just like Maggie, he'd been waiting for the cosmos to smash apart their happiness, because it wasn't fair that two people could be so damn content.

"It's going to be fine," he repeated for them and tried to rub away the chill in Maggie's hand.

"It will be," she confirmed and twined her fingers with his, squeezing tightly for the nearly thirty agonizing minutes it took for the limo to fight crosstown traffic and then head to the Maxwell's store in the Thirties.

There were a few uninvited paparazzi swarming like vultures around the main entrance to the store. As Maggie and Owen stepped from the car, the reporters got in their faces with their cameras, and Owen put himself in front of Maggie to protect her until the store's security guards charged forward to restore order. Even as they were escorted away, the paparazzi snapped photos and shouted out questions about the family feud and the marriage. Their Romeo and Juliet tale had apparently grabbed the interest of the tabloids in a major way, and while neither of them relished the attention, the press surrounding their marriage kept the story of Maggie's efforts to turn around the stores in the public eye, which was a good thing.

If some of those tabloid readers felt compelled to check out that story for themselves with a visit to the stores, all the better, he thought as they entered and rode the escalators up to the floor with the Savannah Courtyard restaurant and the Winter Wonderland on the other side, which would be ready to open in another month. A temporary wall decorated with all kinds of Christmas pictures and photos of children with Santa had been erected across the floor to keep that area under wraps for the moment.

At the entrance to the restaurant stood Maggie's father, the mayor, and several Broadway stars along with a half a dozen or so newspaper people and reporters from two of the local television stations. Opposite them was a select group of long-time Maxwell's customers who had received special invitations to the grand opening and a dozen or so of the most senior Maxwell's employees.

As they approached, Owen took a spot beside Maggie's dad but away from the action, wanting to stay out of the limelight.

Maggie greeted each of the guests, the press, and her employees, and then returned to the entrance to the restaurant and offered him an anxious smile.

He laid a hand at the small of her back for support and whispered in her ear, "You can do this."

She nodded, faced the people gathered there, and forged ahead with her speech. "I want to thank you all for being here with us for the grand reopening of the Savannah Courtyard. This is a project that's dear to my heart, since I remember coming here often as a child with my mother. Those are memories that I will forever cherish, and I hope that you will be able to make such happy memories for yourselves and your families in this very special place."

The crowd clapped, and a few louder catcalls came from the back and the group of Maxwell's employees. Turning back to her father, Maggie held out her hand and drew him forward to help her cut the ribbon. Cameras flashed to commemorate the moment, and as the ribbon fell away, Maggie and her dad invited the guests to enter and sit down for the high tea that had been specially prepared for the occasion.

Owen hung back, waiting for everyone to enter, but when only a few reporters remained, someone called out from the press group, "Mr. Pierce. Rumor has it that your father threatened to disown you for marrying Ms. Sinclair. Is that true?"

Owen peered into the crowd to see from where the question had come and recognized one of the more determined paparazzi who had somehow gotten past security. Although the guards had now recognized the man and were moving in, Maggie held her hand up and stopped them, a questioning look on her face.

She walked to stand beside Owen, and he laid his hand on her back. She was stiff, her upset apparent. Before she could say anything, the same paparazzo shouted out at her, "You stand to lose the stores and your family homes, don't you, Ms. Sinclair? So isn't your marriage just a charade? A business deal so you both get what you want?"

Shock ripped through his gut at the reporter's words. *Lose her family homes?* he thought and faced her, incredulous. Her blue eyes were clouded with pain and fear, giving credence to the nasty words.

He shook his head but knew now was not the time or place for discussion. Faking a smile, he urged her closer and brought his lips near hers.

"Mrs. Sinclair-Pierce?" he said, inviting her to respond.

Maggie took up his cue, forced a smile to her lips, and said, "Mr. Pierce, what do you think? Is this marriage just a business deal?"

He loved her bravado and knew exactly what was needed to get past the awkward moment. He bent his head and said aloud, "I never mix business with pleasure, and you, my love, are nothing but a pleasure."

He kissed her, but it was impossible to ignore the tension in her body, and in truth, he was feeling much the same way. The reporter's ugliness had done its job, sowing seeds of distrust that he hoped they could weed out before they took root.

Behind his closed lids, he registered the bursts of light that said the moment had been captured forever much the same way the memory of this moment was being burned into his brain and every cell of his body.

As they finally eased away slowly, Maggie's blue-eyed gaze was slightly unfocused and almost bewildered, as if she didn't quite know what to make of what had just happened. Despite the unease growing inside him, he tried to kill the nastiness planted within her.

"I love you, Mrs. Sinclair-Pierce. Forever and always."

When they faced the remaining reporters, the paparazzo who had asked the questions was voluntarily slinking away with his tail tucked between his legs, apparently well shamed by the answer they'd provided to his question.

Maggie recaptured her composure and escorted the last of the reporters into the Savannah Courtyard, and Owen followed her in and sat at a table that had been set aside for family. Bryce Sinclair sat with Mrs. Patrick, who was wearing her Sunday best. Tracy, Connie, and Emma were also there, and he was surprised that he hadn't noticed them before now. Of course, most of his attention had been on his wife.

He greeted everyone and took a seat beside Connie, who immediately leaned over and said, "That was some show you put on there."

"No show, Counselor. I love my wife," he said, even if he was upset about the possibility that the reporter's words about Maggie losing her homes was true.

A reluctant mutter of acceptance came from Connie while Emma remained silent, although he could feel her intense gaze on him. Tracy, on the other hand, was smiling like the Cheshire cat, apparently pleased by what she had seen.

A server came around and laid out the items for the high tea, and all the while, Maggie's chair remained empty as she worked the crowd, making sure every guest shared a moment with her. She took photos with each of the customers who had been invited to join them. Her smile was brilliant, but Owen saw beyond it to the brittleness around her lips and the stormy blue of her eyes. She was upset without a doubt, but any discussion would have to wait for later, so he turned his attention to the guests around him.

Maggie smiled again and again for the cameras, wanting to make sure every invitee felt as if they were special. Plus, she needed to be away from Owen as the questions the reporter had asked ricocheted around in her brain, creating uncertainty and distrust.

She chatted with Mildred Evans, the woman who had once been a server in the Savannah Courtyard when Maggie's mother was alive and who was now the supervisor of the kitchen.

"Your mother would be so pleased with what you've done, Maggie," the older woman said.

"Thank you, Mildred. This would not have been possible without you. My mom would be so happy to still have you as part of our family," she said and embraced her.

Mildred returned the hug and was just stepping away when her father walked up to them.

"Everything was fabulous, Mildred. Elizabeth would have so enjoyed everything your staff prepared," her father said.

"Thank you, Bryce. That means a lot," Mildred said with a sniffle and excused herself to go check with her people.

Her father eased an arm around Maggie's waist and leaned close to her. His familiar scent, sandalwood soap and peppermints, teased her senses a second before he dropped a paternal kiss on her cheek.

"Your mother would be very proud, Maggie. This place looks better than it ever did."

Tears shimmered in her gaze as she looked at her father. As one escaped, she swiped at it and said, "I appreciate that, Dad."

"It's more than just that, Maggie. You were right about everything. I'm sorry I didn't listen to you before. If I had, things might not have gotten so bad," he said, emotion making his voice gruff.

She laid a hand on his cheek and stroked the sandpapery rough skin. "It's okay, Dad. We're doing it together now. It'll work out." Or at least she hoped it would. She glanced back toward where Owen was sitting with her friends, smiling and chatting with them. Only she could see the hardness in his gaze and the jerkiness of his movements.

"You didn't tell him, did you?" her father asked, tracking her gaze.

She shook her head and looked away. "I didn't want to think about it, so much so, I drove it out of my mind, and it never occurred to me to mention it."

Her father hesitated for a second. "Maybe he felt the same way about the situation with his father."

She wanted to believe that, Lord how she wanted to, but somehow, the nagging doubt had settled in and was refusing to let go. As another customer walked up to thank her for a wonderful time, she smiled and snapped a selfie with the woman as her father strolled back to the table with Owen, Mrs. Patrick, and her friends.

—◦◦◦—

Owen sat patiently, waiting for Maggie to finish up. He was alternately hurt, angry, and anxious about the reporter's comments. Hurt and angry that she hadn't trusted him enough to tell him about the mortgages on her family's homes. Anxious because she was sure to ask questions about his father's threat.

It seemed like forever before the high tea wound down and Maggie finally came over to their table. She hugged everyone and then tiredly plopped into the chair, exhaustion evident in every line of her body. All the worry and work leading up to this event and the big moment had clearly taxed her, as had the incident with the reporter.

"We should go so you can get some rest," he said.

She shook her head. "Not until everyone's gone."

He understood and did what he could to offer support as another couple of hours passed while people finished the meal and lingered to chat and take photos. It was nearly seven o'clock by the time the last of the crowd dispersed, leaving only those at the family table, and he pressed her again.

"Time to go home. You look beat," he said.

She finally gave in. "Yeah, I am tired. Thank you all for coming."

"It was lovely," Tracy said.

"We wouldn't have missed it for the world," Connie added.

"Everything was fabulous," Emma chimed in.

Mrs. Patrick gushed with similar sentiments. "Your mother would be so proud. She loved this place and you've brought it back to life again," she said, tears in her eyes.

Maggie's father, eyes also misted with tears, echoed his earlier comments. "Good job, Maggie. You were so right about reopening the Courtyard."

Maggie hugged her father tightly. "Thank you, Dad. That means the world to me."

"Ready when you are, Maggie," Owen said.

She looked at him but didn't smile. Didn't take hold

of the hand he held out to her. The blue of her eyes was clouded with worry, and fine lines of tension bracketed the tight smile she gave him.

"Let's go, Owen."

Chapter 30

Maggie should have been joyful at seeing the Savannah Courtyard restored to its former glory and hearing her father's acknowledgment of what she had accomplished. But as she climbed into the limo beside Owen, the tension between them spiraled into an ever-tighter coil with each block that passed. As the limo pulled up in front of the town house, she sprang from the car and rushed inside, wanting privacy for the discussion that couldn't be avoided.

Owen entered their home at a more leisurely pace and casually tossed his keys into the dish on the foyer table, but tension radiated from every inch of his body.

She struck first, lunging at him with her question. "When were you going to tell me?"

A stony scowl on his face, he parried with, "I might ask the same of you."

She hated that he deflected her query but answered anyway. "I hadn't really thought it was something you needed to know when we first started dating."

He arched a midnight brow, his dark-gray eyes glittering with icy shards of silver. "You stand to lose homes that I know are very special to you and now to me, and you didn't think I needed to know? Or is it that you didn't trust me enough to tell me?"

Guilt sunk its claws deep, because she couldn't argue with part of his assessment. She should have told him,

but not telling him had nothing to do with not trusting him. She'd had full trust in him until the reporter's
nasty questions.

Dragging a hand through her hair, she looked away
and said, "It happened well before our bargain, and I had
driven it to the back of my mind because I didn't want to
think about it. I didn't want to consider that I wouldn't
succeed and that I'd lose those two pieces of my heart."

———✸———

Pain sliced through Owen at what she didn't say. That
she didn't trust him, for starters. And that, unlike the
stores and the homes, he wasn't something she might
regret losing with her actions. Sucking in a deep breath,
he held it for a second, and then the words exploded
from him. "How bad is it?"

She shrugged, shook her head, and started to walk
away, but he grabbed her arm to stop her flight.

"You can't run away from this, Mags," he said.

She jerked her arm free and faced him, chill anger in
her crystal-blue gaze. "Don't you dare manhandle me,
Owen Pierce."

"How bad is it?" he repeated more calmly, although
he was feeling anything but calm.

Tilting her chin up in a defiant gesture that had
become so familiar, she said, "If the stores can turn a
decent profit, I can recoup what I put in and pay off
the first few balloon payments on the shore home. After
that, I can pay off the loans on this town house."

"And if they don't turn around?" he pressed.

"I'm pretty much wiped out except for this brownstone, but I can't sell it off and have enough to pay off

the mortgage on our Sea Kiss home. I could call in the notes with my family's company, force them to liquidate some holdings to cover the loans, but I don't want to do that. It would cost too many people their jobs."

Wiped out, he thought and couldn't imagine ever putting himself in that kind of position. But then again, by marrying her, he stood to lose more than just money. He stood to lose all that he'd known for most of his life, just like she did.

"Why, Mags? Why would you risk everything—"

"Why would you, Owen?" she challenged. "The reporter said your father threatened to disown you for becoming involved with me. Is it true?"

It would be the perfect time to tell her. To spill his guts about the deception that had allowed them to be together, but the words got trapped in the tangle of emotions he was feeling over her lack of truthfulness. Over her lack of trust in him. Over his fear of losing her and how powerless that made him feel. As powerless as the young child who had watched his mother walk away and never return.

"You know my father. The way he is," he said, leaving it to her to put the pieces together, even if she assembled them wrong.

—∾—

Maggie stared at him hard, trying to decipher what he wasn't saying, since it was clear he was keeping something from her. "I know the way he is, and I thought I knew you too, but I don't, do I?"

His lips thinned into a razor-sharp slash that cut into her as he said, "I guess we don't really know each other all that well, do we?"

Emotion clogged her throat as she asked, "What else is there, Owen? What else aren't you saying?"

He started to speak, but then he stopped abruptly, looked away, and shook his head. When he faced her again, his features had softened somewhat, and pain filled his gaze.

"I love you, but there are things…" His voice trailed off, and he seemed to be fighting himself over something before he finished with, "Don't believe everything you hear, Mags. Believe in me, in us."

For weeks, she had lost herself in the happiness they had shared and the certainty she'd possessed that their love was real and true. That happiness had driven away fears about everything else that was so uncertain. The way their love was suddenly uncertain because of their failure to communicate. To be honest with each other.

She stepped closer and cradled his cheek. She met his gaze directly and said, "I didn't mean to keep it from you. I want us to be totally honest with each other."

A maelstrom of emotions swept over Owen's face like a sudden summer storm. It was impossible for her to miss that he was struggling with something, but then his features smoothed into a mask that hid whatever he was thinking.

"Please understand that the situation with my father… is difficult. There are things I've done…that I've *had* to do to handle it."

Her hand trembled on his cheek, and she slowly pulled it away. She shot him a questioning look, hoping to break past that falsely calm mask, since it was clear there was more he wasn't saying, but he remained silent. Stoic.

"I'm a little tired. I think I'm going to turn in early," she said and, without waiting for him, trudged up the stairs.

———～～～———

Maggie's steps were slow, almost like those of a much older person, Owen thought.

He wondered if she was waiting for him to follow and decided that she wasn't. She needed time away from him, much like he needed distance to handle the day's troubles and revelations.

He walked over to the dry bar in the living room and poured himself a bourbon. Plopping down on the couch, he loosened his tie and slipped off his shoes and suit jacket. After a sip, the smooth warmth of the liquor slid down his throat and chased away a little of the chill in his heart.

He told himself she hadn't really lied to him, although her omission felt like a lie.

Glancing around the room, he tried to put into perspective all that she stood to lose.

So much that was important to her, he thought, and the dull pain came into his heart that she might not include him in what she might lose. But why would she? Why would she think that when he had supposedly signed on for better or worse? Through sickness and in health, they'd promised, only she probably wouldn't feel that way if she found out about his deception.

But she hadn't been totally honest with him either, he rationalized. Even though she'd said that she'd driven it to the back of her mind, it had to have been there front and center every day. You just didn't forget something like that.

Anger brewed as he sipped his drink again and worked through everything she'd just told him. But even with that anger, he was trying to figure out what he could do to help her save those things that were so important to her.

He leaned back against the comfy cushions on the couch and put his feet up. He closed his eyes for a moment as fatigue settled into his bones. It had been a long day and tiring on multiple levels. As he lay there, he went over and over the words they had exchanged until he grew drowsy.

Long minutes later, he heard a footstep on the stairs and waited, wondering what she might say, hoping she'd ask him to come up, but she didn't.

He lay there, gut twisting, telling himself to let go of anger and hurt and try to make things right. Only he couldn't, and he stayed there, grateful when sleep finally claimed him.

—⁓—

Maggie paced back and forth in their bedroom, replaying that night's fight. It could have been uglier, but they were both too civilized to let it get out of hand. She almost wished they had lost that civility and gotten to the truth. The whole truth, because she knew there was more between them that hadn't been said.

And she knew she was as guilty as he.

She hadn't lied when she said she'd driven the mortgages and everything related to them to the back of her brain. She had wanted to focus only on turning the stores around, because if she did, the dominoes would fall into place and the problem of the mortgages might be one that just went away. But the dominoes could just as easily tumble down another route. One where she lost the stores and her Sea Kiss home and even this brownstone.

Maybe even Owen.

It had been impossible to miss his incredulity at the thought that she had risked everything to save the stores. And yet, hadn't he supposedly risked as much to marry her? If his father disinherited him, wouldn't he lose his place in the business? All that he'd worked for his entire life? His future?

Unless he really hadn't risked it. Unless there was more that had driven him to their bargain that he wasn't saying.

That niggling thought rose up and spread its poison inside her, creating doubt and mistrust. Making her wonder just what it was that Owen couldn't trust her with.

She marched down the stairs, intending to confront him, but halfway down, she realized he was passed out on the couch. Seemingly asleep although she couldn't be quite sure. Even in rest, a narrow slash of a smile was on his lips and he looked haggard. Despite her anger, empathy won out, since she was as exhausted.

She walked over to the couch, grabbed a throw from the back of it, and spread it over him. Leaned down and brushed back a lock of errant hair that had fallen onto his forehead. She watched him for a minute, wondering if she should wake him, but then decided it was better for them to have a little distance tonight.

Lumbering back up the stairs, she told herself it was better this way. They were both too tired, and continuing the discussion now could only rile the situation. It might risk having them both say things that would cause even greater hurt.

It was better they both get some rest and revisit the discussion in the morning. Clear the air about what had happened with calmer minds. But as she reached the door to her bedroom, she laid her hand on the jamb and stared at her empty bed.

In all the weeks of their marriage, she'd never been alone in that bed. She hoped it wouldn't be the first of many nights without him.

Maggie sat at her home office desk, reviewing the financial numbers from the last two months and the two weeks since the Savannah Courtyard had reopened. But thoughts about her personal life intruded, and she set aside the papers and contemplated the frost that had clung to her and Owen since their argument that night.

They hadn't fought again, but there was certainly still hurt and more creating a chill between them. They were guardedly polite with each other, and at night, they still made love but not as often. Even when they did, there was restraint there, as if they were both afraid of revealing too much in those most intimate of moments.

She didn't know how to get past it, how to restore the happiness and joy that they'd experienced before, but she knew she was tired of the way it had been for the last two weeks.

Maybe later, when he got home, she'd try to talk to him about it. For now, she dragged the papers before her again and went back to examining the financial reports for the stores. Store sales were up slightly at the suburban locations but way higher at the flagship store that had been the biggest drain on the company. The

Savannah Courtyard looked like it would cover the costs of operations and repay the monies spent on the renovation in only a couple of weeks. After that, it would be making a small profit.

In a few days, the Winter Wonderland would reopen with another big ceremony. The print ads and television commercials started airing tomorrow, together with the social media campaign that included videos from their employees and photos and stories from their customers.

It all looked to be going in the right direction, and if it kept up, this holiday season might be enough to right the ship and keep the stores afloat. She dared to dream that it would also be sufficient to make the payments to keep her from losing the Sea Kiss home and her town house.

The beep of the security system alerted her to Owen's entry, and she shut down her laptop and hurried to greet him. She didn't want to continue with this guardedly polite way of living together, and she was willing to set aside her own fears and doubts to set things right.

Owen had just dropped his briefcase by the table in the foyer when Maggie came down the stairs, a hesitant smile on her face. Her blue eyes, the barometer of her emotions, were a turbulent indigo as they had been the last couple of weeks.

His heart seemed to skip a beat as she waited on the last step but then stepped into his arms and tucked her head against his. The embrace melted some of the icy fear that had been in his gut for weeks and gave him hope they could go back to the way they'd been before their fight.

"I missed you," she said and kissed him, the touch of her lips hesitant at first but growing more fluid, warmer, as he returned her greeting.

"I've missed you too. I'm sorry I'm a little late, but the Upper East Side project has gone south." After an early easy start on the redevelopment, they'd hit snag after snag, including a lawsuit from the owner of a nearby apartment complex who claimed the construction of the much taller building would result in the loss of his air rights. While legal actions like this were too commonplace and often settled out of court, the litigation had brought construction to a standstill while they tried to reach a compromise. Every day that they weren't working was money lost. Money he couldn't afford to lose in light of the deal he'd made with Maggie, as his father had reminded him with both an email and a surprise personal visit.

"Anything I can do to help?" she asked and started a slow massage of the knotted muscles on his neck and shoulders.

"That feels good." He closed his eyes and dropped his head forward, savoring the feel of her hands on him, relaxing in rough spurts until the last of the tension had disappeared. He looked at her and smiled. "Thanks. That really helped. Have you eaten?"

She nodded. "Connie and I went out for dinner, but I ordered some penne to bring home for you. I can heat it up if you want."

"I want," he said, truly famished. He'd spent the day running between assorted constructions sites and the lawyers and hadn't had a chance to eat.

"Get yourself some wine while I heat it up," she said

and brushed a kiss across his cheek, the caress so easy and freely given that he hoped things were heading back to normal between them.

He did as she suggested and poured them both glasses of a nice cabernet franc Jonathan had recommended. The bottle was from a relatively unknown vineyard in Washington State, but a first sip confirmed that it had been a good choice. The taste was smooth with overtones of some kind of berry.

As Maggie set the breakfast bar for him, he handed her a glass over the counter. "Try this."

She took a taste and smiled. "Delicious."

"Jon recommended it. Yet another of his many talents," he said and was a little surprised by the nuanced jealousy in his voice.

Maggie immediately picked up on it. "You have your own talents. Very special ones, I might add," she said and, after a moment's hesitation, glanced at him with a gaze so heated, he had to take a sip of his wine to cool the ardor her look had ignited.

"Glad you like them," he teased back, relief settling into him that there seemed to be a change from the reticence that had hovered over them since the fight.

She left him only long enough to take a big bowl out of the microwave and place it before him. Then she scooted around the counter and sat on a stool beside him, watching as he ate the first few bites hurriedly. When the initial bite of hunger had subsided a little, he glanced over in her direction and said, "It looks like you had a good day."

"A good two months to be exact. It looks like some of the changes are working."

"That's good to hear, Maggie. I'm sure it's a big relief for you."

"But not for you. Your father won't be pleased with the turnaround."

No, he wouldn't, but Owen would deal with that in time. "I'm not sure there's much that would make that miserable old man happy."

He shoveled more food into his mouth, but the discussion made it difficult to enjoy what was otherwise a very tasty penne in vodka sauce.

Maggie smoothed a hand across his arm as it rested on the counter. "I didn't mean to upset you."

He shoved in one last forkful of pasta before swiveling around on the stool to face her. "You didn't. Upset is just a natural state of being when it comes to my dad. So what will you do next? After the holiday season?"

———————

Maggie had already made detailed plans for the spring season, but even if they managed to turn a decent enough profit for the winter season, continuing the progress would probably take the infusion of a good chunk of any profits they made. She hoped she'd have enough for that and for paying off the debt on her homes.

"I've talked to another designer for a special line just in time for Easter. We're also discussing having a huge flower show on the main floor to invite people to come in and chase away the winter blues. After that, another exclusive designer line for beachwear. Hopefully, we'll have the money for all that, and don't read this as my asking for another loan. You've already done more than I could have expected, and I fully intend to pay you back as we agreed."

He cupped her cheek and smiled. "I always thought you would do it, Maggie. I'm happy that I could help," he said, his voice filled with pride, helping to dissipate some of the concerns she'd had the past couple of weeks.

Since it was so easy to talk to him about business things and she'd come to rely on his sharp mind in the nearly two months they'd been married, she said, "I've been toying with a few possibilities. Like getting the shareholders on the board to allow us to issue some more shares to sell now that I can show investors we're not necessarily a losing proposition. I'm just worried they might want my dad and me to divest ourselves of some of our shares and lose our majority position as payback for allowing us to do that."

He made a face. "And give up more control of your baby to those board members?"

He'd hit her concern right on the head. Before, when it had been a possible way to save the company, she would have relinquished that control, but now she had a touch more leeway if the holiday season shaped up as well as the current numbers were predicting.

"What would you do?" she asked, wanting to show him that she was able to set aside her fears and trust him.

He searched her features as if to confirm that she was serious. When he saw that she was, he shrugged, took a sip of his wine, and a second later, whipped a pen out of his suit jacket pocket and began doodling on his napkin. She watched as he sketched something with swift strokes of his pen, and before her eyes, a building took shape on the paper.

He pushed the napkin in front of her. "You could redevelop the Main Line store. The area needs more hotel and residential choices. The lower level or two would be retail, maybe even another Savannah Courtyard. The demographics for that area would eat up a place like that."

She examined the design, picturing the location. There certainly was enough land and parking on that property for the kind of changes he had proposed. With multiple universities in the area, as well as nearby businesses, hotel rooms were always in high demand. Likewise reasonably priced residential units, like condos or apartments.

"This definitely looks like an interesting possibility. Even if we had to close the store while we did it, we could transfer the employees to our nearby locations. It might take them longer to get to work, but I wouldn't want to lose some of our better people."

"Is that a royal 'we' or did you really mean 'we' as in 'you and me'?" he asked, his gaze trained on her face, his eyes clouded with the doubt and fear that had crept into their relationship over the last few weeks.

She gestured between the two of them and said, "You and me. Together, right?"

Owen offered her a hesitant grin and nodded, liking the thought of the two of them working on that project and others. He ignored the little voice in his head that was shouting out a warning about his father and the lie and how it could all go to shit in no time flat.

"Together. I'll do some rough estimates on what something like this would cost. See how long it would take for the project and what kind of financing we'd need. It may have to wait until I get this issue with the Upper East Side project resolved."

"Is it causing that much of a problem for you?"

"Enough of one," he said, but held back, considering for the moment whether this would be the right time to tell her about the lie he'd told his father. But as he met her gaze, so filled with concern and love, he feared that it was too soon to tell her. Maybe a little later, once she had fewer doubts about his motives and understood that he'd done it for love. For her.

"It'll be fine. Lawsuits like this happen all the time. It's just that between the delay and the legal costs, it's becoming more expensive than I expected," he said.

"If there's anything I can do to help, you'd let me know, right?" she asked, her tone innocent and trusting. Which only made him feel like more of a shit for not confessing his lie and doubling down on it.

"I'd tell you. How about we take this upstairs? Maybe get a fire started?" he said.

Her blue eyes widened, and desire darkened them to the fathomless blue of the ocean at night. She licked her lips and said, "Did I ever tell you about my fantasy featuring you, me, and the fireplace?"

Pressure built in his gut as he imagined just what it was. "No, you didn't."

She grabbed hold of his hand and urged him from the stool. She shot him a siren's smile and said, "I guess it's time I show you."

Chapter 31

IT SEEMED LIKE WEEKS SINCE THEY'D MADE LOVE IN FRONT OF the fireplace, satisfying the erotic dream that had provided so many sleepless nights before marrying Owen. She hadn't slept much that night either, since they'd cuddled and talked late into the night before passion had risen again and needed satisfying.

They'd fallen asleep barely before dawn and been late to work, but it had been worth it. Their talk and that passionate night had restored the happiness that they'd shared in the first few months of their marriage.

In the week since that night, they'd barely seen each other. She'd had one emergency after another crop up at the stores, and Owen had been in the throes of settlement discussions regarding the lawsuit on the Upper East Side project. By the time both arrived home each night, they'd drop into bed exhausted.

Luckily, it looked like she'd be home tonight at a regular hour, and she was hoping Owen would be as well. Engaging the video app on her phone, she called him, and it took a few tries for him to answer. When he did, his exhaustion was evident in the dark circles beneath his eyes and drawn features.

"How's it going?" she asked, hoping that the settlement negotiations were going better than he looked.

"Some progress, but I'll be late again. We'll be done

here by five, but then I have to head back to my office to catch up on everything else I've neglected."

She wanted to remind him she'd been one of those things he'd neglected, but in all fairness, she'd been just as busy the last week.

"I understand. Take it easy. I'll be waiting for you at home."

He smiled, but it was halfhearted and didn't reach his eyes. "Later" was all he said and disconnected the call.

She'd be done by five as well, and if he couldn't make it home, she intended to bring a touch of home to his office to make life a little easier for him. Jumping on the internet, she tracked down a menu for one of their favorite spots near his building and picked out a few items that would work well as takeout. She called the restaurant and placed the order, asking for it to be ready by five thirty. It would only take her fifteen minutes or so to do the crosstown walk and head up to the low Fifties and Owen's office.

With that plan in place, she returned to her own pile of papers, eagerly anticipating the impromptu dinner with her newlywed husband.

―⁂―

For long moments after ending the call with Maggie, Owen stood outside the conference room, contemplating just how much he missed his wife after a week of barely seeing each other. He hadn't really given much thought to what a marriage between two workaholics might be like, but he was certain that this wasn't what he wanted for his relationship with Maggie. Marching back into the conference room, he faced his lawyer and the opposing counsel who were still quibbling over the consideration Owen was willing to pay to resolve the legal action. He slammed his hands on the table, drawing the attention of one and all.

"Let me make myself clear, in case I wasn't clear before. We both know the games that get played in our industry, but this is my final offer. If your client wants to dicker and continue to hold me up, that's fine. I have a building over on Eighty-Ninth, right next to the one your client just bought, and I understand you'll need some variances from your neighbors for what you have planned."

"Is that a threat?" his opponent's attorney asked, a stony look on his face.

"It's a fact. I'm going back to my office now, because I have a work to do," he said and didn't wait for either of the attorneys to reply before exiting the room.

He sat down at his desk and quickly scrolled through his emails, doing a triage of those that seemed to be the most urgent. Half a dozen or so emails later, it was half past five o'clock, and he couldn't imagine staying late again tonight. Especially since he knew Maggie might be home already.

Gathering up the papers on his desk, he was sorting them into piles based on importance when his father marched into his office. He stood there in his black suit, holding on to the chair before Owen's desk, looking like a crow sitting on a fence.

Owen hoped that whatever he wanted wouldn't take too long, because he was eager to get home and be with Maggie. He marshalled his control and, with a faked pleasant smile on his face, said, "Good evening, Father. What can I do for you today?"

"You can tell me you've settled this nonsense about the project, and if you haven't, you can tell me what you plan to do about the money we're losing every day that we're not working on that site."

His father's voice had risen with each word, and although there were valid concerns about cost overrun due to the delays in construction, it was clearly about more than that.

"We can weather this, and in any case, I'm sure this will be settled shortly," he replied in tones far calmer than he was feeling.

"Just like you thought this business with Maggie would be over quickly?" his father chastised. His voice grew louder as he jabbed a finger in Owen's direction and said, "Fuck her, marry her, and get her properties. That's what you said you'd do."

The loud crash of something hitting the wood floor and glass breaking outside his office drew both their attentions.

Maggie stood at the door, her face pale as a sheet. A clear shopping bag from a nearby restaurant lay on the floor next to a broken wine bottle in a pool of red, like blood spilled on the floor.

The look she shot Owen was one of agony and disbelief.

As she bolted away from the door, he hurtled from his chair to chase after her, pushing past his father. Ignoring the look on his face that actually had more traces of guilt than pleasure.

Chapter 32

MAGGIE'S BODY AND BRAIN HAD GONE NUMB, SHUTTING down from the pain that had torn through her as she'd heard Robert Pierce's hurtful words.

Fuck her. Marry her. Get her properties.

Owen grabbed her, only she didn't really feel his hand on her arm. Or the one he cupped to her cheek as he gently urged her to face him. She didn't see the fear and sorrow on his face as he said, "It's not what you think, Maggie."

"What I think? What am I supposed to think?" she said, her voice soft because it was difficult to speak past the lump in her throat. Because it was difficult to draw a breath due to the ache in her heart.

Owen glanced around, and she tracked his gaze. She realized that they'd drawn the attention of everyone in the office. Some turned away, guilty at having been caught watching, while other, less thoughtful ones remained with their heads above the edges of their cubicles like prairie dogs poking out of their warrens.

Embarrassment wove its threads through her pain, and when Owen grabbed hold of her other arm, she lashed out to pull free, hitting him across the face as she did so. Drawing blood.

"Don't touch me," she said, her voice choked with emotion.

"Maggie, please," he said.

But she didn't want to hear another of his lies. She wanted to run. Escape, because if there was only one thing left to her from this marriage, it was pride. Head held high, she blanked herself to the inquisitive glances as she sped away from him and through the office. She somehow made it to the elevator, thinking, *Just put one foot in front of the other. One little step at a time*, as she willed herself not to break down as she left him behind.

As she left her heart behind.

—✦—

The coppery taste of blood filled his mouth, but he deserved that and more.

He took a handkerchief from his pocket and dabbed at the blood. He ignored the mix of curious and pitiful glances from the office staff and glared at them to get back to work. Turning, he walked toward his office where his father stood at the door, an almost gleeful expression on his face. Pushing past him, he marched to his desk and dropped down heavily into his chair.

As his father returned to stand before him, Owen met his wily gaze and said, "Are you happy now, Father? Are you pleased with what you've accomplished?"

His father shook his head. "What *I've* accomplished? *I* wasn't the one who lied, Owen, both to me and to Maggie. I wonder why I didn't see the truth of it before."

No, his father hadn't been the liar. He had done that all on his own, not that it made his father's role in the whole situation any less repugnant.

"I lied to you. I won't deny that. But I never lied to

my wife about loving her. I do love her, and I'm not going to give her up. I refuse to let myself become a bitter, twisted, hateful old man like you."

His father's face paled before an angry red mottled his cheeks. "The Maxwells and Pierces were never meant to be together. Accept that and get on with your life."

"I will *never* give up on Maggie. And she's a Sinclair, in case you forgot."

His father muttered something unintelligible and surged to his feet. "Call the lawyers. Put this chapter of your life behind you and move on."

Owen was going to call a lawyer, but not for what his father thought.

He was not going to give up on Maggie without a fight.

Maggie kept it together during the short walk back across town and to her office, where she closed the door behind her as she started to shake and her stomach did a roll she barely managed to contain. Racing to her private bathroom, she dropped to her knees by the toilet and threw up what little was in her stomach from lunch. She sank back onto her haunches, still shaking, and finally released her fragile hold on her emotions.

Great sobs racked her body as grief overtook her until she was so spent, she could barely hold herself upright and curled into a limp fetal position.

Be strong, Maggie. Be strong, she told herself. She had a lot to do. People who depended on her. She couldn't allow herself to fall apart, even if her world had just shattered into pieces.

———

Owen tried calling Maggie for what seemed like the hundredth time, but as it had before, the phone rang and rang before going to voicemail. The same happened at the direct line at her office as he tried that number yet again.

Swallowing his pride, he reached out to the one person who might know just where Maggie would go and be able to make sure she was okay.

He dialed Connie.

She answered almost immediately, making him wonder if she already knew, and if she did, if he was in for a verbal beatdown, not that it mattered. The only thing that mattered was making sure Maggie was fine.

"Hey, Owen. What's up?" Connie asked with no apparent animosity.

He wasn't about to mince words. "I fucked up and I hurt her, Connie. I need your help to make sure she's okay."

Like bullets from a gun, her words were rapid-fire and heated. "What did you do, Owen? Why would Maggie be that upset?"

He closed his eyes and replayed the whole ugly incident in his head while telling Connie what had happened. Connie was silent for a moment, barely enough for him to take a breath, before she attacked.

"You're a fucking fraud, Owen. She trusted you. Loved you. How could you be such a shit?"

He got her anger. Understood it. Would accept it. But right now, his one and only concern was his wife.

"Just shut up, Connie. I called for your help. For

Maggie's sake. She's going to need a friend, and I need to know she's okay. Do you know where she might go?"

"Not home. Not until you get your ass out of there, which you better do ASAP, get it?"

"I get it," he said and rubbed his hand across his face, feeling so tired. So defeated.

"I know where she might be. I'll find her and take care of her," she said. There was a longer pause after her words this time, making him wonder if Connie had finally heard what was really in his heart. "Are you okay, Owen?"

He didn't think he'd ever be okay again if Maggie couldn't forgive him. And while he wanted to wallow in his self-inflicted pain, he wouldn't for long. He wanted Maggie. He'd give her the space she needed to think about what had happened. But he intended to do whatever he needed to prove to her that he loved her. That he could be trusted.

"I love her, Connie. Nothing is ever going to change that."

To his surprise, her friend said, "I know, Owen. Just give her time to heal, and don't give up. That's all I ask."

"I won't," he said and hung up the phone.

―――⁓―――

Scrubbing away the tears, Maggie rose slowly, gingerly, feeling like she was ninety. At her sink, she ran the cold water and rinsed out her mouth, but the bitter taste of disillusionment clung powerfully. She splashed her face repeatedly until the chill water brought artificial color to drive away her pallor and washed off the evidence of her tears. The woman who stared back at her from the mirror looked older. Almost as haggard and lifeless as Owen had earlier.

Owen, she thought and tamped down the pang of need and worry that erupted at the recollection of his handsome face, ravaged by guilt and sorrow. While he said he loved her, she couldn't quite imagine how he could if he could hurt her like he had. Or maybe hurt was only possible if you did love. Maybe like yin and yang, one couldn't exist without the other.

Maybe Emma was right about love and marriage and the whole happily ever after being a happily never after. That thought caused even more tears to stream down her cheeks. She dashed them away with her hands, bent, and washed her face again.

A hesitant knock came at her door.

"Are you okay?" Connie said from behind the thick wood.

As she stared into the mirror and lifeless, faded-blue eyes stared back, it occurred to her that she might never be okay again. But then she reminded herself that she had to be okay, if not for herself for all the others who depended on her.

She walked to the door and opened it, trying to keep her actions deliberate. Controlled. She needed control now more than ever.

Connie winced as her gaze traveled over Maggie's features, and before her friend could say anything, she said, "I'm fine."

"You don't look fine."

While she appreciated her friend's concern, she wondered at her unexpected visit. "Why are you here?"

Another wince and a trace of guilt crept onto Connie's face. "Owen called me. He was worried about you."

Maggie bit her bottom lip so hard, she worried she'd draw blood, but it wasn't enough to contain her anger.

"Worried? About me? That's rich. Did he tell you what happened?"

Connie nodded. "He told me, and I have to say—"

"Don't," she urged with a sharp slash of her hand. "Don't say that he's sorry. That he didn't mean it. That…" She sucked in a deep breath and held it, using it to dam up the flood of emotions threatening to break through.

"Maggie," Connie said and reached for her, but Maggie stepped away, feeling so fragile that she feared she would break with even the slightest touch.

"Please, let's not talk about this. You're my lawyer. You'll know what to do."

Connie's head whipped back with surprise. "You want lawyer me to do what?"

"Lawyer you. Figure out what to do about the prenup. The marriage."

Her friend clearly recognized that at that moment, any additional discussion was futile. "Okay. Whatever client Maggie wants. Now I want to find out what friend Maggie needs."

From a well deep behind the dam she had erected, gratefulness spilled over her. Fighting back tears yet again, she embraced her friend tightly, holding on to her like a drowning man would a life preserver.

"It'll be okay, Mags. Trust me. It'll be okay," Connie crooned and stroked her back.

"I know," she said shakily, hoping her friend was right. Hoping that the pieces of her heart could somehow knit back together. Hoping, as she had for her friend Tracy, that none of the pieces would be lost along the way, leaving her less than whole.

Chapter 33

AFTER CONNIE HAD CALLED HIM TO SAY SHE'D FOUND Maggie and would take care of her, Owen had given Maggie a day to let her anger simmer down before reaching out to her again.

She'd refused to speak with him.

He'd tried every day since then to contact her, but she hit Reject on her cell phone, and her assistant refused to put through any of his calls. He had been hoping to see her at the gym and approach her, but she hadn't shown up.

He kept on trying, leaving her voicemails to explain. Letting her know that he still loved her and was sorry for the hurt he'd caused.

On Friday morning, he was about to badge through the security area in his building lobby when a man blocked his way.

"Owen Pierce?" the man asked.

Owen nodded, and the man slapped an envelope against his chest. "You've been served."

Owen grabbed hold of the envelope as the man hurried away. He cleared himself through the turnstile and walked to the elevator, opening the envelope as he did so. As he realized what was contained in the envelope, he staggered onto the elevator and grabbed on to the handrail to keep steady.

Divorce papers.

The ding signaling he'd reached his floor barely registered. He stumbled off. Somehow, he mustered his strength to walk to his office, where he closed his door, sat, and picked up his phone. He called Maggie again. As it had before, it went to voicemail. As he had before, he tried to explain.

"I never meant to hurt you, Maggie. It was the only way I could think of to keep my father out of our relationship, and I know now it was a stupid way to do it. Thoughtless, but please believe me when I say that I love you and want to be with you. I won't sign these divorce papers. I won't give up on us."

He ended the message and tossed the envelope on his desk. He'd arrange with his lawyers later to deal with the divorce papers. Right now, he intended to find a way to confront Maggie face-to-face and not in front of a crowd of lawyers.

Maggie glanced at her cell phone as it rang.

Owen. Again.

She'd lost track of how many times he'd called. Of how many messages he'd left, pleading with her to understand. Trying to apologize for his actions when there was no way any apology could ever be enough to assuage the pain of his betrayal. To make her feel alive again.

When her mother had died, her father had buried himself in his work because, in a way, a part of him had died that day as well. At only eight years old, she hadn't understood it. Hadn't understood the real meaning of "burying yourself" in anything. She understood it now.

For the last week, since the breakup with Owen, she had immersed herself in every aspect of what was happening at the stores, especially the goings-on in the Savannah Courtyard and the Winter Wonderland. Even though Christmas was still nearly two months away, the floor was filled with families coming by to check out the restaurant and the various activities they offered daily until Santa's arrival in less than a week. He would arrive earlier than was usual, beating out the Thanksgiving Day arrival of the Macy's Santa, but they needed whatever edge they could get, especially since she refused to open on Thanksgiving Day, like so many retailers did. She truly believed that families deserved to be with each other on that holiday, and they were making it a point in various ads and offering other coupons and special events both before and after in keeping with their theme of families being together and building memories.

She smiled with satisfaction, since it seemed to be working, judging from the many shoppers on the floor. As she rode the escalator down the six stories, she took note of the shoppers in the other departments. When she reached the main floor, the babel of New York City filled her ears with the different languages of the tourists as well as New Yorkers strolling through the gaily decorated aisles. All seemed to be better with Maxwell's, a far cry from the state of her personal life.

She exited the store onto Fifth Avenue, and a brisk wind swept up from downtown, chilling her with a bite that warned winter would soon be on the way. Tucking her lightweight fall jacket around herself, she skipped the cab ride and decided to walk back to the Chrysler Center and her meeting with Connie.

Lawyer Connie, who would hopefully have some answers for her on what to do about the prenup and Owen.

Owen.

She told herself that his constant phone calls were the reason he hadn't left her thoughts over the entire week, as much as she had tried to drive him out the way an exorcist would a demon. The truth was that he had sunk his claws deep into her heart, and she couldn't shake him loose, maybe because a part of her didn't want to. A part of her wanted to believe what he'd said in his voicemails.

Lord, how she wanted to believe, but the forgiveness thing was a lot harder to do than she had expected.

Pressing on as the wind pushed her along, she hurried down Fifth until the big public library with its famous lions was across the street. *Patience and Fortitude*, she thought, recalling how her mother had told her the names of the lions on a long-ago visit. Both virtues she needed to deal with the current state of her life.

The wind died down on Forty-Second Street, unlike during the winter months, when it sometimes blasted down the wide thoroughfare, piercing through clothes and deep into your bones. Within a few minutes, she was strolling past Grand Central Terminal and crossed Lexington Avenue over to the Chrysler Building.

In the lobby, she took a moment to chat with the security guard, asking him about his newborn baby, trying to make believe that life was back to normal. After, she whipped out her building ID and swiped herself through the turnstile to walk through the building and over to the annex, where her friend's law firm was located. She headed up in the elevator and to the law office, where the receptionist quickly ushered her into a large conference room.

A conference room that was surprisingly empty.

She had just shucked her jacket and taken a seat when Connie entered, looking both flustered and pale.

"Are you okay? You don't look well," Maggie said, concern for her friend replacing her own worries as she rose and hugged her.

"Not feeling quite right. I think I caught something," she said, splaying a hand over her stomach.

"I'm sorry you're not feeling well. Are you up to the meeting today?"

Connie's expression soured more intensely. "I was, but I just got a call from Owen's attorney. He wants to reschedule. Says something urgent came up at the last minute."

Anger flared to life, and she dragged her fingers through her hair. "Sounds like bullshit to me."

"Possibly, or maybe he's trying to convince Owen not to fight us," Connie offered.

"Fight us? Does Owen really think that's possible?" she asked, incredulous at her husband's—soon to be ex-husband's—brass.

Connie shrugged and motioned for her to take a seat even though irritated energy had her wanting to pace. She plopped down onto the thick cushion of the leather chair and shook her head. "I don't get it. What could he possibly want? There's no way he can get the properties unless I default on repayment, and I sure don't plan on doing that."

"I'm not sure the properties are what he wants," her friend said. Then she immediately tacked on, "He wants you. He wants a reconciliation."

With a more vehement shake of her head, Maggie said, "Not going to happen." But inside, the little voice that kept on recalling Owen's anguished face started shouting again for her to forgive. To not let anger make her lose the love of her life. It was that voice that made her say, "Do you think that's what I should do?"

Even though Connie's face had paled to a sickly green, her friend still managed to get out a heartfelt, "I think you need time to think about what you want. To think about what's in your heart."

She trusted Connie's advice both legally and personally, as difficult as it was to know what was really in her heart. There was still too much pain and anger there, but she nodded and said, "I'll try, Connie. Why don't you go home and get some rest?"

"I think I may do just that," her friend said and bolted from the room like a student excused for summer break.

———

"I don't think they'll be patient for much longer," his lawyer said.

Owen sighed and replied, "I understand. I just need a little more time."

"Little being the operative word, Owen. They're going to push back sooner rather than later."

"Got it, Mel. I'll be back to you shortly," he said and ended the call. Despite his promise to the attorney, he had no idea on how he would accomplish the "sooner," even though he'd been trying for the last two days to see her face-to-face since his phone calls were being ignored.

"Daydreaming again?" his father asked as he strolled in, smiling.

He'd been smiling a lot lately, making Owen wonder how it was that his misery could make his father so happy. Something snapped loose inside of him with that.

"How can you be so cavalier? How can you enjoy seeing my pain?"

In the blink of an eye, his father's entire demeanor changed. Hands clenched, he charged Owen's desk, surprisingly swift and seemingly stronger.

"Pain!" he yelled and pounded his own chest with his fist. "You don't know the first thing about pain or loss. You don't know what it is to lose the love of your life. Not once, but twice." He emphasized it by putting up two spindly fingers that he almost shoved in Owen's face.

The shock that filled Owen was quickly followed by an epiphany. He now understood why his father had said that Maxwells and Pierces didn't belong together.

Images raced through his brain of his father smiling at Maggie's mother as they'd run into each other on the beach. Of his father giving excuse after excuse for not going to the Sea Kiss house after Maggie's mother had died.

His father had loved Elizabeth Maxwell, Maggie's mother.

"The feud? Losing Maggie's mom was what it's really been about all this time, isn't it? Not the properties. Not the betrayal."

Like a balloon with a pinhole, his father deflated before his eyes and dropped into the chair wearily, hands hanging loosely at his sides. With a feeble bob of his head and a voice made rough by his agony, his father said, "Bryce Sinclair and I had been friends since childhood. It was only natural we go into business together, and as we grew more and more successful, we began to move in higher social circles. That's where we met Elizabeth Maxwell."

His father paused and sucked in a rough, almost violent breath before pushing on with his story. "I fell in love with her the moment I met her, but I knew I had to be richer, more successful, for someone like her to consider someone like me."

Owen wanted to say that life was about more than riches and success but knew it would only add salt to a wound that hadn't healed in nearly forty years. Instead, he came around his desk and sat on its edge. He laid a hand on his father's knee and offered a supportive squeeze.

"What happened?" he asked, although he could guess. While his father was busy working and making money, Bryce Sinclair had been wooing Elizabeth.

His father gazed up at him, his gaze shimmering with pain. "Sinclair beat me to her, and after, he gifted her some properties we had been working to acquire for our business."

"So you broke off your partnership with Sinclair and married my mother," Owen supplied, needing to hear the entire story.

"I couldn't continue to work with a man I couldn't trust. As for your mother..." His father looked away and shook his head. "I was wrong to marry her on the rebound. I didn't love her the way she deserved."

Again, it was all Owen could do to hold back from saying that they'd deserved better from him. That they'd deserved more love and less bitterness. Less judgment.

"You said you lost love twice," he said.

A halfhearted shrug met his statement. "I never

stopped hoping Elizabeth would be mine, even after Maggie was born. But it didn't happen, and I contented myself with just knowing she was there, right next door. Right across those hedges I put up to try to keep their happiness out of sight."

But Elizabeth Maxwell Sinclair had died in child-birth nearly eight years after Maggie's birth, and the more Owen thought about it, that was when his father's acrimony had really taken a turn for the worse. Without his saying a word, his father must have realized Owen needed to know more.

"Elizabeth had a difficult pregnancy with Maggie. She was told not to try having another child. The doctors warned her she'd risk her life if she did, but Bryce let her do it anyway," his father said in softer tones. But a second later, he pounded his thigh with his fist and grew agitated again. "Bryce should have protected her. Kept her safe. Instead, he let her get pregnant, and he let her die."

Since Owen assumed Maggie was a great deal like her mother, he knew that if Elizabeth had wanted to do something, very little would keep her from accomplishing her goal. Which only disheartened him, because it seemed like Maggie was dead-set on ending their marriage. But for now, he needed his father to understand what he wanted more than anything.

"I love Maggie. She is the love of my life, and I don't want to lose her. Can you understand that?"

His father raised eyes shimmering with tears. "Forget about her, Owen. Get on with your life. Don't be like me."

He had never wanted to be like his father, unhappy and unpleasant. Seemingly angry at the world for the state of his life. Longing for the impossible, he now knew. Only getting Maggie back wasn't impossible. Difficult, but not impossible.

"I won't give up, Father. I want her to be my wife. I want to have a family with her. I want to grow old with her."

His father shook his head. "You're more like me than I thought, I guess, and I pity you for that."

Owen didn't know how to reply to that or to his father's pain, but he knew it was time for the feud to end.

"It's not too late to change, Dad. It's not too late for the two families to have a future together. A happy future, and I'm going to try to make it right with Maggie. Maybe you should think about making it right with Bryce Sinclair."

He'd expected the anger he'd gotten in the past, but this time, he only got a tired "I'm not sure that's possible any longer."

"Try, Dad" was all he said.

With a slight incline of his head to give his assent, his father rose woodenly from the chair and walked out.

Owen wasn't sure what his father would do, but he had to follow that same advice and try as well.

He loved Maggie too much not to give it his best shot.

Chapter 34

AFTER MAKING SURE CONNIE WAS IN A CAB AND ON HER WAY home, Maggie headed home herself, but all the while, she kept asking herself why Owen was trying to delay the inevitable. She couldn't stay with a man she couldn't trust, and she could no longer trust Owen, even if deep inside, she still had feelings for him. The fact that he still roused her emotions warned that she wasn't over him, but how could she be? It was barely over a week since she'd overheard his conversation with his father. Less than that since Connie had reluctantly had him served with the divorce papers.

Her friend's reticence had surprised her, as had Connie's belief that maybe Maggie was being too hard on him. That maybe she should really give him a chance to explain what had happened. She even suspected that, given the chance, Connie might have orchestrated a way for the two of them to talk at today's meeting, but of course, Owen hadn't bothered to show up.

She was so lost in her thoughts as she approached her brownstone that she didn't notice the figure sitting on her front stoop. She stepped back, worried that she was about to become another crime statistic, but as the person rose from the shadows, her front porch light illuminated his features.

"Owen," she said aloud as relief of one kind filled her, only to be replaced by another emotion. "What are you doing here?" she said, her tone curt and no-nonsense.

"I came to talk," he said and shifted to allow her to reach her door.

She opened it and stepped inside but barred his entry. As she did so, the brighter light from inside bathed his features, letting her see the misery on his face. The dark circles under his eyes and sharp lines around his mouth and eyes seemed to have been etched there overnight. His pain moved her, but letting him inside was too risky for her heart.

"We have nothing else to say to each other, Owen."

"Please listen to me, Mags," he pleaded, hands outstretched before him.

"Only my friends call me Mags, and right now, you're not a friend. To tell the truth, I'm not really sure what you are other than a liar," she said a little more forcefully as anger awakened within her.

Seeming resigned to accept that name, Owen nodded and said, "I did lie. To my father. It was the only way I could think of to keep him off my back so that we could explore what was happening between us."

"You lied to *me* every day we were together, Owen," she said and tapped her chest for emphasis. "Every day that you let that lie continue…" She paused to take a breath and fight back the tears welling up in her eyes. She would not cry in front of him. She would not let him know just how much he'd hurt her.

"I never wanted to lie to you, Maggie. I love you. I want to be your husband. It's why I did what I did," he said, his entire body drooping. His features looked worn-out and defeated.

In some part of her, sympathy rose up, but it wasn't strong enough to overcome all the hurt and anger and disappointment roiling in her heart. "I'm not sure I can believe you anymore, Owen. I'm not sure I can stay in a marriage based on a lie."

Owen looked away, and his full lips thinned into a sharp line. He ran a hand through the tousled waves of his dark hair and, with a shake of his head, faced her again, determination alive on his face.

"It's not a lie. I married you because I love you. I never lied about that. Maybe we should have talked more about the feud before the marriage. Talked about why our fathers were fighting."

"We don't know why," she reminded him.

Owen nodded and said, "Earlier today, my father told me the real reason for the feud, and it wasn't the properties that caused the fight. He was in love with your mother and wanted to marry her, but she was in love with his best friend and partner. When she died, he lost her again and blamed your father, because he knew that her having another child was very risky."

He paused for a moment to let it sink in.

The revelation surprised her, although it explained the intense rancor that his father had for the Sinclairs while her own father's anger had been more easily resolved. But that didn't explain one thing.

"Why are you telling me this now, Owen? What does this have to do with us?"

"It has everything to do with us, Maggie. If it hadn't been for that feud, you and I...we would have happened long before now. Without lies. But more importantly, I won't be like my father, old and bitter and pining for the love of my life because I let her get away. I won't let you go, Maggie. I love you, and I'm going to fight for you."

Before she could react, he kissed her, hard. Demanding. Letting her know just how badly he wanted her. For a moment, one crazy, illogical moment, she responded to his entreaty before pushing him away.

"I have one more thing to say to you, Maggie. I love you, and I always will."

With that, he turned and walked away, leaving her standing at her door, watching him disappear into the dark autumn night.

She closed the door and leaned back against it. Laid her fingers on lips that felt almost bruised from the force of his last kiss. *His last kiss*, she thought, and the ache in her heart came again, making her wonder how she could live without him. Without the passion they shared. And the humor. And having him as a sounding board, because he just seemed to get her in ways no one else ever had.

Only she had been utterly truthful when she told him she couldn't believe him and that she couldn't stay in a marriage based on a lie, even if it had been a lie told so they could be together. A lie told to satisfy an unreasonable father.

From what little she knew of Robert Pierce, life with him hadn't been pleasant for the boys. She suspected that every day for Owen had been a difficult one because of their relationship and his father's expectations. A part of her felt for Owen and could even maybe understand the reason for the subterfuge. He had stood to lose all that he'd known in his life. His father. The business and everything that went with it.

But did that justify lying to her?

That she was as confused as she was maybe confirmed

Connie's opinion that she needed more time to think about everything. To get over the hurt and anger, to be able to deliberate more rationally. To not let hurt and anger overwhelm her the way it had overtaken Owen's father.

Moving away from the door, she dropped her keys into the dish on the foyer table, and the bowl of seashells on the table beside the couch caught her eye. It reminded her of that first night here with Owen and the cracked shells and broken glass strewn across the floor. She had worried that night about how her life could shatter into pieces if she became involved with Owen and it went wrong. Sadly, her worries had come to fruition, she thought and sank into the cushions of the couch. She laid her head back and thought about all that Owen had just said. About his not giving up on her.

Could I ever forgive him? she wondered, and the little voice in her head urged her to forgive and forget. To listen to his pleas and apology and move on with their relationship. But she was still hurting too much to consider it at that moment. The problem was, she wasn't sure if that hurt would ever go away.

Worse, she didn't know what to do if it didn't.

———

Owen had offered her his apology and promised to fight for her, but he also understood that she needed time away from his constant presence to think about all he'd said.

By the time Wednesday rolled around, Connie was still pressing his attorney to set up a meeting, and Owen was beginning to lose hope. If there was one ray of light in his life, it was that they'd settled the lawsuit with the other Realtor, and the Upper East Side project was back in operation. With that resolved, he decided to take a break from Manhattan and go lick his wounds in the peace of their Sea Kiss home.

Jonathan had been in Sea Kiss for weeks thanks to his staycation and plans to develop a facility in that area. Owen worried about intruding if Jonathan had someone female there with him, but he took a chance. He needed to get away, and he could count on Jonathan to be supportive and offer him advice on what to do about Maggie.

Speed-dialing him, Jonathan answered on the very first ring.

"How's my favorite brother doing?" Jonathan said lightheartedly.

"I'm your only brother," Owen reminded him, deadpan. "If you're done sharing the house with your harem, I was hoping to come down later."

"Dudley's a boy, so I'm not sure he counts as a harem. Besides, I've been staying at a local inn to avoid any issues with our father. How is it going with Maggie? Any developments?"

Owen had talked to his brother right after the blowup, but other than a couple of texts, he hadn't said much more on the subject. "Nothing, Li'l Bro. It's why I want to get away. I need to think about what to do. How to handle the possibility she's really serious about going ahead with this divorce," he confessed.

"Is Connie still pushing your attorney?" Jonathan asked, and the chill in his voice at the mention of Maggie's friend couldn't be missed.

"I thought you and Connie had patched things up? You sure looked friendly enough the night of the wedding."

A strangled cough greeted his statement before Jonathan clumsily changed the subject. "What time should I expect you?"

"I'm assuming you're still busy being domestic, so I hope a nice dinner will be ready when I get there. Probably around seven. I'm not expecting much traffic."

"I'll risk father's wrath to have dinner ready for you at the house. See you later, Big Bro."

"See you later," he repeated and packed up his briefcase with the few papers he might or might not get to while he was in Sea Kiss. But as he gathered the materials, the envelope with the divorce papers and his lawyer's memo with the copy of the prenup caught his eye.

Cautiously, like a snake charmer taming a cobra, he reached for the documents. He picked them up and juggled them, pondering whether to bring them. If Maggie didn't answer his next entreaty or return one of his many calls, it was time to consider setting her free. Not that he'd be free of what he felt for her, but maybe, just maybe, with enough distance and time, she'd change her mind and come back to him.

He tucked the papers into his briefcase and grabbed it. He turned on the out-of-office message on his email program and advised his secretary that he'd be gone for a few days and didn't want to be disturbed.

In half an hour, he was home and tossing clothes into a small duffel. He locked up and headed to the garage to get his car. When the attendant wheeled it around, grinning at being able to drive the unique prototype, Owen forced a smile at the young man, not wanting to spread misery the way his father did. He tipped the attendant, slipped into the driver's seat, and dropped his briefcase and suitcase onto the floor of the passenger area.

Eagerly, he pulled out of the lot and headed toward the tunnel, praying that it would be a speedy trip, because he needed to get to a place where he could reflect and maybe even heal a little. His refuge during both difficult and good times had always been the house in Sea Kiss.

His happiest memories were tied to that place.

Building sand castles with Maggie.

Summer days spent surfing with Jonathan.

Memorial Day parades and fireworks on the Fourth of July.

His first kiss with Maggie.

Marrying Maggie.

Would it still be a refuge with so many memories of what he'd lost through his stupidity? he wondered.

Hands clenched on the wheel, he fought back against that negativity and drove, eager to get to the one place, other than with Maggie, that had always felt like home.

~~~

Maggie fell into bed exhausted. The sleepless nights and days filled with obligations were taking their toll. Luckily, with the arrival of Santa in their Winter Wonderland on Fifth Avenue and all the suburban locations, her last major appearance for Maxwell's was done. Now, it was just a matter of waiting to see how November went before their huge Black Friday events. Hopefully, it would all be enough, because if it wasn't, she didn't know how she would fulfill the terms of the prenup in order not to lose any of the suburban locations to Owen and, after, the shore home and town house.

Although Connie had done a wonderful job of making sure the terms would be fair even if the marriage failed, something that none of them had envisioned, a deal was a deal.

A deal based on fraud, one little voice in her head chided while another recognized that the terms had been more than equitable. No one else would have given her the kind of loan that Owen had provided. He'd been her white knight all along, but she had never imagined that she'd have to sacrifice something way more precious than the properties or the family homes she was bound to lose if things didn't work out.

She'd given him her heart, and she wasn't quite sure how she'd ever get it back. Or even if she wanted it back, she finally acknowledged. The last two weeks without him had been nearly unbearable. She missed his subtle humor and the way she could talk to him about virtually anything. She missed sleeping beside him and waking up to his dimpled grin in the morning, and she'd be a total liar if she said she didn't miss making love with him.

She did. A lot.

He touched her as no one else ever had and maybe ever could.

His last call to her had been so different from his earlier ones pleading for forgiveness. Asking her to reconsider. Unlike his earlier voicemail messages, she'd kept this one and had listened to it more than once in the last couple of days. Almost absentmindedly, she reached for her phone and, with a few swipes, replayed Owen's message.

"Good morning, Maggie. I miss waking up and

saying that to you. Opening my eyes to see you beside me was always one of the best parts of the day for me."

He'd paused then, and she understood. What followed his morning greeting had always been way too amazing for words.

"Work was tough yesterday. I had all kinds of craziness going on, and I couldn't wait to get home, only my place doesn't feel like home. It never did. Nothing without you could ever really feel like home."

Damn it, she thought as tears welled up in her eyes, and she let them spill down the sides of her face.

"I know you're still angry, and I get it. I deserve that anger and more. What I did was unforgiveable, and yet, I hope you can find it in your heart to forgive me. Have a good night, Maggie. I know my night will be filled with dreams of you."

Just like her nights had been filled with dreams of him, but despite that, she wasn't sure that forgiving him was the right thing to do. But forgetting him was impossible. It was like he'd woven himself into her DNA and being without him made her feel incomplete. If that's what love did to you, maybe Emma was right not to believe in falling in love. Who would willingly make themselves so vulnerable? So needy?

But as she placed the phone back on her nightstand, she hesitated and replayed the voicemail message again. She told herself that if she listened to it enough, she could drive him from her thoughts and her heart.

As sleep claimed her, she heard, "Have a good night, Maggie."

And in her dreams, she did.

Chapter 35

JONATHAN HADN'T PUSHED HIM TO DISCUSS MAGGIE WHEN he'd arrived on Thursday night.

His brother had another fabulous steak dinner ready, and the two of them had eaten and then gone out to the lawn to share more than a few beers, a stiff shot of bourbon, and a cigar in companionable silence around the fire pit.

Jonathan had woken him early the next day, since the waves were picking up thanks to a tropical depression near Florida and it promised to be a good surfing day. They'd hit the surf for most of the morning, riding in set after set of four- to five-foot waves. Afterward, they'd showered, dressed, and headed out for a quick lunch.

The pub on the farthest edge of Sea Kiss was a place known more as a weekend watering hole for tourists and locals alike. During daylight hours, it provided oversize sandwiches better suited to hungry laborers. The pub also offered a nice assortment of draft and bottled beers. No matter the time or day, summer season or not, the place always had the faint aroma of spilled beer and the kind of mustiness that came from being in a building that was close to the water and at least a century old.

His father would never deign to eat in a place like this, but Jonathan and Owen had started coming in with some of the local surfers as teens. At first, they'd been the rich out-of-town Bennys to the "clam diggers" who'd been born and bred on the Shore, but little by little, they'd become accepted as locals.

Over steaming-hot Reubens and a cold pint of an amber ale from a local microbrewery, Jonathan broached the subject of Maggie.

"Have you thought about what you'll do if she doesn't forgive you?" he asked.

Because he didn't have an answer, Owen shrugged, picked up his sandwich, and took a big bite. The rich flavors of the corned beef, Swiss cheese, sauerkraut, and Russian dressing teased his taste buds. He followed it up with a long swig of the hoppy ale.

At his delay in answering, Jonathan ate some of his sandwich, chewing on it thoughtfully before he said, "I know you've tried to explain to her, but I think words aren't enough."

Owen took another sip of his beer and eyed his brother over the rim of his glass. "You mean like flowers or something?"

His brother rolled his eyes and shook his head. "Flowers are for forgetting a date or a minor disagreement."

"Jewelry?" he said, not that Maggie was into gold and diamonds. Except for her grandmother's ring and the wedding band he'd gotten her, she favored simpler, less ornate pieces and rarely wore more than one at a time.

A bigger eye roll greeted his question. "I didn't think you were this dense, Owen," Jonathan said and drank a good portion of his own beer.

The comment stung a little, especially coming from his brother. "Says the man who hasn't had a relationship that's lasted more than a month unless you count your state of war with Connie as a relationship."

A serious expression crossed Jonathan's face, and he muttered, "Connie and me... It's way complicated."

Owen laughed. "Seriously, Bro? More complicated than what's happening with me and Maggie?"

"Seriously," Jonathan replied and motioned with his glass in Owen's direction. "A long time ago, someone told me that the smallest of acts was better than the biggest of intentions."

"A good sentiment, but what's that got to do with the current situation?" he asked, leaning back in the booth and pushing away the plate with his half-eaten sandwich, since the conversation had killed his appetite.

"You want to make things right by her, but how will you make it right? What could you possibly do that would say to her that you really love her? That you never intended the marriage to be about the business deal you guys made. That you wanted it to be about the two of you."

He shook his head and sipped his beer, pondering what his brother had said. Thinking about what he could do, although he'd already been prepared to do the one thing she said she wanted, namely, setting her free.

Jonathan leaned closer and peered at him intently. "You okay, Bro? You're looking a little pale."

Maybe because he couldn't imagine giving her up, even though a part of him knew that might be what he needed to do. No small act at all but possibly the only right one. He jerked his head in the direction of the pub's entrance. "Do you think we could go? I really need some time alone to think."

"Sure, Bro," Jonathan said and signaled the waiter for the check.

Connie had insisted that a few days in Sea Kiss with her, Tracy, and Emma was just what Maggie needed to relax a little and prepare herself for the meeting with Owen and his lawyer on Monday. But as they turned down the street for her Shore home, memories assailed her. There had been so much joy connected with the house, but now there was also the memory of her marriage, which brought nothing but sorrow, as did the thought of possibly losing the property.

"It'll be all right," Connie said and squeezed her hand gently, but as they slowly rolled past the Pierce home, Owen's Lightning sitting in the drive warned that getting away from those memories would be harder thanks to his presence just yards away. As Jonathan's Jeep pulled into the drive, Connie's sharp curse confirmed her weekend might not be so easy either.

"Maybe we should go back to the city," Maggie said.

Connie shook her head vehemently, sending the short caramel strands of her hair flying about. "No way. We cannot let them drive us away from something we both love. We'll just have to ignore them."

Which they tried to do as they exited their car at the same time as the two men hopped out of the Jeep. No greetings were exchanged. Only the slightest shift of Maggie's glance in that direction confirmed their presence as they hurried inside.

Mrs. Patrick was immediately at the door, arms open to hug them both and offer her sympathies. "Now, now, my girls. Things will work out."

Maggie buried her head against the old woman's

shoulder and barely contained her tears. She had already cried enough.

"I've made you a nice lunch. We can all sit and eat," Mrs. Patrick said.

They dropped their overnight bags by the staircase and dutifully followed the housekeeper to the kitchen.

The table had been set for five, although they weren't expecting Emma or Tracy until later. At her questioning glance, Mrs. Patrick said, "Emma rescheduled her afternoon appointment. She'll be here in a few minutes, so we can all have lunch together. Tracy is driving in from Princeton. She should be here shortly as well. Won't that be nice?"

It would, and Maggie was very grateful, since it wasn't like Emma to upset a customer by canceling. As for Tracy, she had not only been busy with counseling and trying to rebuild her marriage, but also had decided to put her college degree to work at a nonprofit foundation that worked to improve schools in impoverished areas.

"It will be very nice," she said and entered the kitchen. Because busy hands kept her brain from thinking too much about her current situation, she immediately went to work helping Mrs. Patrick plate the dainty finger sandwiches they'd be having.

Connie joined in as well, but as Maggie pulled some pickles from the jar, her friend's face once again turned an off-colored green, and she excused herself.

"She's feeling a little under the weather, is she?" Mrs. Patrick asked, her keen-eyed gaze on Connie's back as she raced toward the bathroom.

"She's been sick since Wednesday. Thinks maybe it's something she ate."

A disbelieving cough from the older woman had Maggie staring at her and then back toward where Connie had gone.

"You think it's more?" she asked.

"I think you girls have been through a lot lately. I'm sure she'll be feeling better in no time," Mrs. Patrick said.

But Maggie was certain that the old woman was keeping something to herself. She focused on placing the sandwiches on the decorative tray, and when Connie returned a few minutes later, healthy color pinked her cheeks again, relieving Maggie of worry about her friend. By the time they finished prepping lunch half an hour later, the doorbell was ringing and both Emma and Tracy strolled in. Emma looked a little frazzled, while Tracy had a new air of confidence and calm about her.

They all hugged, and as they sat down at the table, relief washed over Maggie as her gaze skipped across the faces of the women seated around her. No matter what happened with Owen, she knew she would never be alone with friends like this at her side.

———

Since the night of that first kiss when they were eighteen, it had been torture for Owen to know that the object of his desire was just yards away. Back then, in his naïveté, he'd thought that all it would take for him to reach her was to find the break in the privet hedges and walk over.

He hadn't put much stock in the family feud back then. To an eighteen-year-old, it seemed implausible that two old men could hold a grudge for so long. But they had, and what had seemed so simple at the time had turned out to be way more complicated over the years. Especially now, Owen thought as he stood at his bedroom window and stared across to the great lawn behind Maggie's house.

With the autumn weather being unseasonably warm, Maggie and her gaggle of friends had been out on the lawn during the afternoon as well as down by the beach. Because of that, Jonathan and he had stayed far away, both of them wanting to steer clear of any interaction with the women.

Dusk cast shadows as the sun set to the west of the houses, and light from the french doors leading into the Sinclair home spilled onto the patio and lawn, broadcasting the silhouettes of the women inside. As he watched, a lone figure stepped out and slowly ambled across the patio and down to the lawn.

Maggie.

Her arms were wrapped around herself as if to ward off a chill, but with the weather being so balmy, he got the sense it was more to hold herself together. He understood, since he'd felt as if his life had been coming apart in little pieces in the two weeks since their breakup.

He hated that he'd made her feel like that. Hated that he couldn't find a way to make things better, until his brother's words rattled around in his head.

The smallest of acts is better than the biggest of intentions.

He'd been racking his brains since lunch, contemplating just what he could do, but only one thing came to mind. It wasn't a small act at all, but it was the right one, his heart and brain told him.

Shuffling over to his briefcase, feeling the weight of his decision like an anchor around his neck, he opened it and withdrew the divorce papers. He grabbed a pen before he could hesitate and signed them so his attorneys could take the final steps to dissolve the marriage. He was about to stuff the divorce papers back into his briefcase when his copy of the prenup caught his eye. Like the flash of a lightning bolt, it came to him what he had to do and not impersonally through his lawyer. Maggie deserved more than that.

He gathered up the documents and raced down the stairs. He sped past his brother who was sprawled on the couch, tapping away on his laptop.

"Where are you going?" Jonathan asked as he rushed by.

"To see Maggie," he said and pushed on, not that Jonathan tried to stop him.

He dashed across his lawn and through the break in the privet hedge. Hurried down her lawn and toward the boardwalk, where he had seen she was headed.

Maggie was sitting by one of the dunes, knees drawn up. Her arms were wrapped around her legs, and her head was buried against her knees. As she heard his approach, she lifted her head, and the tracks of tears on her face glimmered in the fading light of day.

It broke his heart that he had put those tears there.

She jumped up and swiped hurriedly at the moisture on her cheeks. Squaring her shoulders, she tilted her chin up courageously. "I don't want to talk to you, Owen," she said, her voice trembling.

"I know, and I won't bother you again. I understand why you want to end our marriage. No marriage should begin with a lie. That's why I want to give you this," he said and handed her the signed divorce papers.

Her hand shook as she reached for them. She took hold of the papers, opened them, and glanced down to where he had scrawled his signature. Her head shot up in surprise, and she tried to speak, but nothing came out, so he kept on going.

He held up the prenup so she could see what it was, and as puzzlement replaced shock, he tore the document up into pieces. "That's because a marriage shouldn't be based on a business deal."

She shook her head in disbelief. "But what about the loan? The lawyers?"

"I always believed in you and that you could turn the stores around. The prenup was just a formality."

With a deep breath, he waited for her to react. Waited for her to say anything, but she just stood there mutely for long seconds, and with each heartbeat that passed, hope died in him. But he wouldn't go away without one last try.

"I love you, Maggie. I have since we used to play on the beach together. That first kiss just confirmed it. I've thought about you, about us, every time I saw you in the years after that. The day I married you was the happiest day of my life, and this is the saddest, but I understand, Maggie. I really do, and I hope that in time you can forgive me."

At her continued silence, he tucked the pieces of the prenup into his pocket, turned, and walked away.

Maggie stared at his retreating back before peering down at the signed divorce papers. Before reliving the moment he'd torn up their prenup.

So much had stood between them before their marriage, but they'd still managed to fall in love. Now, when yet more had risen between them, she'd lost her faith in him and his love. She'd lost her trust in the truth of his love.

With one swipe of his pen and a few quick rips of paper, Owen had restored her faith and her trust. The one thing still keeping them apart was her pride, but she only had to call up the vision of Owen's bitter and unhappy dad to know where twisted pride could lead her.

She bolted up the few steps from the beach to the boardwalk and saw him striding across the lawn and toward the hedges. Waving the divorce papers, she called out his name.

He stopped and turned, a wary look on his features, but he stayed in place so she could catch up to him.

"You hurt me, Owen, but I was wrong as well. What we had…what we *have* is about more than properties and feuds. It's about love, and we got started on the wrong foot."

He narrowed his gaze and considered her. "Tell me what you want, Maggie. If it's for me to go—"

She ripped the divorce papers in half and handed him the two pieces. "What I want is for us to start over. Marry me because you love me, Owen. That's the only reason I'll accept for being married to you."

"I love you, Maggie. Marry me," he said, then he wrapped his arms around her and hauled her close for a kiss filled with the promise of so much. He kissed her over and over, and it was only when she was out of breath and nearly dizzy with joy that he broke the kiss.

As they turned, arms around each other's waists, it

was to find their family of sorts gathered on the lawn, smiling. Jonathan, Connie, Emma, Tracy, and Mrs. Patrick all stood there, clearly delighted with what they were seeing.

They walked toward the group together, and as they got there, Maggie shared a knowing look with Owen.

He grinned, dimples winking at her, and said to Emma, "Do you think you could plan a small, intimate wedding for immediate family for next weekend?"

Emma shook her head with mock outrage. "I'm not sure. Do you plan on making it stick this time?"

Owen peeked at her, smiling, and said, "Forever this time, Emma. No doubt about it."

His hands shook as badly as if he had never made love with her before.

Owen wanted to make this night special. Wanted every kiss, every touch, to show her just how extraordinary she was to him. To show her how much he loved and adored her.

He ran his hands down her back, his touch as light as if she were a piece of fragile crystal. He bracketed her waist with his hands before inching upward to cradle her breasts.

"You are so very beautiful. So special to me," he said, his voice hoarse with emotion.

Maggie trembled at his words and leaned into his caress, needing his touch like nothing she had ever needed before.

She splayed her hands on his chest and swayed

toward him, her knees growing weak as he tenderly tweaked her nipples and bent his head to kiss her.

His kiss was gentle, an invitation to more, and she answered, opening her mouth and accepting the slide of his tongue. Tasting him and pushing her hips against his erection as damp and heat erupted between her legs.

"I've missed you," she said and reached between them. She encircled his erection and stroked him, dragging a rough groan from him.

"I can't wait, Maggie."

"I don't want to wait either," she said and took hold of his hand. Guided him toward her bed.

They fell down on it together, kissing and touching. Passion building with every breath and caress. Each heartbeat pounding out a declaration of love until it was a continuous rhythm without beginning or end.

He joined with her, and they climbed higher and higher until, with a final thrust, they tumbled over the edge together, their love stronger now that it had been tested and survived the challenge.

Chapter 36

ONLY THE CLOSEST FRIENDS AND INTIMATE FAMILY WERE invited to the Saturday afternoon wedding where Maggie and Owen intended to reconfirm their vows. About two dozen people gathered on the lawn on an unseasonably warm mid-November day as the minister walked down to the arbor decorated with various fall flowers, foliage, and fruits. Like ducklings following their mother, the guests chased after him and then drifted to the rows of seats beside the center aisle and took their places.

The bridal party had already gathered at the arbor, along with Maggie's father, waiting for Maggie and Owen to walk down the aisle together. There was just one thing missing, or rather, one person still missing.

As Owen scanned the people gathered outside, his lips thinned into an anguished line.

Maggie squeezed his arm and rose on tiptoes to brush a kiss across his cheek. Lovingly, she wiped away the slight trace of lipstick from his skin and said, "I know we both hoped your father would show up after my dad talked to him, but maybe we were being unrealistic."

He nodded and said, "Maybe." He gazed at her, his dark eyes filled with love, and his features brightened as he said, "Are you ready to do this, Mrs. Sinclair-Pierce?"

"I am, Owen. I've never been more ready."

Owen motioned to the two waiters at either side of the french doors, and they opened the doors so Maggie and he could once again begin the journey to their life as husband and wife. But as they stepped out onto the patio, motion from the privet hedges caught their attention, and they stopped their stroll down the aisle.

Owen's father slipped through the gap in the hedges and stopped to straighten his jacket before marching straight up to them.

He wasn't smiling, Maggie thought, but then again, there was a softness to his normally dour expression that hinted at a possible change of heart.

"Father. I'm glad you could make it," Owen said, his voice thick with emotion.

His father dipped his head in greeting and stared hard at Maggie. "You're the spitting image of your mother, Maggie. She was a beautiful woman and bright as anything too. I know she would have kicked me in the pants for being a fool for so long. I'm sorry for all the hurt I've caused. I hope you and Owen have a long and happy life together."

He turned to walk down the aisle to a seat but stopped short as he realized his old friend and partner had approached and stood just a foot away.

"Bryce," Robert Pierce said with a hesitant nod.

Maggie's dad held out his hand. "Robert. We're all very glad you could make it."

Robert glanced at the three of them and then at the gathered guests. "I guess it's time to do this thing right, Bryce," he said and eased his arm through Owen's.

Bryce Sinclair smiled at his old friend. "I guess it is," he said and slipped his arm into Maggie's.

She looked up at her husband, smiling while tears streamed down her face. He was grinning too, his gaze watery as he said, "Let's do this. It's long past time for the Sinclairs and Pierces to be together."

"Damn straight," his father muttered, and as one, they walked down the aisle for the start of their new life.

Read on for a sneak peek of
At the Shore book 2

What Happens in Summer

by *New York Times* and *USA Today*
bestselling author Caridad Pineiro

Available soon from Sourcebooks Casablanca

Prologue

Sea Kiss, New Jersey

PLAYING IT SAFE WAS FAR WORSE THAN TAKING A RISK ON what you wanted.

Jonathan Pierce knew just what he wanted.

He grabbed hold of the gnarly branch of the decades-old wisteria vine that climbed the side of the Sinclair mansion and boosted himself up. He'd made the journey so many times this past summer, he could do it blindfolded.

He scrambled up the vine, finding the familiar foot- and handholds until he vaulted up and over the second-floor railing and landed on the balcony as silent as a cat burglar. The balcony ran the length of the immense oceanfront mansion, with elegant french doors offering views of the sea.

The first darkened doorway was Maggie Sinclair's room. He rushed past it quietly; Maggie belonged to his older brother, Owen. Not that Owen had acted on it yet, but Jonathan had known for years that the two were meant to be together, family feud be damned.

The next doorway was usually Maggie's dad's, but the old man had stopped coming down to the Shore as often as he once had, so it was a good bet that room was unoccupied.

Reaching the third room, he saw the curtains wafting in the summer breeze and the dim light from behind the partially closed french doors. He smiled and his heart raced with pleasure.

Connie was waiting for him. Ever responsible, ever loyal Connie had broken her own rules to fall in love with him. Or at least he thought it was love. It definitely was on his part. With barely a week left before the girls all went back to school, he intended to let her know just how he felt.

He slipped carefully through the open doors and shut them behind him. He'd gone no more than a step when she launched herself at him, laughing and kissing him as she said, "What took you so long?"

"I missed you, too," he said, knowing it was more about the separation to come in a week and not about the long hours since last night.

He bent his head and kissed her, his touch tender and caring, and she answered in kind, her lips soft and coaxing.

Although Maggie had been bringing her friends to the Jersey Shore every summer since they'd met freshman year in college, he'd never really paid much attention at first. He'd had his share of girls from his high school class fawning over him.

But when Maggie and her friends had come back the next year, he had finally, gratefully, noticed what a real woman should be. Like Connie—all luscious curves, plus proud, smart, and independent.

As impatient as he might be to make love to her tonight, he wanted her to know how much this meant to him, how this wasn't only a summer romance for him.

He leaned over her, his gaze locked on her face. He wanted to say the words—Lord, how he wanted to—but they stuck in his throat and so he let every kiss and touch tell her what he couldn't voice.

———∿∿∿———

Connie's heart thudded almost painfully in her chest as she wondered how, in a week's time, she could leave him. The ache deepened beneath her breastbone and she put her hand there and rubbed to assuage the hurt.

What had started as a summer fling with a funny, smart, and beautiful boy had turned into something so much more, with an incredibly amazing man. Falling in love with Jonathan hadn't been in her game plan, but he was just too hard to resist.

She *should* have resisted. He was a Pierce. She wasn't a Sinclair, but Maggie was like a sister, and that stupid family feud was still going strong, as far as she knew.

He was going back to Villanova in a week and she'd be returning to Princeton. The colleges were not all that far apart, but if she was to execute her game plan, she had to stay in the game, which meant studying and more studying. Not nights spent in bed making love and days spent daydreaming about the nights. But like Eve with Adam, now that she'd had a bite of such delicious forbidden fruit, she didn't know how she could go on a Jonathan-free diet.

At the moment, she could just admire his sun-streaked light-brown hair waving wildly around a masculine face with chiseled features. A sexy dimpled grin was on his lips and his eyes glittered with a blue as enchanting as a Sea Kiss summer sea.

That ache in her heart rocketed to life again, together with an almost unbearable lightness in her soul. For so

much of her life she'd been driven to accomplish more
and more, but with Jonathan, she could just be herself.
No goals or responsibilities. Just…happy.

And so, in the blink of an eye, her game plan altered.
She could see it all so clearly, only now Jon was there
beside her at each step. Finish college. Head to law
school. Pass the bar. Get a job in a big New York City
law firm so she could help her family financially, as well
as others who had legal problems and couldn't afford
representation. Become a partner. Marry Jonathan. Or
maybe marry Jon and then become a partner. She didn't
want to wait too long to be with him forever.

Not that she'd ever pictured getting married to anyone
before, since her home life hadn't been anything great.
But for Jonathan, she'd make an exception.

As she snuggled into the curve of his arm and pil-
lowed her head on his broad shoulder, she sighed and
said, "I can't believe the summer's almost over."

He grunted his reply in a too-typical male way.
"Sucks." But then he surprised her by adding, "I'd like
to keep on seeing you once you're back in school."

She smiled, pleased by his admission, and glanced up
at him. There was a contented smile on his full lips and
the first hint of a dimple. The hard line of his jaw had a
bit of blond stubble from an evening beard. She ran her
hand up to brush away a lock of his hair.

"I'd like that, too," she said.

His smile broadened and the dimple fully emerged,
drawing attention to that luscious mouth. She couldn't
resist reaching up to skim a kiss along that dimple and
the corner of his lips.

"What was that for?" he asked.

She wanted to say because he made her happy, but she hesitated. She'd seen what could happen to a woman whose happiness depended on a man, as she'd watched her mother lose herself and her dreams.

"As a way for you to remember me until we visit each other at college," she said instead.

Tension crept into his body, impossible to miss. Enough to worry her. She pulled back from him. "I thought you wanted us to see each other. At least, that's what you said a minute ago."

A chagrined look passed across his features, stirring the worry inside her.

"I do, only…I won't be at college this year. I'm not going back to Villanova."

She searched his face, finding it hard to believe, but he appeared deadly serious.

"What do you mean, you're not going back? Did something happen? Are you transferring to another school?"

She was freaking out and Jonathan understood. To someone like Connie, college meant everything, including the stability she'd not had in her early life because her father had abandoned her family. But he wasn't like her. The whole predictable route that she and her friends—and even his brother—were taking was not the path he wanted to follow.

"I liked Villanova—the people, the place, even some of the classes—but the whole college thing is not for me."

Shock registered on her features and she shook her head, either not comprehending or, worse, not wanting to. "What do you mean, it's not for you? So what do you plan to do? Spend the rest of your life surfing? Or working at the bar?"

Her words were too much like those his father had shouted at him when he'd told him a week ago of his decision. His father, a bitter, angry old man who never had a kind word for either of his sons.

Her words, the look she gave him, stoked the anger in his belly. He tried to keep it banked, because he understood where such anger could lead. In as calm a voice as he could muster, he said, "I have plans, Connie. They're just different from yours."

"Was I ever in your plans? Or was this just a summer hookup?" she said, the upset evident in her gaze, but his own pain was just as alive. Just as sharp.

He snorted a breath and said more roughly, "You act as if I'm the one who wanted this to be just fun, but who's the one who didn't want her friends to know she'd been seeing me?"

She laid her hand over his heart. "It's not what you think."

The pity in her tone unleashed something inside of him. Something ugly and hurtful. "Don't tell me what I think, Connie. I think you're ashamed of me. That I'm not good enough for someone like you."

Now, that is rich, Connie thought. For someone like him, who'd grown up with a silver spoon in his mouth, to think that she, who'd grown up on the edge of poverty, would think he wasn't good enough. But in a flash of insight, it occurred to her that their differences had nothing to do with money.

"I care for you, Jon," she said, unable to fully commit because the idea of falling in love and changing her game plan was still too new. "But I know what it's like to want a man you can't rely on. A man who doesn't fulfill his responsibilities. I won't have that in my life. I *can't* have that in my life again."

Angry color blossomed on his features and his hands clenched at his side. "If that's what you think I am, I guess it's a good thing the summer's over so *this* can be over."

He marched to the door and stood there for a long moment. The delay gave her hope, then he turned back to face her. "I love you, Connie. My bad. I should have known better than to give my heart to someone like you."

His words cut deep and that ache in her heart became almost unbearable. Her throat choked up and she almost couldn't breathe. She couldn't get the words out as he stormed through the french doors and slammed them shut. But somehow through the pain and the tears that slipped unheeded down her face, she said what she hadn't been able to before.

"I love you, too."

Chapter 1

JONATHAN PIERCE STARED HARD AT THE MIRROR, WONDERING what Connie Reyes might see tonight when she and her friends came over for dinner. What she might think after so much time had passed.

The teen she had known seven years earlier was gone, replaced by a man who had known his share of hardship and success. Barely perceptible laugh lines that hadn't been there that last summer bracketed his mouth and eyes. A thin scar above one brow was thanks to a crash while testing a new vehicle prototype on the Bonneville Salt Flats. Another jagged white line on his jaw was courtesy of shrapnel when a hydrogen fuel cell had unexpectedly exploded in their lab.

He looked away and leaned heavily on the edge of the vanity, noting the other assorted nicks and scars on his hands. They were the hands of a man who had lived life to the fullest and made himself what he wanted to be and not what others expected. He knew he'd sometimes hurt people with his choices, especially his older brother, Owen, who'd had to shoulder the burden of the family business as well as their father's ire whenever one of Jonathan's escapades caught the attention of the media.

He'd gotten used to the interest the press had in him. After all, he was the renegade son of a wealthy family. A self-taught inventor who had sold his first small invention for millions. He was revolutionizing the motor vehicle and battery industries with his innovative designs, unconventional methods, and fearless experiments.

He had brought idea after idea to life with detailed research and hard work. There had been failures along the way, but that had only made the successes that much more enjoyable. He had celebrated those successes with his team, his brother, and a bevy of actresses and models who were only too keen to be seen on the arm of a rebellious multimillionaire who might soon be a billionaire if his company's stock prices continued to climb.

Only…none of those women could hold a candle to Connie.

Connie, who he would see in just a few hours, thanks to his brother. Owen had finally decided to fight for Maggie Sinclair, but Jonathan hadn't anticipated that Owen's courtship would result in him having to be involved with Connie again.

Smart and beautiful Connie, he thought with a sigh and a shake of his head.

He'd managed to avoid her for the last seven years. Sure, he'd seen her occasionally from afar when Maggie and her friends had come down to Sea Kiss. Or every now and then when he'd gone to some business event in the city.

He'd tried to tell himself he didn't like the sleek professional woman she'd become. That she wasn't prettier than ever. He tried not to imagine peeling off those elegant business suits to reveal the real woman beneath. But he was lying to himself.

He had never really gotten over Connie Reyes and doubted he ever would. You never forgot your first and only love.

—∿∿—

Connie Reyes splayed her hand across the nervous butterflies in her stomach that were beating their wings so violently, she felt like throwing up. She was tempted to beg off from dinner with the Pierce boys, only Maggie needed her moral support and Connie never disappointed a friend. Especially Maggie, who was like a sister.

"You feeling okay?" asked Emma Grant, her other BFF, as they followed Maggie onto the patio and to the long row of tall privet hedges that separated the two Jersey Shore mansions.

"Just fine," she lied, but it was clear from Emma's meaningful stare that her friend suspected something was up.

She tamed the flutters much as she did when arguing a case before a judge and trudged along behind Maggie as they eased through the hedges and approached the entrance to the Pierce mansion. They had barely reached the front porch when Owen threw open the door, a big, friendly smile on his handsome face.

He welcomed them warmly, but Connie couldn't resist mumbling to Emma, "Said the spider to the fly." She still wasn't sure this thing between her friend and Owen was a good idea.

Emma jabbed her in the ribs, and luckily, it seemed as if Owen either hadn't heard her comment or, if he had, was choosing to ignore it. She gave him props if it was the latter, since it indicated he was truly trying to be nice for Maggie's sake.

They quickly walked through the foyer and living room and back to the dining area. Thanks to the open-concept renovation someone had done to the Victorian mansion, she could see Jonathan was in the kitchen, an apron over his jeans and T-shirt. The T-shirt hugged his broad, muscled chest and laid bare the powerful muscles of his arms. His light-brown hair still had the kiss of the sun and was tied back from his face, revealing the sharp lines of his features.

He looked older, but still so handsome. It was impossible to forget the way he'd held her in his arms, a dimpled smile on his lips, his sea-blue eyes bright with humor and love. With that memory, the flutters in her stomach were replaced by an ache in the region of her heart.

As they walked into the kitchen area, Jonathan looked up and smiled. He sauntered from beyond the island, over to Maggie, and hugged her. "Nice to see you again, Maggie."

He embraced Emma next, playfully teasing her like he might a kid sister. "How's the world's best wedding planner doing?"

Emma grinned back, totally at ease. "Busy making the world less safe for confirmed bachelors like you."

When it came time to greet Connie, his demeanor changed drastically. He kept his distance and provided her with only a quick nod and a forced smile. "Connie."

He might as well have dug a knife into her gut, the pain of his actions so sharp, so hurtful, that she lost control and responded out of anger, something she rarely did.

"Jonathan. I almost didn't recognize you. It's been so long since I've seen your face in the tabloids." Her friends' muffled gasps chased her words.

About the Author

New York Times and *USA Today* bestselling author Caridad Pineiro is the author of more than fifty novels and novellas and has sold more than one million books worldwide. Caridad writes romantic suspense, military romance, contemporary romance, paranormal romance, and vampire suspense. Caridad is also a Jersey girl who loves to travel, cook, and spend time with family and friends.